# CHAINED TO THE STREETS 3

**Lock Down Publications and
Ca$h Presents
Chained to the Streets 3
A Novel by J-Blunt**

Chained to the Streets 3

**Lock Down Publications**
**Po Box 944**
**Stockbridge, Ga 30281**

**Visit our website**
www.lockdownpublications.com

Copyright 2020 by J-Blunt
Chained to the Streets 3

First Edition August 2020
Printed in the United States of America

**Lock Down Publications**
**Like our page on Facebook: Lock Down Publications @**
www.facebook.com/lockdownpublications.ldp
Cover design and layout by: **Dynasty Cover Me**
Book interior design by: **Shawn Walker**
Edited by: **Jill Duska**

## Stay Connected with Us!

Text **LOCKDOWN** to 22828 to stay up-to-date with new releases, sneak peeks, contests and more…

## Submission Guideline.

Submit the first three chapters of your completed manuscript to ldpsubmissions@gmail.com, subject line: Your book's title. The manuscript must be in a .doc file and sent as an attachment. The document should be in Times New Roman, double-spaced and in size 12 font. Also, provide your synopsis and full contact information. If sending multiple submissions, they must each be in a separate email.

Have a story but no way to send it electronically? You can still submit to LDP/Ca$h Presents. Send in the first three chapters, written or typed, of your completed manuscript to:

**LDP: Submissions Dept**
**Po Box 944**
**Stockbridge, Ga 30281**

*DO NOT send original manuscript. Must be a duplicate.*

Provide your synopsis and a cover letter containing your full contact information.

Thanks for considering LDP and Ca$h Presents.

J-Blunt

# Chapter 1

"Y'all know how we do. We runnin' in and fucking er'body up. Everything breathing gotta go," Flacco lectured to his goons as he whipped the truck through traffic.

"On my B's, I'm smoking er'thang." Mili grinned from the passenger seat, massaging the AR-15 in his lap.

When Flacco looked in the rearview mirror, the sight in the back seat made him smile. Rosé and Duke were checking the clips on their pistols. Murder was written on the young Bloods' faces. In a few moments, Milwaukee, Wisconsin would be the next city to feel the wrath of The East Saint Louis Nightmare.

Five minutes later, Flacco parked the truck in front of Lucky's house in Franklin. It was a little after ten p.m. and the suburban neighborhood was peaceful. But not for long.

The four Bloods mobbed out of the truck, all of them armed with automatic weapons as they trotted towards the house. They were almost to the porch when a noise from behind made Flacco turn around. Desmond and Lucky were climbing from a black Ford Fusion. Flacco knew who Desmond was immediately. The men locked eyes, exchanging hostilities in the blink of an eye. No words were needed to describe the seriousness of the situation. Flacco pointed the AK-47 a moment too slow.

Desmond lifted his pistol and allowed the gun to do the talking.

Pop, pop, pop, pop, pop, pop, pop!

Mili took three bullets to the back, collapsing on the first step of the front porch. Flacco was able to dodge the volley of bullets headed for him and he returned fire with his AK-47.

Brrrrreaaaaatttt! Brrrrreaaaaatttt!

Desmond and Lucky ducked behind the car as the Ford was riddled with high powered rounds from the rifle.

"Get them niggas! They behind that car!" Flacco ordered.

Duke and Rosé turned their weapons on the car and began spraying as the Bloods surrounded the vehicle. Desmond glanced at Lucky. His older brother met his stare. There was so much that they wanted to say, but they were outnumbered and Desmond had the only gun. The chances of them making it out alive were slim.

Gunfire from outside got the attention of the shooters from Detroit inside Lucky's house. Quincy and Demon reacted quickly. They didn't think twice as they grabbed pistols and ran towards the front porch. They went outside and saw the men dressed in red with red bandanas covering their faces shooting at a black car parked at the curb. There was also a man in red lying on the front porch moments away from death. Demon put the pistol to his head and sent him to meet death faster.

Pop!

While Demon was executing the Blood on the porch, Quincy took aim at Duke and started blasting.

The Blood never knew what hit him as bullets to the back made his body jerk and fall to the ground.

Flacco looked towards the porch, watching Mili get shot in the head by Demon. Duke got flashed by Quincy. Their mission was busted. A good general knew when it was time to retreat. The only thing he could do was regroup and try again later. He spun the chopper towards the porch and let death fly while making his way toward the SUV.

Quincy was able to duck out of the path of the rifle rounds, but Demon wasn't so lucky. The gray-eyed shooter's body twisted as he fell to the ground, hot lead from the AK filling his corpse.

Desmond could hear the extra gunfire and knew more guns had entered the battle. He looked to Lucky. "It sound like somebody else shooting."

Lucky smiled. "Them my li'l niggas."

Desmond poked his head out just in time to see Quincy and Flacco in a gun battle.

Rosé stopped shooting at the Fusion to see what his big homie was shooting at, and that's when Desmond made his move. He lifted the Glock and let it sing.

Pop, pop, pop, pop, pop, pop!

Rosé's body began jerking as the .40 caliber bullets tore into his chest, felling his body on the lawn. After killing Rosé, Desmond turned the pistol towards Flacco as he hopped in the SUV.

Pop, pop, pop, pop. Click.

"Bitch-ass shit!" Desmond cursed, angry that he had run out of bullets.

"Who the fuck was that?" Quincy asked, watching the Suburban speed away.

"I don't know," Lucky said, looking at the bodies sprawled across the lawn.

"We gotta get the fuck outta here!" Desmond said, climbing in the bullet-riddled Fusion.

"Lucky!" Laronda called, stepping onto the porch with the other Detroit shooters, T.A. and Ryder.

Lucky wanted to comfort his daughter, but the neighbors were peeking out of their blinds and slowly coming outside. "Y'all, c'mon. Get in the car. We gotta get the fuck outta here!" Lucky called as he ran towards his rental car.

♦♦♦

Desmond followed behind Lucky's rental car, watching his rearview mirror, hoping he didn't get flagged by the police as he sped along the highway in the bullet-riddled car. He had a brick of heroin under the seat and an empty pistol in his lap. Even though he was working for the Feds and could probably get out from under any charges, he didn't want to have to explain any kind of police contact to Donny and his people.

Twenty minutes later, they pulled up in front of Rachel's house on the north side of Milwaukee. The Detroit shooters, Lucky, and Laronda piled out of the rental car and walked towards the house. Desmond hopped out of the Ford and followed.

"What the fuck was that about?" Desmond asked.

Lucky spun around, anger in his eyes. "Why the fuck is you still here?"

Desmond was surprised by the angry response. "I just saved yo' ass, nigga. Fuck wrong with you?"

Lucky looked at Desmond like he stank. "Fuck wrong with me? Nah, nigga. What the fuck wrong with you? You the one on that bullshit. I ain't forgot what you did. I don't fuck with fuck niggas."

Quincy, T.A., Ryder, and Laronda watched the men, surprised by the arguing.

"What is y'all fighting for?" Laronda asked. "Somebody just shot at us and killed Demon. What the fuck is wrong with y'all? Y'all niggas tripping."

The brothers exchanged angry mugs before Lucky turned to his daughter. "You betta watch how the fuck you talk to me," he lectured.

The teenager rolled her eyes. "Whatever. All I'm saying is we don't got time to be arguing. Can we go in the house?"

"Who out there?" a female called from behind the door.

"It's Lucky, baby. Open the door."

A moment later the door opened and Rachel appeared. She looked surprised to see all the people standing on her porch. "What's going on?"

"Somebody just came to our house shooting and now they arguing," Laronda explained with plenty of attitude as she walked into the house.

Rachel looked to Lucky for an explanation.

"We good. Let them in," he said, nodding towards his shooters. "I'ma be in in a minute."

After everyone went in the house, Lucky turned to Desmond. "What you want me to say? That I'm cool with you working for them people? I ain't. You bogus."

"So, this how we doing?"

"You did some shit I don't agree with, Des. I'm going through my own shit. I got the police on my ass about all kinds of shit. Melissa and her kids got killed. Wacco got at me at the club and a couple of my niggas died. And I'm on the run from my P.O. But you know what I'm not gon' do? Snitch. I'ma take my weight."

Desmond stared at his brother, angered by the accusatory tone but more surprised at everything he was involved in. "I know you mad, but I did what I had to do. But what's up with all yo' shit with the police?"

"I just told you."

"So, you not gon' try to take care of it? You wanna go back to jail?"

"I don't got a fuckin' choice, Desmond!" Lucky snapped. "I tried to do the right thing. I tried, brah. But it seems like everything I do is wrong. It feels like I'm chained to these fucking streets. And I'm not going back to jail. Fuck that. I'm not about to spend the rest of my life in a fuckin' cell. They not gon' let me back out if they get they hands on me. I'm involved in too much."

The brothers went silent for a moment.

"So, who is these niggas dressed in red? They look like Bloods. Did that have something to do with the deal you made?" Desmond asked.

"Nah. I don't know who the fuck them niggas was. But I'ma find out. That deal I made was with Donny, and I guess you know all about it since you killed Polo."

"So that's what the dope is for, huh? You about to hustle?"

Lucky nodded.

"What happened to writing books and starting a business?"

"That shit over, brah. I gotta do what I gotta do to survive."

"Damn, Lucky," Desmond mumbled, feeling sorry for his brother.

"Don't feel sorry for me, nigga. I made my bed. I'ma take my weight. You should follow my example." Lucky mugged him.

Desmond was tired of the shots being taken at him. "I made my bed too. And it is what it is," he spat. "If you want it to be like this, fuck it. I ain't about to kiss yo' ass, nigga."

"And I definitely ain't about to kiss yours, nigga!" Lucky yelled, poking out his chest.

The brothers shared a long stare, an entire conversation being spoken without a word being said.

"I got the brick in the car," Desmond mumbled before turning and walking towards the bullet-riddled Ford. He got in the car and set the kilo of heroin on the passenger seat.

Lucky moved reluctantly towards the car, opening the door, and grabbing the dope. The brothers shared another look.

"So, what's the mission, Desmond? What the Feds want?"

Desmond considered the question, wondering if he should say. There was a time when he trusted Lucky with everything. But now that things between them had changed, he wondered if his brother would give him over to Donny and the family.

"Why you wanna know?"

"So now you don't trust me?"

"I just wanna get my life back, man. That's it."

Lucky gave him a long stare. He was about to speak, but didn't. Instead, he turned and walked away.

◆◆◆

"What's going on with you and D-Money?" Quincy asked when Lucky walked into the house.

Lucky looked around the living room and saw his three hitters sitting on the couch giving him all their attention. Rachel sat on the love seat also, awaiting an explanation as to why her house was suddenly filled with strangers. Lucky didn't have a good answer for anyone and needed time.

"Where is Laronda?" he asked when he didn't see his daughter in the living room.

"She went to the bathroom," Rachel spoke up. "What's going on, Lucky? Who was shooting at you?"

"I don't even know. Some Blood niggas. I don't even got no beef with Bloods."

"Somebody might've paid 'em to get at you," T.A. said.

Lucky thought for a moment. "I only had beefs with Wacco and Polo. And ain't neither one of them niggas paying nobody to get at me. They got they own shooters. I think these Blood niggas is something else. I just got that house. Ain't no way Polo or Wacco found us that fast. Only a few people knew about that house, and most of us is in this living room right now."

Everyone took a moment to think on Lucky's words.

"Is y'all okay?" Rachel asked.

"For the most part. Lost one of my niggas back at the house," Lucky answered.

"Did anybody follow y'all here? Am I safe?" Rachel asked, fear upon her face.

"You good, baby. We took care of that shit," Lucky said, trying to calm her nerves.

"One got away," Ryder spoke up.

Lucky shot him an evil glance. The youngster lowered his head, realizing his mistake.

"We good, baby. I just need to keep er'body here with me tonight until I figure out the next move."

Rachel gave her man a long look. "Okay. I'm going to my room. Come back there when you get everybody situated," she said before leaving.

"How long we gon' stay here?" Laronda asked, walking into the living room.

"I'm not sure. Until we figure out the next move," Lucky answered.

"Where yo' girlfriend go? I want to talk to her."

"She went to her room."

Laronda turned and walked towards the back of the house.

"You never answered me about you and D-Money. How you know him?" Quincy asked.

Lucky considered telling his soldiers the truth, that Desmond was his rat-ass brother. But he knew that would cause more problems and probably get them killed. And as much as he was disgusted with Desmond, he didn't want him to die. "D-Money is a friend of the family."

"Seem like y'all got an issue. What he do?" T.A. asked.

"What you mean?"

"Outside you said he did some bullshit and you don't fuck with fuck niggas. What happened?"

Lucky thought quickly. "Some bullshit that I don't got the energy to talk about right now. Y'all fall back and be easy. Make something to eat if y'all hungry, 'cause we ain't goin' back outside tonight. I'ma go holla at my girl and try to get us another spot to lamp at. The house in Franklin burnt up."

Lucky left his niggas and walked back to Rachel's room. Laronda and Rachel were sitting in the bed talking like they had known one another for years.

"What's going on?" Lucky frowned.

"Nothing. She just telling me more about you," Rachel said, eyeing him suspiciously.

Lucky looked to his daughter. "You better not be on no bullshit. And if any of them niggas ask about Desmond, tell them he a friend of the family and not my brother."

Laronda frowned. "Why?"

Lucky knew that he wouldn't be able to dismiss Laronda as easily as he had done his shooters. "Because Desmond working with the Feds. If them niggas find out, I'ma have to kill 'em all to stop them from telling the boss."

Rachel looked shocked.

Laronda was amused. "Uncle Desmond is a snitch? So that's why y'all was arguing, huh?"

Lucky nodded.

"Damn, Pops," she laughed.

"What the fuck is going on, Lucky?" Rachel shrieked. "You got shot at by some Bloods and your brother is working with the Feds? What about Donny? You don't think he needs to know this?"

"Nah. I got it. I just need to sit down and come up with a plan," he said before turning to Laronda. "Have you heard from yo' mother?"

"Nah. She ain't answering her phone or my texts."

"Keep trying. She needs to know not to go back to the house."

♦♦♦

"What happened? Where er'body else at?" Derek asked after letting Flacco in the house.

Flacco paused to stare at his cousin, trying to think of the words to say. The truth was, he was speechless. He didn't know how to say he'd lost the battle. He'd never uttered those words before. Just thinking about it felt unfamiliar. "They killed my niggas," he grumbled, sinking onto the sofa with a heavy heart.

Derek looked surprised. "All of them?"

Flacco nodded, unable to hide his shock. "All of them."

"How? I thought Lucky was by hisself."

A vision of Desmond killing Mili flashed in his head. "His brother ain't locked up. And they got a couple shooters."

The men sat in silence for a few moments. Flacco continued replaying the shootout in his head. He wasn't expecting to lose a battle. He had never lost one so lopsided until now. All three of his brothers were gone. It was his fault. He wasn't expecting Desmond to be there. He didn't properly plan. His arrogance and anger got his men killed. He would right that wrong. He would avenge his brothers' deaths sevenfold. He was going to gather another team and come back stronger.

"What you wanna do? I got a few niggas that get down," Derek offered.

Flacco mugged his cousin. "You and yo' niggas been tryna get at these niggas all this time and never got close. I got my own niggas. I'ma take care of these niggas. Milwaukee gon' remember the East Saint Louis Nightmare."

J-Blunt

## Chapter 2

"D-Money, what's going on, brotha? Its three o'clock in the morning. Did that work out for you?" Donny asked, sounding like he just woke up.

"I had a problem."

There was a slight pause on Donny's end of the phone. "What kinda problem? Did the chicken touch down?"

"Yeah. That's good. I'm driving into Detroit right now. My car got shot up, so—"

"Don't say nothing else. Pull over and I'ma send Royce to get you. I'll meet you at the cleaning company."

"Yeah. I'll be here."

After hanging up the phone, Desmond parked and waited for Royce. While sitting on the side street, he thought about Lucky. He had a hard time accepting that his brother didn't want to fuck with him anymore. They had been tight their whole life. And when Lucky was in prison, Desmond supported him on every level: letters, visits, pictures, and money orders. Now that Desmond was hurting and at the bottom, Lucky had turned his back on him. That was fucked up and he had a hard time accepting how Lucky was dealing. He would've never turned his back in his brother, no matter what he did. They shared the same blood. The love was supposed to be unconditional. But it was apparent that Lucky didn't believe the same principles.

It took Royce ten minutes to get to Desmond. When the G Wagon pulled to the curb, the Navy SEAL climbed in the passenger seat.

"I heard you had a hard time in Milwaukee." Royce chuckled.

"Man, that's an understatement. I been in a lot of close calls fucking with the army and that was damn near on the same level."

Royce looked surprised. "Damn. What happened?"

"I was making the drop to Lucky when some Blood niggas pulled up. They jumped out with battlefield guns and tried to run in Lucky's house. We jumped out the car and got to banging. Put all them niggas down except one."

"Do you know who the niggas was?"

"Nah. Never seen 'em. They wore all red like they was Bloods and Milwaukee don't got too many Bloods."

"Damn. It sound like Lucky got his hands full across the lake. They gon' have to start calling it Killwaukee."

When they got to the cleaning building, Desmond explained the situation to Donny. The boss man sat behind the desk, opening and closing a gold pocket watch, wearing a disturbed look.

"Damn. I don't like the sound of that. I think that might fuck with the business."

Desmond shrugged. "I don't know. I helped get them niggas off his ass. The shooters that you sent came through too. Lost li'l Demon in that shit. He went out gunnin' though."

"Well, that's what they there for. Casualties are part of war. I'ma give Lucky a holla," the boss said, dropping the watch and picking up the phone to make the call.

"What's good, Donny?" Lucky answered groggily.

Hearing his brother's voice gave Desmond pause. He hoped Lucky didn't say anything that would get him in some bullshit.

"I talked to D-Money. He told me what happened. How you holding?"

"D-Money with you right now?"

"Yeah. He's right here. Why?"

There was a pause on Lucky's end. Desmond held his breath.

"Nothing. He came through for me. Right now, I'm trying to regroup."

"What can I do from my end? Let me know what you need. Some more goons?"

"I don't know. Maybe. First I gotta find somewhere to set up Quincy n'em. I can't go back to my house."

"If money is a problem, just let me know. I'll send you something to get you a roof."

"I'll let you know something tomorrow. Right now, we're just laying low for the night."

"Okay. Do you know who they were or what they wanted?"

"Nah. I never seen 'em before. And they didn't ask no questions. One got away, so I'ma put my ear to the street and see what I come up with."

"Okay. Do that. I'ma let you go. Make sure you get back to me and let me know if you need anything or if you find out who them niggas is."

"You got it, Donny."

After hanging up the phone, Donny picked up the watch again and began opening and closing it. Then he looked to Desmond. "How do you feel about taking another trip to Milwaukee?"

Desmond shrugged. "I'm not excited about it. I told you my plans to eventually fall back from the game."

"I know. But it sounds like they might need somebody with your skills. I don't wanna lose the ground we gained. I've invested a lot trying to gain access to the Milwaukee market. I need to exhaust all resources to keep it."

Desmond thought about Donny's words. Even though he wasn't seeing eye to eye with Lucky, he would still do battle with all the demons in hell to save his life. "I really don't want to go. But if you don't have any other options, I'll do it."

"My man." Donny smiled. "Okay. Let me get your money so you can be on your way. You have been a real blessing to me, man. A real blessing. And don't worry about your car. I'll give you one of mine tomorrow. Royce will give you a ride home."

◆◆◆

Desmond moved slowly, trying not to wake Lasonya as he slid into bed. He had just pulled the covers over himself when she stirred and opened her eyes.

"Hey." She smiled.

"Hey. I tried not to wake you."

"You just got home? What time is it?"

"Almost four in the morning."

"What happened? How did everything go in Milwaukee?"

Desmond shook his head. "Everything that could go wrong went wrong. We got shot at and Lucky's pissed off at me."

Lasonya's eye's popped. "Oh no! What happened? Did anybody get hurt?"

"One of Lucky's li'l niggas. Some Blood niggas I never seen before tried to run in his house and we had to get down."

"Damn. What the fuck is Lucky involved in?"

"I don't know, babe. I'm kinda worried about the nigga, but I guess we not talking no more. Said he don't wanna fuck with me."

Lasonya got mad. "Because you working with the Feds?"

Desmond nodded. "He don't want to understand my side. He only see shit his way and want me to go to jail like he did."

"That's some bullshit, baby. It's not like you in the streets no more. You an army man, not a street nigga. The rules ain't the same. Plus, you stuck by his side all those years he was in jail and didn't have nobody, and this how he do you?"

"I was thinking the same thing."

"Well, fuck him then. Don't kiss his ass."

"I'm not. I just want my nigga with me. I want what's best for him. You know what's crazy? Even though he on this bullshit, I would still go to war for that nigga."

Lasonya kissed his lips. "That's because you're a good man and a good brother. If Lucky don't see it, you don't need him. I'll be your brother, baby. I won't ever turn my back in you. No matter what."

Hearing the supportive words made Desmond smile. "Thank you, baby. Sorry for waking you. Go back to sleep."

"I don't think I can go back to sleep. I'm awake now. Just hold me and tell me how much you love me."

◆◆◆

"How did it go?" Agent Johansen asked when Desmond climbed in the car.

"I made the connection. Had a little problem, but I worked it out."

20

The federal agent shared a look with her partner.

"What does that mean? What kind of problem?" Agent Wright asked.

Desmond let out a breath. "I don't think y'all want to know. Just know that I took care of it and made the drop."

Agent Johansen looked in Desmond's driveway. "Where is your car?"

"I'm getting a new one today."

"Brief us on everything that happened in Wisconsin. Don't leave out anything," Agent Wright spoke.

"While I was making the drop, somebody ran up on us with guns and we had a shootout."

"Who did you make the drop to? I thought you didn't know who you were supposed to meet with."

"I don't. The guy I met with, his name is Quincy. But I don't think he was the leader of the operation. He seemed more like a follower than a leader."

"Quincy. Okay. The next time you meet, we're going to need you to get video or a picture somehow. Tell us about the shooting. Did anyone die this time?"

Desmond nodded.

The agents picked up on his unwillingness to talk.

"How many people?" Agent Wright asked.

"Four."

"Shit!" Johansen cursed. "We're trying to avoid the bodies, Desmond. What the hell?"

"I know. I didn't have a choice. I was trying to save my ass. They came at us with heat. Whatever they got going on in Milwaukee is serious. I got caught up in it."

"Okay. I'll make some calls and see what happened and if you were compromised. For now, just keep doing what you're doing and try to find out who the drugs are going to in Milwaukee," Agent Wright said.

"And stop killing people," Johansen added. "Let's hope that what happened in Milwaukee won't get back to us here, because the director won't like more people dying."

"Okay," Desmond nodded. Then he thought about Lucky. "How much longer do I have to be in this? This is taking a toll on my family and I want to wrap this up as soon as I can."

The agents shared a look. "We almost got everything that we need. We know Donny is the head of the Detroit chapter of the organization. We need to know who is at the top pulling the strings, or at least find out a couple more players in other states. The more people we can bring charges against, the more likely we are to get the people at the top. Right now, all we have is Donny. If you can get us more names, then we can wrap the investigation up sooner," Johansen said.

"Okay. I'll see what I can do. We good?" Desmond asked, ready to end the meet.

"Yeah. We're good." Agent Johansen nodded.

"And stop shooting people," Wright added.

"I'll do my best." Desmond laughed, exiting the car. He was walking towards the house when his phone rang. It was Rich Red. "Richy Rich! What's good, my nigga?"

"D-Money! What it do, fooly? I see you made it back in one piece. What you on?"

"Shit. Lamping around the crib. Shit got crazy in the Mil last night. I had to flex on something."

"On what? Damn, my nigga. You good?"

"Yeah, I'm good. You know a nigga damn near bulletproof." Desmond laughed.

"That's real shit. Listen, I'm going out with my bitch Teona tonight and her friend, Pebbles, askin' 'bout you. I need you to step out with me and slide down on these hoes."

"Damn, Rich. I really was tryna fall back."

"C'mon, D. I been tryna get you to step out wit' me for a minute. Fuck with yo' boy one time. We doing VIP shit. Lil Lava concert with backstage access. After party at Desire. This exactly what you need after that shit you went through last night. Come fuck with me, brah."

◆◆◆

22

Rich Red was right. The concert was exactly what Desmond needed. Lil Lava put on a show that had the crowd rocking and Pebbles kept her ass glued to his crotch the entire performance. When the show was over, they got to kick it with the platinum-selling rap artist backstage. After the concert, if you had backstage passes, the party continued at Desire, an upscale strip club frequented by the who's who in Detroit.

Desmond was chilling in a booth with Pebbles sitting close enough to be his second skin. Rich Red and Teona sat on the other side. A stripper was dancing on the table in front of them while the foursome showed appreciation with dollar bills.

"You never told me where you was from in Flint. Who you fuck with?" Pebbles asked.

"I fuck with my niggas T.Y. and J-Dawg," Desmond lied.

"I heard y'all. MJ fuck with y'all too, right?"

"Yeah. That nigga is a fool. Certified, fa sho'." Desmond laughed, continuing the act. He really didn't have a clue who MJ was.

"Was you at the funeral?"

Desmond looked caught off guard by the question. "Yeah. I mean, nah. I was outta town. I'm not even really from Flint. It's just kinda where I ended up at."

She gave him a questioning look. "Where you from? Originally?"

"Milwaukee. Then I did a li'l time in the army. After I messed up my eye, I landed in Flint."

She nodded. "Teona told me you was in the army. Said you fucked some niggas up that tried to rob Rich Red."

"Yeah. I learned a couple skills."

Pebbles stared at him for a couple beats, expecting him to say more.

"What's up? Why you looking at me like that?" he asked.

"I like your humility. It's different from the niggas out here. Most niggas woulda told me how bad they was. How many niggas they beat up and killed. You got a quiet confidence. I like it."

"I ain't most niggas. I let my actions do the talking."

"I'm 'bout that action too," she said, looking him up and down while sucking on her bottom lip. When she met his eyes again, a challenge shone in her light brown irises. "I don't like niggas that talk and can't back it up."

Desmond chuckled. "I'm not one of them niggas."

She reached her hand into his lap and began massaging his dick through his pants. "I can feel it. But do you know what to do with it?"

Desmond stared into her eyes for a moment, watching the desire to have him grow by the moment. She wanted to fuck him tonight and Desmond was seriously entertaining the thought. Pebbles was bad. Light skin. Hair dyed pink and purple hung to her shoulders. Perfectly arched eyebrows and makeup that looked done professionally. Sensational lips with the top one fuller than the bottom. Her frame was petite with small breasts and a plump booty. She was dressed simply in a form-fitting lemon-yellow dress and open-toed Giuseppe heels that showed a fresh pedicure. If he was a single man, Desmond wouldn't hesitate to take her down. But he couldn't do Lasonya like that. As far as he was concerned, kicking it with Rich Red was part of the mission – at least, that's what he had told Lasonya when he left the house.

"I don't talk how I walk. I just do my thang."

She licked her lips. "How do you like to do it?"

"Back shots all night, baby," he said, wrapping her hair in his fist and pulling her face towards his. He kissed her aggressively, sticking his tongue down her throat. When he broke the kiss, Pebbles looked ready to cum in her thong.

"Damn, D. You got me dripping wet."

He smiled confidently and gave a wink. "I know."

"D-Money! I see you, boy!" Rich Red yelled, smiling and nodding his approval.

Desmond grabbed a bottle of bubbly from the table and lifted it in the air. "Boss nigga shit!"

Rich Red raised a bottle in return. "Boss nigga shit!"

When they left the club, Desmond climbed in the back seat of Rich Red's Audi truck with Pebbles and made out with the dime piece all the way to her house. When the truck stopped, she grabbed his arm. "C'mon."

He declined. "It's not the right time."

She looked stunned that he turned down the invitation. "What?"

"Nigga, you betta get in there and tear that pussy up!" Rich Red encouraged.

"C'mon, D," Pebbles begged, closing her legs and wiggling like she had to pee.

"I never seen a bitch beg for the dick." Teona laughed.

Desmond was stuck. He didn't want to cheat on his girl, but if he didn't go through with it, it might look bad.

"I'ma hit you in the a.m.," he mumbled to Rich as he climbed from the truck.

"Beat it up, my nigga!" Red laughed.

"Ay! What the fuck you think you doing?"

Desmond and Pebbles looked to the right as a tall dark-skinned nigga emerged from a white sedan.

Pebbles smacked her lips. "Adrian, what the hell you doing?"

He continued walking closer, anger in his eyes. "Nah, don't do that. What the fuck you doing? Who the fuck is this nigga?" he barked, mugging Desmond.

Pebbles stepped between them. "Chill, Adrian. Don't do this."

Desmond remained silent, watching the jealous man intently.

"Fuck that. I told yo' ass I was gon' fuck you up and whatever nigga you with. You think I'm playin' wit'chu, bitch?"

Teona climbed from the Audi truck and tried to intervene. "Adrian, get the fuck outta here, nigga! She don't want you no more."

"Shut the fuck up, bitch! I ain't talking to you!"

"Adrian, what you doin', brah?" Rich Red asked. "You clowning, my nigga."

"Oh, you want it too, nigga? I got something for all y'all!" he yelled, going for his waist.

Desmond knew he was going to try something and he was ready. By the time Adrian grabbed the butt of the pistol, Desmond had reached around Pebbles and grabbed his wrist in a tight grip. With his free hand, Desmond reached around the other side of Pebbles and punched Adrian in the mouth. The jealous lover stumbled, but Desmond was still holding his wrist, so he didn't fall. Then Desmond pulled him forward so the men were chest to chest, taking the pistol and holding it to Adrian's balls.

"What's good, my nigga? You want me to put yo' dick in the dirt, stupid-ass nigga?"

The anger and jealously disappeared from the man's eyes, replaced by fear. "I'm good, brah. I-I'm good."

"You know how fuckin' stupid you look right now, nigga? Out here actin' like a clown over some pussy that don't won't you no more. Have some muthafuckin' dignity, nigga. Let her go before yo' stupid ass be dead or in jail. And when you dead or in jail, she still gon' be fuckin'. Boss up, you soft-ass pussy whooped-ass nigga," Desmond lectured, grabbing ahold of Adrian's face and shoving him away. "Don't let me see you no more," the soldier warned.

Adrian stumbled backward, eventually catching his balance. He paused a moment to mug Desmond and Pebbles before jumping in the car and speeding away.

"My nigga is a savage!" Rich Red yelled, geeked up by Desmond's display.

Pebbles stood nearby, unable to speak, eyeing Desmond like he was a superhero.

"You good?" Desmond asked.

She nodded. "Yeah. I'm good. Um…yeah."

"You good, D-Money? You still chillin', right?" Rich Red asked.

Pebbles grabbed his hand before he could speak. "Stay with me tonight. Please. That nigga crazy."

Desmond looked into her pleading eyes and knew he couldn't tell her no. "I got you, shorty," he said before turning to Rich. "Let's try this one more time. I'ma get with you in the a.m., fool."

"In the morning," Rich nodded before hopping back in the truck.

After the women said their goodbyes, Pebbles led him into her house. She lived in a one story two-bedroom flat on Detroit's East side. The living room was plush, decorated with pink furniture, black carpet, and white walls. A 50" big screen was mounted on the wall.

"Nice spot," Desmond complimented.

"Thank you. Have a seat while I change into something more comfortable."

"Wait," Desmond stopped her. "What's up with yo' boy?"

She waved a hand. "Adrian is old news. Right now, it's all about me and you. I got some drinks in the refrigerator. Help yourself," Pebbles said before walking to a room and closing the door.

Desmond sat on the couch and contemplated leaving. Not only was he about to cheat on his girl, but Pebbles also had a crazy ex-boyfriend that might come back with more drama. The last thing he needed was more problems. He had enough already. He also didn't need to drop another body. Wright and Johansen would go crazy if he killed Adrian. What he needed to do was leave. And right when he got up the nerve to call off their night, the bedroom door opened. Pebbles walked out of the room wearing a sexy-ass negligée that made Desmond's jaw drop.

"Damn," he mumbled.

"You like it?" she asked, spinning around and giving him a full view.

Desmond's dick reacted, instantly becoming hard as an I-beam. "You killin' it, baby."

She pranced over to him, dropping to her knees and untying his shoes. "Let me help you undress."

After taking off his shoes and socks, she had him stand and helped him out of his pants, underwear, and T-shirt. When he was naked, she pushed him on the couch and got back on her knees. She grabbed his meat in her fist, looking in his eyes as she took him slowly into her mouth.

"Oh, shit!" Desmond moaned, loving the warmth and wetness of her mouth.

Pebbles continued sucking him while giving him eye contact and using her hand to stroke what she couldn't get in her mouth. After a few minutes, she took him out of her mouth and began licking and kissing the underside of his dick and sucking his balls. When she went back to sucking him again, Desmond was on the verge of busting.

"Damn, baby. I'm finna buss!" he warned.

Pebbles removed her mouth, pulling down the front of her negligée and exposing her breasts while stroking him with her hand. Desmond's seed shot out onto her chest and she used his dick and her free hand to rub his seed all over her breasts.

"This feels so good," she moaned.

Desmond watched as she seemed to get pleasure from rubbing his sperm across her breasts. When she was done, she stood and stripped out of the lingerie.

"You said back shots, right?" she asked, kneeling on the floor and tooting her ass in the air. Her cheeks spread open, revealing meaty cum-soaked bald pussy lips.

Desmond slid off the couch and shoved his dick right into her pussy. When he hit the bottom, he understood why Adrian wanted to catch a body. Pebbles had that fiya!

## Chapter 3

A knock on the door woke Lucky and Rachel from their sleep.

"Come in," Lucky called.

Laronda stepped into the room, tears falling down her face. She tried to talk, but only managed to let out a sob.

Lucky sat up, sensing something seriously wrong. "What's going on, baby girl?"

"My mama. She dead."

"Oh my God!" Rachel cried.

Lucky launched out of bed and wrapped Laronda in his arms. "What happened, baby?"

"My aunty April said the police called her and told her they found her body. Somebody killed her," she sobbed.

Lucky did the only thing he could do and held her in his arms. No words could comfort the loss of a parent. He'd already gone through it. "I got you, baby girl. I got you."

"I wanna see her body. I can't believe she gone. I just seen her," she cried, refusing to accept that her mother was gone. "Can you take me to see her?"

"Okay. We can try to see her. Let me get dressed. I need to use your car, Rachel," Lucky said, throwing on some clothes and grabbing his pistol.

"I don't think you should drive. You're hot, baby. I'll come with you."

They left the house and hopped into Rachel's car. Fifteen minutes later, they parked in front of April's house. Rachel, Lucky, and Laronda walked to the house and rang the doorbell.

"Who is it?" April called from inside.

"It's me, Aunty," Laronda called.

The door opened and a teary-eyed April wrapped Laronda in her arms. "I'm sorry, baby. She gone."

"But I just talked to her the other day. How? What happened?"

There was a kind of horror in April's eye's that made her unwilling to talk about what she seen. "Y'all come in."

Laronda walked in the house.

"Hey, April. Sorry for this shit," Lucky said, wrapping her in a warm hug. "This my girl, Rachel. What did they say happened to Sharday?"

April glanced behind her to make sure Laronda couldn't hear. "I didn't want her to hear," she said, wiping away tears. "Somebody tortured her, Lucky. I had to identify her body. They beat her and burned her," she said, struggling to hold back tears.

"Damn." Lucky shook his head. "Why would somebody do that to her?"

"They don't know. The police said they looking into it."

"Okay. Do me a favor and look out for Laronda for me. I got a lot of shit going on right now and I can't keep her with me. Plus, it's probably good for her to be around family right now."

"Okay. I got her."

"Do you know who Sharday was with before she died?"

"I heard something about her supposed to be going by her friend Anne's house. But I guess she didn't make it."

"You know where she live?"

"Yeah. Over on 23$^{rd}$ and Center. Second house from the corner."

After leaving Laronda with April, Lucky directed Rachel to Anne's house. It was still early, just a few minutes past nine in the morning, so the block was quiet.

"Stay here. I'ma be right back," he told Rachel before leaving the car. After climbing the stairs, he knocked on the door and waited.

"Who is it?" a woman called.

"Lucky. I'm looking for Anne."

The door opened and a short, slim, light-skinned woman answered. She looked Lucky from head to toe. "Do I know you?"

"Nah. I'm Lucky, Sharday's baby daddy. I heard she was coming to yo' house and I'm tryna find out what happened to her."

Recognition flashed in her eyes. "She told me about you."

"Do you know what happened?"

She nodded. "Yeah. She was by my house all day. She made a run and was supposed to come right back. My neighbor, Ken, said he seen some niggas dressed in red snatch her in a black Suburban. Then I heard this morning that she was dead."

Hearing about the Bloods in the black Suburban sent a chill through Lucky's body. *That's how them niggas found out where we live. They tortured Sharday.* "Do anybody know who them niggas was?"

"Nah. Ken said he think they was Bloods. What they wanted with Sharday? She didn't have no problems with no Bloods."

"I'm tryna figure that out. I'ma give you my number. If you hear something else, let me know."

After giving Anne his phone number, Lucky went back to the car. He opened the door and sat down heavily.

"What she say?" Rachel asked.

Lucky took a moment to answer. "I think Sharday got killed because of me."

Surprise shone on Rachel's face. "What? How? What did you have to do with it?"

"The niggas that came to my house shooting kidnapped her. The Bloods. They tortured her to find out where I lived. Damn."

Rachel connected the dots in her head. "But it don't make sense. You don't know no Bloods. Do you?"

Lucky shook his head. "Nah. That's what don't make sense. I don't know who these niggas is or why these niggas looking for me."

"I could ask around at the club. We get all kinds of niggas in there running they mouth."

"Nah. I'ma need you to stay outta this shit. Matter of fact, I'm leaving yo' house today. I might have to stay away from you until I can figure this shit out."

"What!" she yelled, looking at him like he was crazy. "You don't think you overreacting?"

He turned to give her a serious look. "This the second time somebody close to me died because of my beef. I ain't tryna get you caught up in my shit too. We gotta fall back."

Rachel sucked her teeth and drove away from the curb.

Lucky watched her, waiting for her to speak.

"Do I get any say in this, or you just gon' do you?"

"C'mon, Rachel. I'm tryna protect you."

"What if they find out who I am and come at me? You won't be able to protect me if you not with me."

Lucky thought on her words. She had a point. "So, what do you suggest we do?"

"I think you should stay with me."

"And what about my li'l niggas? They my shooters and supposed to be protecting me."

"Then I guess we need to get a bigger house."

Lucky stared at her to see if she was serious. "You for real?"

She took her attention from the road to look him in the eyes for a moment. "I'm dead serious, Lucky. I want to stay with you through all of this. I know we just met, but I'm all the way down with you." After saying her piece, she reached over and interlocked her fingers with his.

Lucky looked at their intertwined hands while giving her words some more thought. "A'ight," he said, kissing the back of her hand. "You my Queen and I'm yo' Slim."

"Except we gon' survive," she added.

"For sure. Now we gotta find another house. Somewhere don't nobody know us, so we won't have to worry about some more enemies finding us."

"I think I know somebody selling a house."

"For real?"

"Yeah. I make a lot of connections as a dancer."

Her words gave him some thoughts. "I got a package from Donny the other day. You know somebody that can help move some heroin?"

"When we get home, I'ma make some calls. I think I can help you out."

◆◆◆

When they got back to Rachel's house, she made some calls. The connections she made proved to be valid. Not only was she was able to find them a house in Brown Deer, but she also put Desmond onto her big cousin, a small time hustler looking for a good plug so he could take the next step in the dope game. Zoe was big and burly with a fluffy Rick Ross beard and tattoos above both eyebrows. He was dressed dope boy fresh in a T-shirt, jeans, and Air Max 95's.

"What's good, brah? These my Detroit niggas Quincy, Ryder, and T.A.," Lucky introduced.

"What's good with you niggas?" Zoe nodded, giving daps, pounds, and handshakes before turning back to Lucky. "Li'l cuz told me you got that diesel. What you tryna do?"

"Shit, we tryna make power moves, my nigga. Got a big table. You ready to eat?"

Zoe smiled and rubbed a hand over his belly. "You see I ain't no li'l nigga, right? I love to eat."

"Good. I got dog food, and a lot of it. I'm tryna build a team and make major moves, but I need help. My niggas ready to do whatever necessary to take us to the top. You don't gotta worry 'bout no fuck shit. We all a hunnit and my niggas 'bout that action. What we don't got is clientele. Get down with us and help us build up the lines. Like I said, we got a big table. You ready to eat like a boss?"

Zoe looked to his cousin. Rachel nodded.

"I'm ready, my nigga. This what a nigga been waiting for. I gotta couple heads on line and I know some niggas that's gon' cop from us if the work is good and the price is right."

Lucky smiled and extended a hand to Zoe. "Let's eat then, my nigga."

◆◆◆

Zoe left Rachel's house with an extra pep in his step and a smile on his face as big as the Kool Aid man's. He bounced to the gray old school box Chevy parked at the curb, envisioning how the trap would look with a new candy paint job and 26-inch chrome wheels. After hopping behind the wheel, he found the perfect song to fit his mood and drove away playing "Glow Up" by Meek Mill. His struggling days would soon be over.

Ten minutes later, he parked in front of a white and gray duplex on the west side. He climbed from the car and bopped towards the house with the same glee he had after leaving Rachel's. He knocked on the door and waited.

"Who is it?" a woman called.

"Zoe!"

The door opened and he was staring in the face of Quitta. She was his nigga Meechy's girl. Her looks were average and she had the body of a dump truck, but his nigga fucked with her. Plus, she was cool. "What up, nigga? Where the weed at?" she asked, stepping aside to let him in.

Zoe pulled three grams of sticky from his pocket as he stepped into the house. "Roll up. Where Meechy?"

"In the back somewhere," Quitta said, snatching the weed.

Zoe walked to the back of the house and found his nigga in the kitchen cooking eggs. Meechy's looks favored Zoe. Both men were big and dark-skinned with face tats. What separated them was Meechy's shoulder-length dreads.

"Zoe, what it do, boy?"

"My nigga, you ain't gon' believe what just happened to me. My li'l cousin just put me onto a move. Niggas having real money."

"Oh, hell yeah!" Meechy said, getting excited. "Who them niggas is?"

"Some Detroit niggas. Nigga just showed me at least a zip of that food."

Meechy dropped the fork he was using to scramble the eggs, ready to make the move. "Where they at? You wanna hit 'em right now?"

"Nah. It's too many of em and I think them niggas really get down. Plus, this Rachel, nigga. If we don't make the right move, she could bring down the ship."

Meechy picked the fork back up and began tending to the eggs again. "So how you wanna play it?"

"I think these niggas really holding and they trust me. They want me to get money wit' em. I'ma slow stroke this bitch. Find out where the stash at, then we gon' take it all!"

Meechy didn't seem impressed. "How long you think that's gon' take? I'm ready to eat now?"

"I don't know. Ain't no time limit. But I'ma put you on to these niggas too. They got work and no clientele. We can use these niggas to eat and when the time is right, make our move."

Meechy nodded. "Damn, li'l nigga. I see you studied my moves and now you tryna play chess, huh?"

Zoe laughed. "That's what we do. Study niggas' moves so you can make yo' own. I got a good feeling about this next lick. If we take our time and do it right, we gon' have that oil money!"

◆◆◆

Flacco pulled into the garage behind his trap with dread filling his being. The L he took in Wisconsin haunted him. He'd lost several soldiers in battles. That was a part of war. But never had he lost a battle so lopsided and had to run away. He knew retreating was the right thing to do. A general couldn't die on the battlefield. They were needed alive because of their knowledge of war. Not everyone was capable of leading. And even though he knew the words to be true, he still felt like a coward for not dying with his brothers. He moped from the garage and into the house. Jordan and a few more Bloods were waiting in the living room.

"What's good, Blood?" Jordan nodded, greeting his OG with a handshake and hug. They had already discussed what happened in Milwaukee and Jordan knew the feelings of their leader.

"You know what it is," Flacco said, looking around the house at the seven men gathered there. It was a mix of young'uns and OGs, all of them eager to hear words from the lips of the East Saint Louis Nightmare. "I know y'all heard what happened in Milwaukee. I thought it was sweet and didn't do my homework. Our brothers' blood is on my hands because of it. I failed my niggas. They trusted me with they lives and I led them to the grave. A part of me wishes

I woulda died with em, but I know I can't do that because I gotta avenge my niggas. That's why I need y'all. I wanna take y'all to Milwaukee and tear that bitch up. Make no mistake about it, these niggas get down and it ain't sweet. But they got something that we don't got:    devotion to our dead niggas. And because of our devotion, we gon' bury all them niggas and everythang they stand for. If y'all wit' me, holla Piru love!"

The men lifted their voices with the unison of a choir. "PIRU LOVE!"

Seeing the devotion in his brothers' eyes and hearing it in their shout filled Flacco with an indescribable joy, making the savage smile. "My niggas!" He grinned. "Jordan, did you do what I asked you to do? We might be in town for a while and we gon' need some spending money."

"You know I got you, big homie." Jordan nodded. "We hittin' Cardale. It's about time that nigga contributed to the cause."

Flacco looked pleased by the choice. "A'ight. Pick two niggas and let's move."

Jordan looked over the crowd of eager faces and settled on two youngsters. "B-dog and Chello. Let's get it."

The young thugs shook hands and celebrated like being chosen was a great honor as they followed their OGs out of the house.

"Y'all got heat?" Flacco asked as the men piled into the Suburban.

Both young'uns pulled semiautomatic pistols.

"Neva leave home without it." B-dog grinned.

"Good shit, li'l niggas," Jordan applauded before turning to Flacco. "We hittin' his baby mama spot. We gon' use her to bring him to us."

Flacco nodded. "Let's get this bitch."

Cardale's baby mama lived in a working-class neighborhood on East Saint Louis's south side. Flacco parked the Suburban a few houses away and the killers cased the scene. It was almost noon and the block was empty, since most people were at work or school.

"A'ight. Check it out," Flacco spoke up. "B-dog, you up. You look young enough not to draw too much attention. Get out and get her to open the door. When you in, lay her down and wave us in. You ready?"

The young shooter looked eager to put in work and prove his worth. "I was born ready, so I won't have to get ready."

Flacco smirked. "Go put in work."

The young Blood hopped out of the SUV and walked coolly towards Cardale's baby mama's house. After climbing the steps, he rang the doorbell and waited.

"Who is it?" a female called.

"Darien. I'm looking for Cardale."

"He ain't here right now. Come back later," she called, not opening the door.

The youngster thought fast. "Well, can you just take this money? He said he was gon' meet me here. I can't wait. I got other shit to do."

The locks clicked and a fine chocolate woman poked her head out. "Who you say you was?"

"I'm Darien. I owe him some money."

She looked him over as if judging whether or not he was a threat. "Okay. Give it to me."

B-dog looked around like he was leery. "You want me to give it to you out here?"

The woman looked around like someone might be watching. "Okay. Come in," she said, opening the door.

B-dog walked past her, pulling the pistol from his waist as he stepped into the house. "Who all in here?" he asked, pointing the pistol in her face.

"Nobody! Just me and my babies. Please, I don't know nothing about what Cardale do. Ain't no money here," she pleaded, on the verge of crying.

"Shut up. Sit down on the couch."

After the woman complied, B-Dog looked outside and waved to his niggas.

"Stay out here. Watch everything and call us if you see something that don't look right," Flacco told Chello before he and Jordan hopped out the suburban.

"Good shit, li'l nigga." Jordan nodded to B-Dog as he and Flacco walked in the house.

"How many people in here?" Flacco asked the woman as he closed the door.

"Just me and my babies. Please, y'all. I don't got nothing to do with what Cardale into."

"You good, shorty. We gon' let you go. This ain't got nothing to do with you. Just call Cardale and tell him something that will make him come over."

The woman began crying crocodile tears. "Please, don't put me in this. I don't want nothing to do with this."

Flacco looked to B-Dog. "Go grab one of them shorties."

The woman jumped up from the couch. "Don't touch my baby!"

Flacco punched her in the mouth, splitting her lips and knocking her back on the couch. "Don't move from this mu'fuckin' couch, bitch!"

"Please! Don't do this," the woman cried.

B-Dog came back a few moments later carrying a three-year-old boy. Flacco pulled a pistol from his waist and put it in the kid's face then turned to the woman. "Call yo' baby daddy and get him here or I'ma blow yo' baby's shit back."

"Okay. Okay," the woman complied, the fear of her worst nightmare in her eyes. "I need my phone. It's in my room."

"Let's go," Flacco nodded.

The woman led the way to the room and grabbed her phone from the bed.

"Leave it on speaker," Flacco ordered.

Her hands shook as called Cardale.

"What up, baby girl?"

"Baby, I need you to come over right now! Something wrong with Lil Cardale. I can't stop him from choking and his face turning blue. You gotta hurry up. Please!"

"Shit! A'ight. I'm on my way. Call an ambulance!"

"I did. I need you here. Hurry up!"

"Okay. I'm getting in the car now. I'ma be there in like five minutes."

"Hurry up!" the woman cried one last time before hanging up. "You did good." Flacco nodded. "Get the other shorty and let's go back in the living room."

The woman grabbed another toddler from a second bedroom and took him to the living room, huddling up on the couch with her kids. Flacco and Jordan watched the windows, waiting for Cardale to arrive. It took less than five minutes for the red Porsche truck to park outside. Cardale rushed from the truck in a panic, never guessing that the entire situation was a set up.

"Shawna! Where y'all—" Cardale called as he ran into the house. When he saw the Bloods in his living room holding pistols, he lost his words and his heart sank to the bottom of his stomach.

"What's good, Cardale?" Flacco nodded.

"C'mon, Flacco. What is this about, my nigga? Why you got my girl like this?"

"Collection call. I need what you got in the safe."

"Okay, my nigga. You got that. Let my family go."

"When I get the paper, yo' people good."

Cardale didn't believe him. "C'mon, Flacco. I know how you get down, brah. Let 'em go now. She ain't gon' call the police and I'ma get you a hunnit G's."

Flacco turned the pistol towards Cardale's family. "I'm done talking. Let's go or I'ma start fucking shit up!"

"Okay, okay! I ain't got no money here. You gotta come with me."

Flacco turned to Jordan. "You stay here with the family. I'm taking B-Dog. I'ma hit you when I get the bag."

"I got you," Jordan nodded.

Flacco and B-Dog hopped in the Porsche truck with Cardale. He took the Bloods to his stash house. Inside was $134,000 and two kilos of cocaine. After the Bloods packed up the money and drugs, Flacco turned to Cardale.

"I need the keys to that truck."

Cardale handed them over.

"You know this ain't personal, right?"

Cardale nodded. "I know."

"Good," Flacco said before turning to B-Dog. "Get yo' gun dirty."

The youngster smiled as he lifted his pistol to Cardale's head. Pop!

While they were leaving the house, Flacco texted Jordan:

*I got it. Take care of them and hit the trap.*

## Chapter 4
### ONE MONTH LATER

Lasonya stirred, the smell of bacon arousing her from sleep. She sat up, looking around the room for Desmond. He wasn't in bed. It was normal for him to get up early and go to sleep late. She stretched and yawned, preparing to get up, when she began feeling lightheaded and queasy. She closed her eyes, hoping the sick feeling would pass. It didn't. Suddenly she got the urge to vomit. She jumped up from the bed, holding her mouth as she raced for the bathroom. She barely made it to the toilet before the contents of her stomach began spilling. She retched and heaved loudly, hurling up last night's dinner.

"Mommy, you okay?" Quaysha appeared, concerned for her mom's health.

"I'm okay, baby. I'm-uh-I'm okay," she managed between heaves.

Quaysha took off running from the bathroom screaming. "Desmond! Granny! Mommy sick and throwing up!"

Desmond ran to the bathroom and found Lasonya kneeling over the toilet. "You good, baby?"

"No," she mumbled before spitting.

"What happened? Did you eat something bad?"

"I don't know. Leave me alone. Get out. You can't be seeing me like this."

Desmond laughed, grabbing a towel and running it under cold water. "You should appreciate this moment. I'm watching you blow chunks and I'm still in love. This is real intimacy and unconditional love," he said, wiping her forehead and neck with the towel.

"Is she okay?" Marcy asked, appearing in the doorway.

"Yeah. I think she ate something bad yesterday," Desmond said, continuing to be the good boyfriend and wiping Lasonya with the cool towel.

"It ain't got nothing to do with what she ate," Marcy said knowingly. "She pregnant."

Desmond's eyes grew wide as two silver dollars. He turned to Lasonya who was laying her head on the toilet. "You pregnant?"

"I don't know. Maybe. I need a test."

Desmond jumped up and gave Marcy the towel, the excitement of being a first-time father lighting his eyes. "I'ma go buy a test."

After he left, Marcy rinsed the towel in cold water and began wiping Lasonya's neck. "How late is your period?"

"Almost two weeks."

"Why didn't you tell him?"

Lasonya didn't answer right away. "I don't know. I wanted to be sure."

"You sure now?"

"I don't know."

Marcy smiled proudly. "Y'all gon' have some pretty babies. Get in the shower. It'll make you feel better. I'ma finish making breakfast. Let me know if you need anything."

When her mother left the bathroom, Lasonya undressed and climbed in the shower. She thought of what it would be like to raise a family with Desmond. He would work hard to be a good father and provide. He was a good man and the love he had for her was real. He'd shown it by the sacrifices he made. And now she would give him his first child. Times appeared to be good. Then the doubt crept in. What if it was really Lucky's baby? What if Lucky told Desmond what they did and he left her? She shook her head, regretting the thirsty move she had pulled. It was unnecessary. Desmond found a way to get free and get back to her. Now everything was in jeopardy.

Damn. She needed to find a way to keep the secret from getting out. The only way she knew was to continue to drive a wedge between the brothers or hope something bad happened to Lucky. He was wanted by the police and had enemies all over Milwaukee. Her baby daddy was one of them. Just then she had a thought. If she could somehow get in contact with Wacco…

◆◆◆

*I'm about to be a daddy!*

It was all Desmond could think as he drove home from the pharmacy. In the passenger seat was a bag full of pregnancy tests. The woman at the store said they sometimes gave false positives and false negatives so he should buy more than one brand. He ended up buying five and was speeding back home so he could hurry up and get the results. He pulled the Chevy Tahoe into the driveway, grabbing the bag of tests and bolting into the house. Lasonya was getting out of the shower when he walked in the bathroom.

"Here. I got five different kinds," he said, shoving the bag in her face.

She looked at him quizzically. "Why you get five?"

"The lady said they sometimes give false positives and negatives. I wanted to be sure."

She laughed. "Okay. Get out so I can take the test."

He looked at her like she had just asked him to take a hit off a crack pipe. "Nah. I wanna take part in every step from here on out," he said, grabbing her shoulders and sitting her on the toilet.

"But I don't gotta pee yet."

"That's cool," Desmond said, opening one of the boxes. "We got time."

Lasonya shook her head. "Gimme the damn test."

Desmond sat on the side of the tub and opened all the boxes while waiting for her to pee. When he heard tinkling in the toilet, he jumped into action.

"Don't use all the pee on that one!" he said, handing her another test.

"We can just wait until I pee again."

"No, we can't," Desmond said, grabbing the remaining four tests in his fists and shoving them between her legs."

"Desmond, what the hell!" Lasonya yelled. "You making me get pee everywhere!"

He continued holding the tests under her stream of piss. "So what? I got it all over my hands and I ain't tripping. We need to know for sure."

After Lasonya finished peeing, he dropped the tests in the tub and washed his hands in the sink.

"You nasty, baby," Lasonya laughed.

"So? You still love me, right?"

"I won't ever stop," Lasonya smiled.

"How long it take?" he asked, studying the tests like they were foreign objects.

"A couple minutes. Have some patience."

Desmond's phone rang, giving him a distraction from the pregnancy tests. It was Donny. "What's up, boss man?"

"D-Money, I need to see you. Can you make it to the cleaning service?"

Desmond noticed Donny didn't have a friendly tone to his voice. "Yeah. You got it. What's going on?"

"I would rather not say on these phones. How soon can you get to me?"

"Um, gimme an hour. I'm wrapping something up."

"Forty-five minutes," Donny said and then hung up.

"What happened?" Lasonya asked, reading the stress on Desmond's face.

"Donny wanna see me. He sounded funny."

Lasonya looked worried. "Do you think he knows about you? What if Lucky said something?"

Desmond thought for a moment. "Lucky wouldn't do that," he said, pausing again. "I don't think."

The lovers shared a long look. Desmond didn't want her to worry, so he looked at the tests in the tub. "Look. Three of them say positive!"

"Congratulations, Daddy." Lasonya smiled.

Desmond leaned forward to kiss her lips. "Thank you, Mommy. I gotta go take care of something. I'ma be back."

Lasonya grabbed his hand, stopping him from leaving. He looked down and seen worry on her face.

"Be careful. And make sure you come back."

"I'm invincible, baby." He grinned before leaving the house.

During the drive to Detroit, Desmond thought about what Donny could want. Whatever it was, it sounded serious. It made Desmond wonder if Lucky had told Donny he was working with the Feds. But would Lucky really do something that could get him killed? He wasn't sure. But if it seemed like something was about to go wrong, he was going to kill Donny and everybody in his path. He had to make it back to his family. Back to his unborn. And after the family was safely tucked away, he was going to kill Lucky.

His thoughts of murder were interrupted by a phone call. It was Pebbles. He put the call on the Bluetooth.

"What's good, baby?"

"You, D. What's up? Why you acting all fly?"

"C'mon, shorty. You know it ain't like that. You know I'm married to securing that bag."

"So that means I don't got no priority? Where do I fit in at?"

Desmond knew this would happen. She would want more time with him, and time was one thing he didn't have. He didn't want to juggle two relationships, especially now that he was about to be a father. "Listen, Pebbles, I fuck with you, for real, but I ain't tryna do nothing serious. Let's just get together when we can."

There was a brief pause on Pebbles's end. "Yeah. I'm on that same shit. I'm married to my check too."

Desmond could tell his words cut her and he felt bad about it. "Look, I didn't mean it like that. Tell you what, how about the next time I'm in the D, I come fuck with you."

"Yeah. That's cool. But look, I gotta go. Hit me when you wanna kick it."

She ended the call before he could say another word. Desmond just shook his head.

When he got to the cleaning service, Royce let him in.

"What's good, Royce?" Desmond nodded, studying the bodyguard to see if his greeting would change.

"You got it, D." He nodded, looking serious. "Boss in the office."

Desmond headed for the back office, noticing a few extra men that he'd never seen before in the building. They all gave him questioning looks. The gun on Desmond's hip began to burn, itching to be used. When he got to the office, Donny was talking to a clean-cut white man.

"Come in, D-Money. I was just wrapping this up," Donny said. "This is my business consultant, Marty. Marty, this is the key to my success and secret weapon," Donny said, smiling at Desmond like a proud father.

"Key to success?" Marty laughed. "Shit, I might need to steal you away."

Desmond gave a practiced laugh. "Sorry, man. I don't bite the hand that feeds."

Donny's smile got bigger. "Okay, Marty. Send me those contracts and the numbers for the Wilson project. I'll have my people take a look at them and get back to you as soon as I can."

After shaking hands with Donny, the white man left. Donny's friendly demeanor walked right out of the building with him. "Have a seat, D," Donny said, nodding towards the chair and pulling the gold pocket watch from his pocket.

Desmond sat down on the edge of the chair, ready to pull the gun and kick ass if necessary. "What's going on, boss?"

"We got problems, D," he said, flipping the watch open and looking Desmond in his eyes.

The gun burned hotter on Desmond's hip. "What is it?"

Donny took his time answering. "It's a rat in my crew."

Desmond remained stoic but on the inside, he panicked. "Who is it?"

"I'm not sure. But I got my people looking into it. I got people all over this city and state. Even in the federal building. That's how I've stayed on top for so long. Somebody is leaking information to the Feds."

*Shit! Lucky gave me up!* Desmond thought. "Are you sure? It seems like you run a tight ship."

"That's what my man in the federal building told me. He's working on getting the identity of the rat. The reason I'm telling you is because I might need you to take care of it for me. Somebody with your skill could take care of it without anybody knowing. I haven't told nobody this, so keep it to yourself."

Desmond nodded. "You got it."

Donny studied Desmond for a moment before closing the watch and setting it on his desk. Then he reached a hand under the desk. "You not working with the Feds, are you?"

The question was serious, and Desmond knew that Donny was probably clutching a pistol. He didn't trust himself to answer, so he began laughing.

Donny looked surprised by the reaction. "What's funny?"

Desmond laughed harder. "You. Am I the Feds? Fuck kinda question is that? As many bodies as I dropped?"

Donny began laughing with him and brought his hand from under the desk, grabbing the watch again. "My bad, D. I had to ask."

"I guess I understand. Having a rat around you is some serious shit."

"Yeah. It is. I'm changing all of our phones to burner phones just in case the ones we got are tapped. And no more saying names or discussing business on the phone."

"You got it, boss."

"Now that we got that out of the way, I need a favor."

Happy to move on from talks of rats and Feds, Desmond agreed. "You got it. Just say what you need."

"That bitch made-ass fag that left my office. I need you to kill him."

Desmond looked surprised. "I thought he was your business consultant?"

"He was. But Marty is trying to get over on me. Sonofabitch is trying to hit me for at least a half mil. I called him to the cleaning company so you could see what he looks like. This meeting was planned."

Desmond nodded. "Okay. I'll need to study him to see how he moves."

"Not necessary. I need this done as soon as possible and tonight he's going to be at a black-tie benefit downtown. My friend, Marty, has a taste for Oriental women and I've arranged entertainment after the party. Make sure they die," he said, snapping the watch closed for emphasis and setting it on the desk. Then his hand disappeared again.

"You got it, boss." Desmond nodded at the desk like he could see through it.

"It's a nice watch, ain't it?" Donny asked, lifting the watch so Desmond could get a good look.

"I guess," Desmond answered, not really caring about it.

"This has been in my family for four generations. Great granddaddy passed it down to my granddaddy. Granddaddy passed it down to my daddy. And my daddy passed it down to me when he died. This is the most treasured thing I own. If I could, when I die, I would take it to the afterlife with me. But since I can't, I'ma leave or with my son and hope he passes it down. One day it might be worth a lot of money," Donny explained, staring at the watch like it was the crown jewel.

"I hear you, boss. But if that's all, I'ma get out of here and get on that business."

Donny smiled. "That's my kinda nigga. Eager to put in that work. That's all, D-Money. Take care of that for me and I'ma owe you forever."

♦♦♦

Desmond left the cleaning service, breathing a sigh of relief as he hopped in the Tahoe. That was a close call. Donny knew the Feds had infiltrated his crew. And had Desmond not done a good acting job, he would probably be dead. The shit was too real. He was about to be a father. He wanted to be around to see his baby born. After pulling out of the lot, he called Agent Wright.

"Hey, Desmond. What's going on?"

"Donny knows you're investigating him."

There was a pause on the line. "What? That's impossible. This mission isn't being shared within the department. The only people that know are on the team."

"Well, somebody on the team is playing both sides. I just left the cleaning service and Donny questioned me about being a Fed and says he has someone in your building. What the fuck is going on, Wright? You trying to get me killed?"

"No, no, Desmond! Hell no. Um... Let me make some calls and see if I can figure out what the hell is going on and who could be the leak."

"Wait! You can't just start calling people and telling them you know. You gotta be smart about it. My life is on the line, man."

"I know. I'm not going to broadcast it. I'm going to call Agent Johansen and we'll come up with a plan. Don't worry, Desmond. We're not going to let anything happen to you. I'll get to the bottom of this. I promise you."

◆◆◆

Marty wasn't a fan of fundraisers. The plates cost too much and there were too many fake people giving fake smiles and fake handshakes. Most of the people in the upper echelon were really criminals. They had broken all the laws in the name of Benjamin Franklin. If you dug deep enough into any of their backgrounds, you would find enough dirt to fill up a six-foot-deep grave. When the event was over, Marty gave out more fake handshakes and smiles before retiring to the back seat of the rented sedan.

"Where we going, Mr. Jacobs?" the driver asked.

"The Super 8 hotel."

The driver smiled in the rearview mirror. "Sounds like somebody is about to have a good night!"

Marty laughed. "Call it a night cap."

Twenty minutes later, the black sedan pulled into the parking lot of the economy hotel. Marty handed the driver a fifty-dollar bill.

"Come back in two hours."

"You got it, boss man. Have fun."

Marty left the car and walked to room #8. After rapping on the door, he waited. Moments later it opened and he was looking at his favorite Korean entertainer. Mai-Tai was petite, only 5'1" and 110 pounds. She wore light makeup on her pretty face and was dressed in a pair of boy shorts with suspenders, a tie, and a pair of heels.

"Damn, sweetie. You are so fuckin' hot!" Marty grinned, stepping into the room and pawing at her body. He kicked the door closed.

Mai-Tai allowed him to grope and feel her body. "Do you want me to fix you a drink?"

"Mmmhhh. Yeah. Please," he mumbled, kissing and licking her neck.

"Okay. Sit on the bed. Get comfortable."

Marty reluctantly let her go and began to undress. He stripped down to his underwear and left on the tie. "We're matching," he joked.

"We are." Mai-Tai smiled, sticking her finger in the glass of vodka and sucking it in her mouth.

Marty looked like he wanted to bust. "Oh, hell yeah! Bring your sexy ass over here!"

Mai-Tai handed him the drink and climbed in bed, kissing his body and rubbing the bulge in his underwear. "What do you want me to do?"

"Whatever you want, baby!" Marty said before slamming the drink.

"Okay. Stay right there," she said and then she climbed out of bed. After locking the door, she went in her purse and pulled out several silk strips of fabric.

"Ohh! I think I like where this is going!" Marty grinned, fidgeting around like a giddy kid about to receive a gift.

Mai-tai tied his hands and feet to the bed posts and used a silk strip to blindfold him. "Would you like some music?"

"Yeah. Sure," he said impatiently, ready for the sex.

Mai-Tai plugged her phone into the radio beside the bed and turned up R. Kelly's "Greatest Sex". She shimmied Marty's underwear off, spread his legs, and sucked her index finger before pushing it up his ass.

"Oh yeah!" Marty squirmed. "That feels so fucking good, baby!"

She continued working the digit in his anus while teasing the head of his dick with her tongue. Marty went wild, moaning and groaning and bucking his hips.

"C'mon and suck my cock. Stop teasing me."

Mai-Tai obliged and went down on him. Marty hollered like a bitch, calling out the woman's name as she delivered pleasure. When he felt his load building, he stopped her.

"I'm about to blow. Grab my tie. Choke me!"

Mai-Tai's hand replaced her mouth and she began whacking his meat while grabbing his tie with her free hand and choking him. Marty gagged as the semen began shooting out of his dick.

◆◆◆

Desmond walked quickly towards the motel office, making sure to stay in the shadows. He was dressed in black, his hands covered by leather gloves. A black surgical mask covering his face, pistol in hand. It was late and there were no guests present. He snatched the door open and stormed into the office, scaring the shit out of the clerk. He had already done his homework, having watched the motel for the last hour, and he knew the clerk was alone. As long as he didn't try to play hero, Desmond was going to let him live.

"Gimme the key to room eight!" Desmond demanded.

The clerk was so scared he couldn't talk, so he pointed to the board behind the desk with the room keys.

"Grab number eight," Desmond told him, walking behind the desk.

The clerk shook as he grabbed the key and handed it over.

"Now turn around and put your hands behind your back."

"Please don't kill me," the young man whined, on the verge of tears.

"Turn around," Desmond told him forcefully.

The man spun around and Desmond pulled out zip ties, tying his hands and feet before pushing him to the floor. "Don't move," Desmond warned before leaving the office and heading for the rooms. When he got to eight, he stopped outside the window. There was a slit in the blind and he could see into the room a little. Marty was blindfolded and tied to the bed while the Asian woman gave him head and fingered him in the ass. The music was playing loudly, but Marty's moans could be heard over R. Kelly. Desmond moved to the door and stuck the key into the lock carefully, trying not to make any noise. He twisted slowly, unlocking the door and easing it open. The Asian woman had moved and was now jacking Marty off and choking him, oblivious to the big man dressed in black that crept into the room. Seeing a man get choked while busting a nut gave Desmond pause, and that's when Mai-Tai looked up and saw Desmond in the room.

"Ahhhh!" she screamed.

Desmond lifted the gun and fired two shots, one in each of their heads before disappearing into the darkness.

## Chapter 5

Quincy pulled to the curb outside April's house, looking around as he parked the Buick Envoy. Milwaukee was way more dangerous than he expected and he had to be careful. All he knew about the northernmost state across Lake Michigan was they had a good basketball team and the NBA's reigning MVP, The Greek Freak. Just a few months later, his image of the city had changed drastically. Milwaukee was full of niggas with short tempers and long clips. When he first signed up to establish Donny's business in the Mil, he expected it to be easy. Donny was a powerful man and Quincy expected that power to extend across the lake and be respected by niggas in Milwaukee. It wasn't. The niggas in Milwaukee didn't get that memo and every time he turned around, it seemed like they were in another gun battle.

After determining the coast was clear, he climbed from the CUV and walked up on the porch of the gray and white house, ringing the doorbell.

"Who is it?" a woman called from inside.

"Quincy. Is Laronda here?"

The door opened and a chubby dark-skinned woman peered down her nose at him. "Who is you?"

"I'm Quincy. I'm looking for Laronda."

"What do you want with my niece? You look too old to be talking to her. You know she's only fifteen?" April questioned.

"Yeah. I know her daddy, Lucky. I just wanted to make sure she was good," he explained.

"Who is that looking for me, Aunty April?"

The woman stepped aside and turned to look at Laronda. "Do you know him?"

Laronda looked surprised to see Quincy. "Yeah. He's Lucky's friend." Then her eyes grew wide with fear. "Is my daddy okay?"

"Yeah. Lucky good."

Laronda looked relieved. "Oh." Then she frowned. "What you want then?"

"I wanted to see if you needed anything. Make sure you was good."

April looked back and forth from Quincy to Laronda, caught up in the show.

Laronda continued to wear a frown. "Yeah. I'm good."

An awkward moment passed between them. Quincy was waiting for the aunty to walk away while Laronda and her aunt waited to see what else he wanted.

"Can you come outside so I can holla at you?" he asked, ending the awkwardness.

Laronda stepped past her aunty and onto the front porch, closing the door behind them. Then she looked at Quincy suspiciously. "What you doing over here? Lucky know you came over?"

Quincy shook his head. "Nah. I came on my own. I told you I wanted to see how you was doing. I just wanted to make sure you was good."

"Why?" she asked, looking at him from head to toe.

Quincy recalled the words he'd practiced during the drive to see her. "I know we never really talked that much, but I dig you, Laronda. Not because you got a bad body or yo' looks. I like who you are and when yo' moms passed, I got to see a different side of you. I know what it feels like to lose a parent 'cause my daddy got killed when I was growing up. That shit was devastating. I didn't know how I was gon' make it without him. But I did. And you can too."

Tears welled up in Laronda's eyes as memories of Sharday played in her head. "It's hard, man," she cried, wiping the tears that spilled down her cheeks.

"I know," Quincy said, wanting to reach out and hug her. "But you stronger than you think you is. And going through this only gon' make you stronger. That's how life works. What don't kill you makes you stronger."

Laronda was silent, wiping the tears as they spilled.

"You hungry? We can grab something to eat if you want," he offered.

She nodded.

Quincy led her to the Buick and opened the passenger door. The unexpected display of chivalry caught Laronda by surprise.

"What you wanna eat?" he asked when he hopped in the driver's seat.

"I don't know," Laronda said, taking a moment to think. "What about gyros?"

Quincy smiled. "Hell yeah. I ain't had no lamb meat in a minute. I don't really know my way around so you gotta give me directions."

"I got you. They got a spot over on Hampton."

Quincy turned on the radio and Webbie's "I Miss You" filled the ride.

"I like this song." Laronda smiled, bopping her head.

"Webbie my nigga. I hated when him and Boosie got into it. I'm one of them loyal niggas that stay down for my niggas. As long as my nigga don't betray me, I fuck wit' 'em the long way."

Laronda nodded. "Lucky be telling me about loyalty. He put it before everything."

"That's how it's supposed to be. That's why I like yo' pops. I think he a real nigga."

Laronda smiled again. "Me too."

"And that was the first time I ever heard you call him Daddy on the porch when you thought something happened to him. What's up with that? I couldn't call my daddy by his name."

Laronda thought on how to answer his question. She remembered Lucky telling her not to tell them about Desmond being his brother and figured it would be better if she kept their personal life a secret. "I really don't even feel like getting into that right now. You got some loud?"

After sparking a Backwood and grabbing a bite to eat, they drove back to April's house and sat in the car talking.

"You kinda cool, Quincy. I never liked you before, but you showed me a different side of you today. Thanks for the gyros."

"You know that wasn't no problem. And the reason you didn't like me was because you didn't know me. But once you get to know me, you ain't gon' have no choice but to love me."

Laronda smiled, liking the cockiness. "I hear you. We'll see. But you don't think it's something wrong with a fifteen-year-old loving you?"

Quincy looked her in her eyes, showing her how serious he was. "I'm only nineteen, but I think you older than a lot of females my age. When you love somebody for real, don't nothing matter. Not age, not color, not distance. Nothing. I ain't sayin' I love you, but I got love for you and I wanna spend time getting to know you. Can we do that?"

Laronda nodded, intoxicated by his words. "Yeah. I wanna get to know you too. I think you real cool."

Quincy's phone ringing broke up their conversation. "Hold on. Let me get this. What up, Zoe?"

"I got some action on line, brah. Where you at?"

Quincy looked at Laronda. "I'm kinda busy right now."

"My nigga, quit bullshitting. This some real money. We need to get at Lucky."

Quincy knew his time with Laronda was over. "A'ight. I'm on my way to the trap," he said before hanging up. "I gotta go get this money, baby girl."

Laronda looked disappointed, but she understood. "I know how it is. Gotta check that bag. Thanks for checking on me," she said, reaching for the door handle.

Quincy grabbed her arm. "Wait. Lemme get yo' number and give you mine. And if you need anything, I don't care what it is, call me."

◆◆◆

Lucky sat down heavily upon the couch, letting out a long breath like he was exhausted. The last few weeks were taking a toll on him. Trying to start a drug empire from the ground up was hard work with long hours. Staying on the grind demanded attention twenty-four hours a day, seven days a week. Some elements of the game involved the same principles as running a business. Advertising and marketing. Dividing the profits from the re-up.

Taking care of the workers and making sure the product was good. He just needed to rest for a moment. He closed his eyes.

Sleep came fast until he was awakened by the phone vibrating in his pocket. He pulled it out and checked the face. It was Ryder.

"What's good, brah?"

"You told me to call you when we started getting low. 'Bout time to make that call."

"A'ight. I'ma get with y'all later." After hanging up, Lucky called Donny.

"What's good, my brotha?"

"You got it. I need to holla at D-Money again."

"Okay. But I'm in the process of getting everybody burner phones. We not using names no more."

"What's going on? You good?"

"Nah. I gotta exterminate a rat. But don't worry 'bout that. I'll handle it. Look, I'm outta town right now but I'ma make a few calls and try to get that taken care of. What you want? Same way?"

"Yeah. We doing okay, but we ain't ready for nothing heavy."

"Say no more, my dude. I'ma get on that."

After ending the call, Lucky thought about his brother. Donny said he was about to exterminate a rat. Did that mean he found out Desmond was working with the Feds? Lucky wanted to call him, but they hadn't spoken in a month. A part of him missed Desmond. They had been close all their lives. And while he was in prison, Desmond made sure he was straight. Visits, pictures, money wires, everything a nigga doing time needed to be content. For the support, he would always love his little brother. But he couldn't respect him being a snitch. It hurt Lucky to cut his brother off, but he felt he had to. He couldn't accept telling. No way. No how. But he hoped his brother was okay.

"You look tired."

Lucky looked up and saw Rachel coming from the bedroom wearing a bathrobe. "I am. This hustling shit ain't as easy as it looks."

Rachel sat down next to him. "That's because you trying to do everything. What about yo' li'l niggas from Detroit? Why don't you give them bigger roles?"

"I don't think they ready yet. They was flunkies back in the D. Giving them slots could make my job even harder. I already have to keep checkin' on 'em. If something goes wrong, it's on me."

Rachel shrugged. "Well then, I guess you're going to keep busting your ass trying to do everything."

"Yeah. That's how it's looking."

She looked towards the kitchen. "Where are your little shadows, anyway?"

"I left them at the old house. They like staying in the trap. That's what they used to."

Rachel wrapped her arms around his neck and leaned in for a kiss. "So, you telling me that it's just me and you in our big-ass new house?"

Lucky's hands found their way inside her robe, fondling her breasts. "Yeah. What you wanna do about it?"

Rachel straddled his lap, opening her robe. "I gotta get ready for work in a li'l while, but I got time to take care of my man," she said, kissing him on the neck while going for the button on his pants.

Their petting became hot and heavy as clothes began to fly. Lucky had just stood up to take off his pants when his phone rang.

"Damn," he cursed.

"Don't answer it," Rachel said, wanting him.

"I got to," Lucky told her, pulling the phone from his pocket. It was Quincy. "What up, Q?"

"I need you to come to the spot. Got some niggas that you might wanna meet."

Lucky watched as Rachel got on her knees, pulled down his pants and began giving him head. "Mmmhhh. Damn, baby," he moaned. "Who is them niggas?" he asked, wanting to get off the phone and fuck his girl.

"They CSG."

When Lucky heard the clique's name, it was like someone had taken all the lust from his body. "CSG?" he questioned, making sure he heard him right.

"Yeah. Nigga named Fred. He outside with Zoe. What you want me to do? I'll get down on that nigga right now if you want me to."

"Nah, don't do nothing. Stall him. I'm on my way," Lucky said, hanging up the phone and pulling his dick from Rachel's mouth.

"What you doing?" She frowned.

Lucky pulled up his pants and buttoned them quickly. "I gotta go, baby. This is important," he told her before bolting from the house.

It took him twenty minutes to get to the trap. He made sure to park in the alley so the CSG nigga wouldn't see him coming. He walked in the spot and found his hitters in the living room.

"Where them niggas at?"

"He left with Zoe. They'll be back though," Quincy answered. "He wanted a hundred grams and I told him we was waiting for it to come. He said he was gon' come back."

"Did y'all tell Zoe that I'm beefing with CSG?"

"Nah. All this finna be a surprise," Quincy said as his phone rang. He checked the screen. "This Zoe right here."

Lucky pulled the pistol from his waist and walked to the back door. "Come outside with me. Tell him to pull up in the alley."

Lucky waited next to the garage with Quincy and watched as the black Cadillac Escalade pulled into the alley. They stayed out of sight, watching to see how many people were inside. Zoe was the passenger; Fred was the driver. When the engine was cut, Lucky and Quincy moved quickly, opening the door and climbing in the backseat.

"What the fuck?" Zoe flinched, going for his pistol. When he saw Lucky, he relaxed. "Fuck wrong with you, brah? Can't be creeping up on niggas like that."

"You good," Lucky said, keeping his pistol concealed and turning to Fred. "What you need, brah?"

Fred spun in the seat and looked at Lucky. Recognition immediately shone in his eyes. "Shit!"

Lucky lifted the pistol. "Where Wacco at, nigga?"

"Lucky, what you doin', brah?" Zoe asked.

"This don't got nothing to do with you, my nigga. Fall back," Lucky told Zoe before turning to Fred. "Tell me where he at, bitch-ass nigga!"

"C'mon, Lucky. That shit don't got nothing to do with me. I'm just tryna eat, my nigga."

Lucky shoved the pistol in his face. "I ain't playin' with you, nigga! Where the fuck is Wacco?"

"He ain't in the city right now!" Fred yelled, scared for his life.

"Where he at?"

"He left this morning. He went to California."

"When he come back?"

"I don't know. He go to a meeting every couple months with the Family. Couple days probably."

"Where he live at?"

"I don't know."

"Quit lyin' to me 'fore I buss yo' shit, nigga!" Lucky threatened, pressing the barrel of the gun in his eye.

"C'mon, Lucky! I really don't know. He don't let er'body know where he live. He don't fuck wit' me like that. I'm out here tryna do my own thang. I ain't serving packs for that nigga. I get my own money. I'm just tryna find a good plug."

"Tell me something, nigga, or I'ma fuck you up. How do I get to Wacco?"

Fred thought for a moment. "If I tell you, you ain't gon' kill me?"

There was betrayal in Fred's eye. He wanted to talk. Lucky lowered the pistol. "It betta be valid. Don't tell me no fuck shit."

"On my mama, this shit valid. I ain't gon' play you, brah. I know how you and yo' brotha get down. I'm just tryna eat, my nigga. This CSG shit just a way for me to get money. I ain't loyal to them niggas. I'm loyal to gettin' money. I just want a plug. I heard about yo' work and you rocking the city. I wanna fuck with you."

Lucky eyed Fred, judging his words. "Okay. I'ma fuck with you. How can I get Wacco?"

"He got a li'l bitch over in them Green Tree Apartments. I got a li'l bitch over there and I seen him a couple times. He also got a piece of that tattoo shop, Hawkstar, on the South Side. They be having meetings there. Headquarters for us is on 39th, but he barely be over there because the young shooters keep it hot. Am I good?"

Lucky nodded. "Yeah. We good. What you wanna cop?"

Fred relaxed. "I'm tryna catch a hunnit grits."

"Seventy-five hunnit. Give it to Zoe."

Fred pulled a fat stack of cash from his glove compartment. He counted off seventy-five hundred and gave it to Zoe. When he turned towards the backseat to confirm the transaction, Lucky lifted the pistol and shot him in the face.

"Oh shit!" Zoe yelled, wiping Fred's blood from his face. "What the fuck, Lucky?"

Lucky watched Fred's body collapse against the infotainment center and begin shaking. "That's yo' check for bringing this nigga to me. I need y'all to clean this shit up for me. Make sure y'all get rid of the body and set this truck on fire."

Lucky stood at the curb as the Chevy Tahoe pulled up. He and Desmond exchanged a long look through the windshield. On the outside, his face remained neutral. On the inside, he was smiling. Even though he wasn't going to show it, Lucky was happy to see his little brother.

"What's up, Lucky?" Desmond nodded.

"You got it," Lucky said flatly, tossing a bag filled with money on Desmond's lap as he climbed in the truck.

Desmond handed him a brown paper bag. "We still doing this?"

Lucky mugged him. "You still working with the Feds?"

Desmond shook his head and the brothers sat in silence for a moment.

"How is Laronda?"

"She good. Starting to come around."

"Send her my love. You ever find out who killed Sharday?"

"Them Bloods. That's how they found my house."

Desmond looked surprised. "Who is them niggas?"

"I don't know, but I'm looking into it."

"You need me?"

Lucky shook his head. "I got it. I'm about to get at Wacco too. End all this bullshit."

Desmond continued to look surprised. "For real? How you find him?"

"You don't wanna know. Just know that I'm 'bout to end that. He in Cali right now meeting with the Family. But when he get back, I'ma get on that."

Desmond thought for a moment, recalling a conversation he had with Donny. "Donny in Cali, too. He said something about a meeting with his family."

The brothers shared a look.

"His family or the family?" Lucky asked.

"He said his family."

"You think these niggas related?"

"Nah. But I bet they connected. This shit is crazy."

"What the fuck is Donny doing? You think he using us to get at Wacco?" Lucky asked.

Desmond thought about killing Marty. "I wouldn't be surprised. Donny is a schemer."

The brothers got lost in their thoughts again.

"When I talked to Donny, he said it's a rat in his mob. Was he talkin' 'bout you?"

"I don't know. He know somebody working with the Feds, but he don't know who it is."

Lucky shook his head. "And this is what you want?"

Desmond shrugged. "I don't got no choice."

Lucky mugged him, deciding the conversation was over and reaching for the door.

"Lasonya is pregnant," Desmond blurted. "You about to be an uncle."

The news made Lucky pause. He looked at Desmond and saw the joy of a first-time father in his eyes. Then a vision of Lasonya bent over Trev's sink making fuck faces while he hit it from the back flashed in Lucky's mind. "You sure it's yours?"

Desmond looked like he got punched in the face. "What kind of question is that? Yeah, I'm sure."

Lucky wanted to tell Desmond about their escapade, but couldn't. The revelation would crush him. So instead of ruining the moment, Lucky smiled. "Congratulations, brah."

Desmond saw through Lucky's smile, recalling the argument they had before the shootout with the Bloods. Lucky knew something. "What happened? You know something that I don't?"

Lucky couldn't take Desmond's stare nor look him in the eyes while he lied, so he looked away. "Nah, brah," he said, reaching for the door handle.

Desmond grabbed his arm, determined to find out the truth. "Before them Bloods ran up, you said she wasn't all the way one hunnit and I fell for it? Is that why you questioned if her baby is mine?"

Lucky looked over and saw the anger and determination in Desmond's eyes. He was looking for the truth, but Lucky knew Desmond couldn't handle it. And he couldn't be the one to give it to him. "I didn't mean nothing by that. I just wanted you to be sure the baby was yours. That's all."

The brothers shared a long look before Lucky climbed from the truck.

♦♦♦

The Family was one of the biggest crime syndicates the United States had ever seen. The drug empire spread across twenty-five states, from the east coast to the west coast, growing bigger every year. Billions of dollars in drugs and money were funneled through the organization. The goal was to create a single drug supplier in the U.S. The visionary behind the nationwide empire was Billy Washington, a.k.a. Wild Bill. He wanted to see a day when every dollar spent on drugs in the United States would come through his people. When that moment happened, he would be the most powerful man in the United States. Controlling the drug market meant unlimited money and unlimited power. His organization would be bigger than the government. He would have armies at his disposal, ready to do his bidding. He would be the next black president.

The Family was meeting in the ballroom at the Hilton. Seated around a thirty-foot table were the twenty-five representatives from each state. It looked more like a United Nations meeting than a meeting of drug dealers. The doors were guarded by Wild Bill's security, making sure that the only people in the room were with the organization.

"Good morning, ladies and gentlemen," Wild Bill spoke up, bringing the people present to attention. "Thank you all for showing up to our quarterly meeting. I've gone over the numbers submitted and the accountants are busy making sure that our profits are up and losses down. I'm also honored to introduce the newest member to the family, representing our Louisiana chapter, Big Slim."

A tall dark-skinned man with the slim build of a basketball player stood and nodded. He was about to sit back down when Wild Bill stopped him.

"Please, say a few words to your brothers and sisters."

"Uh, okay. I'm just happy to be a part of the Family. I'm ready to complete the vision and do my part."

"Don't forget about the money. It's good, ain't it?" Wild Bill joked.

Big Slim nodded and smiled. "Yeah. The money is good. Can't forget about the bag."

"All right. Now that that's out of the way, does anybody have any grievances?"

A fat, balding white man rose to his feet, staring daggers at Donny. "Yeah, I got a grievance. This sonofabitch violated the code and I wanna piece of him!"

"Salvatore, cool it, man!" Wild Bill warned. "We have rules."

Donny remained seated, keeping his cool. "That's a hell of an accusation, Salvatore."

"Don't give me that smug look, you bastard. My man Marty died in your neck of the woods and I know you did it. Don't think I don't know about your plan to creep into other family members' territories, you sleazeball."

"Salvatore!" Wild Bill yelled. "If you make another unsavory comment towards Donny, you will be taxed and fined. Final warning."

Salvatore sat down angrily, staring daggers at Donny.

"Donny, what is our New York brother talking about?" Wild Bill asked.

"His associate was found dead in a hotel room in Detroit, but I already assured him I didn't have anything to do with it."

"Why was he in Detroit?"

"I have no idea. But I assure you, I will look into this incident."

"He lyin'," another member of the Family spoke up.

Wild Bill peered down the table. "You have somethin' to say, Wacco Tony?"

Wacco stood and looked directly at Donny. "Donny is lying."

"And what evidence do you have?"

"My city is talking. Heard we got some Detroit natives doing business. That's Donny all day."

Donny finally lost his cool and stood. "You got some nerve talking about I'm a liar! What about yo' people you tried to send to Detroit a while back? Sent 'em all back in caskets, fuck boy."

"Bitch-ass nigga!" Wacco cursed, leaping onto the table and running at Donny.

"Zay! Primo! Stop them! Get them out of here!" Wild Bill yelled to his guards.

The guards arrived at the conflict just as Wacco swung a foot at Donny, trying to kick him in the face. The older man took a step back, dodging the leg whip. Wacco jumped from the table, trying to continue the attack when the guards hemmed him up.

"I'ma catch you, Donny. That's my word. And when I find out who yo' people is, I'm sending all they asses back to Detroit in sandwich bags!"

"Wacco and Donny, both of you are out of order! Leave this meeting right now. I will see both of you later."

After the troublemakers were removed from the mix, Wild Bill tried to restore order. "Ladies and gentlemen, what you have just seen is unacceptable behavior and it will not be tolerated in these proceedings. We will not behave like thugs and hoodlums. The only way we will be taken seriously is if we carry ourselves in a serious manner. Am I clear?"

When no one spoke, the visionary continued. "Now, as I was saying before I was unceremoniously interrupted, does anyone have any more grievances to air?"

## Chapter 6

"Oh, shit! Yeah, D! Pull my hair!" Pebbles moaned.

Desmond wrapped a handful of her purple and pink locks in his fist and tugged while drilling her phatty from behind. Her fleshy cheeks bounced and jiggled against his pelvis every time he thrust forward. Pebbles took the D like a champ, keeping her face down and ass up.

"Spank me, D-Money! Slap some money on my ass, baby! Get some money!"

"Oh yeah! I got you. Hold on." Desmond laughed as he stopped hitting it and grabbed his pants. There was a little more than five hundred dollars in the pocket. He pulled the cash out and began spanking her with it. "You like that? Huh? You like that?"

"Yeah, baby. Fuck me and make it rain on me."

Desmond slipped his dick back inside her walls and began beating the pussy up while holding the bills high in the air and letting them rain down on her back. After all the money was on her body and the bed, he grabbed her hips and continued the drill session.

"Oh yeah, D! Mmmhhh! Oh yeah!" she moaned.

When Desmond felt his nut building, he pulled out and flipped her onto her back, spreading her legs apart and taking a moment to look at her pussy. It was bald, the lips fat and glistening with her juice.

"C'mon, D. Gimme some more," she begged, grabbing his dick and trying to shove it in her box.

"Wait. I'm looking at that pussy. Yo' pussy fine as you."

Pebble's hand went to stroke her clit. "It is pretty, ain't it? And my pussy bad, too. I want you to beat it up. Beat this pussy up."

Desmond leaned forward and slapped his dick against her pussy lips.

"Oooh!" Pebbles moaned. "Do it again."

Desmond slapped his dick against her pussy a little harder.

"Keep doing that shit. Spank my pussy with yo' dick," she moaned.

Desmond began rapidly tapping his dick against her pussy and Pebbles went wild. "C'mon, D. Fuck me right now. I need that dick."

He slipped the head in, teasing her by only giving her a few inches. She began lifting her hips off the bed, trying to get more.

"Gimme some more, D. Stop playing. Fuck me," she demanded.

Desmond felt he had teased her enough and was ready to get it. He held her legs wide apart and dove deep until their pelvises were touching. Then he began long stroking, watching his dick come all the way out until only the head was inside and then disappear all the way in.

"Oh yeah, D! Oh my God! Oh my God!" Pebbles moaned, throwing her pussy up at him while pinching her own nipples. A few minutes later, she was cumming and screaming his name.

"Oh shit, D-Money! I'm cumming, baby! Oh shit!"

Seeing her pleasure was what Desmond needed to reach his peak. He tried to hold off for as long as he could. Right when he was about to bust, he snatched his dick out and stroked himself, busting on her stomach.

"Damn, girl. You got that wet wet," he panted, lying down next to her.

Pebbles lay on her back with her legs still open, rubbing cum on her stomach. "Oh my God, D. Damn, you know how to fuck, nigga."

The lovers lay still, collecting their breath.

"Where you really from?" she asked.

Desmond turned to look at Pebbles only to find that she was already looking at him. "What?"

"Where you really from? And don't gimme that Flint shit."

"I told you I'm from Milwaukee."

"How long you been in Flint?" she asked, watching him like she knew he was lying.

"What's up with all the questions?" he asked, uncomfortable under her stare.

"You got this mysterious vibe about you and I wanna know more. And I caught you in a lie."

"Yeah, right," he laughed. "I ain't lie about shit."

"You lied about MJ. You said you knew him. He died five years ago. You said you just got here after you messed up your eye." She pointed to his wound. "That don't look like it happened five years ago."

Desmond had fucked up. If Pebbles told the wrong person that he wasn't from Flint and it got back to Rich Red and his uncle, shit could get real dangerous real quick. He had to flip the script. "What kinda games you playing, shorty? You tryna set me up or some shit?" Desmond asked, acting offended.

The sudden change surprised Pebbles. "What? Set you up? No. I just wanted to know where you was from."

"By asking me some shit to try and trap me? That's bullshit. If you wanna know something, come at me like a real bitch. I ain't no fuck boy you can play mind games with. You comin' at me on some entrapment shit like you the Feds."

"Well, I'm sorry. I didn't mean it."

Desmond sat up and reached for his clothes. "Matter of fact, stop asking questions about me."

"Why? Did I do something wrong?"

"Yeah. You asking too many muthafuckin' questions."

She sat up and grabbed his arm. "Wait, D. Damn, baby. I'm sorry. I didn't mean to make you mad."

He yanked his arm away and slid into his boxers. "When I fuck with you, I don't wanna be stressed out. I don't wanna be tested or played with. I go through enough in the streets."

"Okay, D. I said I'm sorry. Take off your clothes and get back in bed."

Desmond stood and put on his jeans. "I'm good. I got some shit to do. I'ma get up with you in a minute."

Pebbles folded her arms over her chest and watched as Desmond got dressed and left without another word. He hopped in the truck and mobbed out.

During the drive, Desmond thought about his performance. He had overreacted and he knew it. But he needed to teach her a lesson. And he also needed a reason to leave. He didn't want to spend the night with Pebbles and have to explain himself to Lasonya.

"Damn," he cursed aloud, wishing he hadn't allowed her in his thoughts. Thinking of Lasonya hurt because he knew she had fucked off while he was locked up. Lucky knew too. He saw it on his brother's face yesterday when he asked if Desmond was sure the baby was his, not to mention Lasonya was all of a sudden trying to drive a wedge between the brothers. She didn't want Lucky to tell on her. The only question he didn't have an answer to was who she cheated with. He wanted to press Lucky for a name, but he knew Lucky wasn't feeling him right now and probably wouldn't tell him. He thought about confronting Lasonya as well, but he didn't think he would get far with that either. She was too good a liar. After all, she had already convinced him to have a baby with her to cover up the possibility of her being pregnant by someone else. But Desmond was no fool. He was going to keep his knowledge of what she did to his chest and wait for Lasonya to slip. And when she did, that was her ass.

The ringing of his phone pulled him from thoughts of fucking up his girl. He pulled the phone out and saw a text from Pebbles.

*I'm sorry. Call me.*

He looked up from the text just in time to see he had swerved into oncoming traffic. A semi truck's horn blasted and Desmond was momentarily blinded by headlights as he yanked the steering wheel hard to the right. The Yukon tires squealed as the SUV swerved back into the right lane and almost hit another car. Desmond yanked the steering wheel again and smashed the brakes. The front tire popped as the truck came to a stop in the middle of the street. When Desmond realized he wasn't dead, he let out a breath of relief and pulled to the side of the road. He got out and checked the back of the truck for a spare tire. There wasn't one.

"Bitch-ass shit," he cursed, looking around and trying to decide his next move. There was a gas station a block away. He hopped back in the truck and drove there to see if he could get service. A young female stood behind the counter.

"I need a tire."

She looked at Desmond like he'd spoken Spanish. "Uh, we don't sell tires. We sell gas."

"Is there a tire shop nearby?"

She shrugged. "I don't know. We sell gas."

Desmond shot her a mug before walking back outside and calling Rich Red.

"D-Money, what's good, boss?"

"I got a flat tire. I need a ride."

"A'ight. Say no more. Where you at?"

It only took Rich Red ten minutes to get to the gas station. He pulled up in the Audi truck with the music up. Don Q's "Clarity" filled the night with music. "D-Money! What it do, fooly?" he yelled.

"Who don't got a spare tire in the back of the truck?" Desmond fumed as he climbed in the passenger seat.

"Apparently you!" Rich laughed.

Desmond shot him a look. "I need a ride to the crib. I'ma come and get the truck tomorrow."

"All the way to Flint?"

"Yeah, nigga. That's where I live."

"Fuck that shit, my nigga. You can chill at my crib. Get yo' truck fixed in the morning."

Desmond thought about Lasonya. "Man, I need to get to the crib. Quit bullshitting, nigga."

"Nigga, you act like you got a bitch at the crib or something. Fuck with me tonight. I got you in the morning."

Desmond couldn't tell him that not only did he have a woman at home, but an entire family. So, he relaxed in the passenger seat and kicked it with Rich Red.

◆◆◆

"Who the fuck you was just talking to?" Breed spazzed, grabbing Evet by the throat and pushing her against the wall.

"Stop, Breed! Let me go, nigga!" the woman yelled, struggling to free herself from his grip.

Breed reached an arm back and slapped her across the face, sending her falling to the ground. "Bitch, quit tryna flex! Fuck you think you fuckin' wit'? Gimme that mu'fuckin' phone."

Evet threw the phone at him. "Take it and leave me the fuck alone!"

The phone hit Breed in the chest and fell to the floor. Even though it didn't hurt, it pissed him off as if she had punched him in the face. "Oh, you wanna throw shit?" He chuckled, balling up his fists as he approached.

"Get away from me! Get the fuck away from me!" Evet screamed, laying on her back and lifting her feet in the air to kick at him.

"C'mon, Breed. Chill, dawg," Chauncey said, coming over to grab his boy.

"Get'cho hands off me, nigga!" Breed snapped.

"C'mon, brah. You tripping. Leave that shit alone and let's go."

"Nah, fuck that. This bitch think she slick. I know that was a nigga on this phone. Who was it, bitch?" he yelled, dodging kicks as he approached.

"Stop, Breed! Leave me alone!" she yelled, continuing to kick the air.

Breed caught one of her feet and pulled her to him and dove on top of her. They rolled on the floor a couple of times before Breed was able to climb on top and pin her down. He straddled her and wrapped his hands around her throat. "Yeah, bitch! Talk that shit now." He grinned sadistically as he choked her.

"Breed. Stop. I can't. Breathe." Evet struggled, gasping for air.

"Ay, Breed! Chill, Nigga! You 'bout to kill her," Chauncey said, bending down and trying to pull Breed's hands from her throat.

"Move, nigga! Let me go 'fore I kill this bitch! You betta let me go!" Breed yelled, squeezing harder.

Evet's face turned blue and she looked close to death.

Chauncey backed away. "A'ight, nigga. A'ight."

Breed loosened his grip on her throat and grabbed the phone from the floor. Evet choked and coughed as air rushed into her lungs.

"What's the password to unlock it?"

Evet continued choking.

Breed kicked her in the arm. "Fuck is the password, bitch?"

"Yo' birthday," she gasped.

Breed opened the phone and found some text messages. "Who the fuck is Vel?"

"Nobody. Gimme back my phone."

Breed pulled a pistol from his waist and pointed it at her. "Who the fuck is Vel, bitch?"

Evet looked at the gun, terror gripping her body. "Just somebody I know."

"He got some money?"

"Yeah. A li'l bit."

"Where he live?"

"Please, Breed. Don't do this," she begged.

"Nah, bitch. You just told him you was finna get up wit' him and because you wanna be a li'l hoe, Vel gon' pay. Now get yo' ass up before I shoot yo' stupid ass. You finna take me to this nigga's house and help me rob him."

Desmond kicked it with Rich Red, riding around the city doing deliveries. They ended up at an apartment building on Detroit's upper east side.

"Come in with me, Money. This my nigga Vel's spot and he keep some bad thotties on deck."

Desmond followed Rich into the building. They stopped outside an apartment on the second floor and knocked.

"Who dat?" a man called from inside.

"Rich. Open the door, nigga."

When the door opened, a short, chubby, light-skinned nigga stood smiling. "'Bout time you got here, nigga. Where my shit?" Vel asked, stepping aside to let them in.

"I had to grab my nigga, D-Money. His car fucked up."

Desmond nodded to Vel as he followed Rich Red into the modestly furnished apartment. "What it do?"

"You got it," Vel acknowledged before turning back to Rich. "Where my shit at, boy?"

Red went in his pocket and threw a bag with fifty grams of heroin on the table. "Where my money? And where the hoes at?"

"My li'l stripper bitch, Evet, on the way with her buddy. Shit, I thought you was her," Vel said as he handed Rich a stack of money.

"Oh, we chillin' then. Let's see what these hoes 'bout," Rich said, copping a seat.

"Where yo' bathroom?" Desmond asked.

"Right in the back. Ain't no shittin' in my bathroom, brah," Vel warned.

Desmond gave him a look. Vel busted out laughing. "I'm just fuckin' wit' you, brah."

Desmond was walking to the bathroom when his phone rang. It was Lasonya. "Hey."

"Hey, baby. When you coming home?"

"I won't be able to make it back tonight. The truck got a flat and I'ma stay with Rich and get it fixed tomorrow."

"No, baby," she whined. "You don't got a spare?"

Desmond walked in the bathroom and closed the door. "I was thinking the same shit when I checked. But Donny didn't have one in there. I'ma make sure I get one tomorrow."

"Aw, man. Okay. Make sure you come home when you can. I miss you, baby."

"Yep. I will."

"Okay. I love you."

Desmond wanted to laugh. "Yep."

"Desmond, did you hear me? I said I love you."

"I heard you."

"You not gon' say it back?"

74

He let out a breath, thinking of a response. He didn't have the time to go back and forth with her about saying "I love you". "I gotta go, Lasonya. I'ma be home tomorrow," he said and then ended the call. "She loves me," he cracked, standing over the toilet, about to take a piss.

A loud noise came from the front of the apartment, making him freeze. He listened for a moment and could hear yelling. He pulled the pistol from his waist and opened the bathroom door.

The voices got louder as he crept towards the front room. He hugged the wall at the edge of the hall and began listening.

"Who all in the house, nigga?" Chauncey asked.

"Just us," Rich Red said, keeping his hands where they could be seen.

"Rich Red? That's you, bitch-ass nigga?" Breed asked, smiling like he won a prize.

"Aw shit," Rich cursed when he recognized Breed's voice.

Breed moved closer, pointing the pistol in his face. "I been waiting to catch yo' bitch ass again. Where yo' bitch-ass guy at that popped my nigga, Marco?"

When Desmond heard one of the robbers say Rich Red's name, he wondered if it was the nigga that got away at Teona's house. He didn't want to run in the living room blind, so he pulled out his phone and used the reflection on the screen to peek around the corner.

And that's when his phone rang. Lasonya's name popped on the screen. The jackers looked towards the hallway and caught a glimpse of the phone before Desmond could pull it back.

"Who is that?" Chauncey asked.

"Bring yo' bitch ass out here!" Breed yelled, pointing his pistol towards the hallway and applying pressure to the trigger.

Desmond remained frozen, unsure how to react. He had lost the element of surprise. If he showed himself, he would be gunned down. If he started shooting blindly around the corner, he might hit Rich. Not seeing another way out, he did the only thing he could and ran to the bathroom. He locked the door behind him and went for the window.

"Who the fuck back there?" Chauncey threatened, pointing the pistol at Vel.

"D-Money. Some nigga named D-Money."

"That nigga killed Marco!" Breed yelled and started shooting at the walls, hoping a bullet went through and hit Desmond. Then he crept over, ready to bust, only to find the hallway empty. He ran to the only closed door in the hallway. He kicked open the door, his pistol ready to blaze. The bathroom was empty, the window open.

"Bitch-ass nigga!" he cursed before running back to the living room. "Fuck them niggas, brah. We gotta get this nigga," Breed said as he ran out of the apartment. Once outside, he looked up and down the block, trying to find Desmond. The big man had already disappeared into the night.

"What the fuck was that shit, brah? We left the money," Chauncey yelled angrily.

Breed continued looking around. "Fuck that money. That was the nigga that killed Marco."

"Shit, he gone now. Let's get the fuck outta here."

After one last look around, Breed ran for the getaway car.

Desmond stood in the shadows of the apartment building across the street, watching as Breed and Chauncey hopped in the car. There was a female already in the car. It took all of his discipline to stop himself from killing them. He didn't know what kind of nigga Vel was and if he would snitch. Plus, the apartment was already hot because of Breed shooting inside and Desmond didn't want to add to the heat by dropping bodies outside. But one thing was for sure: he was going to kill Breed.

## Chapter 7

39th and Clarke was alive with activity. The sun had gone down over an hour ago, but nobody moved to go inside. The weather was nice and there wouldn't be many days like this since fall had arrived a few weeks ago. Groups of men stood in front of houses on the sidewalks. Women and children sat on porches enjoying the warm autumn air. Everybody was busy doing their own thing, so nobody noticed the black Intrepid with tinted windows parked near the stop sign. Three men sat in the car lurking. They were watching a blue and black house near the middle of the block. It was CSG headquarters. Up on the porch were six CSG members.

"Dog, the bitch Rihanna just inboxed me!" Pistol said, staring at his phone in unbelief.

"Quit bullshitting, nigga," Cam laughed. "Rihanna don't fuck wit' yo' type, dirty-ass nigga."

Pistol showed him the phone screen. There was a small picture of an attractive brown-skinned woman in a bathing suit. Cam's eyes bugged when he read the message next to it.

"Yo' bum ass ain't used to baggin' bad bitches." Pistol laughed. "I'm finna fuck the shit out this bitch!"

"Lemme see!" Mikey yelled, grabbing the phone. "Damn! Bro got Rihanna on deck!"

Pistol snatched his phone back and messaged her a response. "I'm finna see what this bitch doing right now. Definitely can't wait to slide through."

"See if she got some friends, nigga!" Bill yelled.

"Let me get in first, nigga. Damn, ole thirsty-ass nigga."

Everyone on the porch laughed.

"Fuck you, crummy-ass nigga," Bill sulked.

Pistol's phone chimed. It was a response from Rihanna. "Oh, hell yeah! She want a nigga to come through. I'm out this bitch!" he yelled excitedly. "I'ma holla at you niggas in a minute," he said, showing his niggas love before walking towards his Cadillac CTS parked at the curb.

He hopped in the car with bad bitch pussy on his mind, not paying attention to the black Intrepid that began following. He pulled up to the corner store and ran inside to grab some condoms and blunts. When he came back out, the occupants in the Intrepid jumped out holding heat.

"Get'cho bitch ass in!" Flacco demanded.

Pistol looked around like he was thinking about screaming for help or making a run for it.

Jordan slapped him with the pistol and grabbed him by the shirt. "Get'cho bitch ass in the car, nigga!"

Pistol collapsed in the back seat. Jordan jumped in with him and closed the door. B-dog jumped behind the steering wheel.

Flacco got in the passenger seat and slapped the dashboard while looking around to see if anybody had witnessed the kidnapping. "Let's go, li'l nigga."

"What's going on, fam? What y'all want?" Pistol asked, his voice squeaking with fear.

"Where Wacco?" Jordan asked, keeping his pistol pointed at their hostage.

"I don't know. Ain't nobody seen him in a minute."

Flacco spun in the back seat, mugging their captive. "Before I finish with you, you gon' tell me everything you know."

The Bloods took Pistol to an abandoned house that had been made into a den of torture. They dragged him to the basement, cuffed his arms behind a brick pillar, and began the interrogation.

"Where is Wacco?" Flacco asked.

"I told you, I don't know. Ain't nobody seen him."

Flacco nodded to B-Dog. The young hitter grabbed a brick and walked behind Pistol. He lined the jagged brick up to Pistol cuffed hands and cocked his arm back. Then he swung the weapon at the hostage's hands.

"Ay, brah! What you doing? I said I don't - aaaahhhh!"

Multiple bones in both of Pistol hands were shattered and broken as he collapsed to his knees.

"Where the fuck is yo' boss at, nigga? Tell me something," Flacco said.

"I don't know," Pistol cried. "I told y'all I ain't seen him."

"Hit him again," Flacco ordered.

B-Dog cocked his arm back and smashed the brick against Pistol's hands again.

"Ahhhh!"

"You betta tell me something, nigga. How do I find Wacco?"

"I don't know, brah! On my mama, I don't know!" Pistol cried, tears dripping down his face.

Flacco walked behind their victim and squatted to take a look at his hands. Blood dripped from his mangled fingers. "Yo' hands fucked up, li'l brah. Shit only gon' get worse. Tell me something."

"I'm telling you, fam. I don't know shit. I swear to God, I don't know."

Flacco took the brick from B-Dog and walked to stand in front of Pistol. The cuffed prisoner stared up at the Blood leader with a pitiful look. Flacco had no pity. He cocked his arm back and hit Pistol in the face with the brick so hard that it broke in half. Pistol's neck snapped to the side as the lights went out. He fell at an awkward angle, face hitting the floor, his arms still cuffed to the pillar. Blood began gushing from the wound on his cheek and the side of his face began swelling.

"Damn! You fucked that nigga up." Jordan laughed.

"I'm tired of playing with these niggas. I don't got time for this shit," Flacco huffed.

"This the third one that we took and we still can't get to this nigga," B-dog said.

"Somebody gon' eventually tell us something," Jordan said.

"Maybe we asking the wrong questions," Flacco said, unzipping his pants and pulling out his dick.

"Fuck you doing?" Jordan asked, stepping away from his nigga.

"I'm waking him up," Flacco said as he began pissing on Pistol's face.

The captive stirred as the urine sprayed him in the face. It took a few moments for him to realize he was being pissed on. "What the fuck?" he groaned, trying to get away from the stream of body fluid.

"Who knows how to find Wacco?" Flacco asked, shaking the dribbles from his piece.

"I-I don't know. Damn, nigga. You pissed on me!"

Flacco pulled a pistol from his waist and pointed it in Pistol's face. "I'm gon' do a lot worse if you keep lying to me. Who know how to find Wacco?"

"King. That's his right-hand man."

"What he look like and what kinda car he drive?"

"He a tall, skinny, light-skinned nigga. He got King tatted on his forehead. He drive a white BMW."

Flacco nodded. "The truth has set you free."

Pop!

◆◆◆

Hawkstar tattoo shop was near and dear to Wacco. It was the first business he started when he got his money right. It was also where he and the CSG lieutenants gathered to meet. In a back room of the shop, Wacco sat around with four senior members of CSG: King, BG, Cyco, and RIP.

"Somebody knocking our niggas off. They found Fred burnt up in his Cadillac truck. Tone and CJ both got tortured before they died. Somebody hunting us," Wacco said, looking at all his members.

"I ain't heard nothing, but I been telling them niggas to stay on point," King said.

"Same here," BG spoke. "We kicked a lot of niggas out the hood, so it could be anybody. I think this the kinda shit that happens when you get the streets bloody."

"I think it's more to it," Cyco spoke up. "They tortured two of our niggas. That ain't no regular war shit. You torture a nigga when you tryna get something out of him. Information. I'm thinking like you, Wacco. I think somebody hunting us. And they looking for something specific."

"Or somebody," King added.

The members became silent for a few beats.

"It might be some Detroit niggas," Wacco said. "When I was in Cali last week, I found out this Detroit nigga ain't been playin' fair. Nigga named Donny."

"He part of the Family?" King asked.

"Yeah. But he might want get back for that move we pulled a couple years back when we tried to get in Detroit. It's bad blood."

"You think he making moves in the Mil?"

"I don't know. I'm just letting y'all know all the possibilities. All of y'all with slots gon' have to keep a low profile. Do what y'all do, but make sure y'all keep a couple hitters. And keep y'all eyes open," Wacco warned.

"I'ma holla at a few other niggas and put my ear to the street to see if they heard something. Niggas can't keep they mouth closed, so I know somebody gon' know something," BG said.

"Do that," Wacco nodded. "If y'all ain't got nothing else, y'all can ride out. I know y'all prolly got shit to do. King, hold on. Lemme holla at you."

When the other lieutenants left, King addressed the top dog. "What's good, brah?"

Wacco stared him in the eyes for a few beats. "Carla."

When he heard the name, King smirked, his facial expression giving him away. "Listen, Wacco. Shit just happened, brah."

"Don't gimme that shit, brah. That's my sister and you like my brother. You know she got a baby with Cyco and you got a girl. Y'all gon' start some shit that's gon' fuck over a lot of people."

"C'mon, Tony. It ain't like that, my nigga. Carla like my sister, too. And Cyco my nigga. Shit just got outta hand. We fucked around a couple times. It ain't nothing serious."

"Stop fucking around. Both of y'all. I ain't finna have CSG split up because you and my sister on some sneaky shit."

King and Wacco had a will-testing stare-off.

"A'ight. You got it, Wacco. It's over."

Wacco continued to stare at his second in command, letting him know he was serious. "I'm serious, King. That shit over!"

"A'ight. We done. That's my word."

"A'ight. Let's get up outta here. I got a run to make. I'ma fuck with you later," Wacco said, embracing his brother in arms.

"You know it's love," King said before gathering his shooters and leaving the tattoo shop.

Wacco walked up front to get his shooters. "Jason. Big. Let's ride," he said as his phone rang. The number was blocked. "Hello?"

"Hey," a woman said.

"Who is this?"

"This Lasonya. Yo' baby mama."

Hearing her voice made Wacco pause. "Hold on, y'all," he told his shooters. "What's up, shorty? I wasn't expecting to hear from you."

"I know. How you doing?"

Wacco walked over to an empty booth and sat down. "You know how it is in Milwaukee. Nigga tryna stay alive. What's up with you though? How is the baby?"

"We good. I don't know if you know, but we left Milwaukee."

The news surprised Wacco. "Nah, I didn't know. Where you at?"

"In California. We staying with some family. Shit got too crazy there."

"Yeah. You and yo' people was in a lot of shit. Where yo' man and his brother at?" he fished.

"Desmond in a military prison. You know Lucky still there. I heard y'all had a couple run-ins."

"So that's why you called, huh? You tryna help yo' people set me up?"

"Nah. I don't fuck with Lucky like that no more. That nigga disrespectful."

Wacco thought for a moment. "So why is you calling? What you on? I know you ain't just being cool."

"I am. I been thinkin' about what you said when you came by my mama's house. I wanted to send you a picture of Quaysha. I'ma text it to you."

"Yeah. Okay. Do that. But I know you, Lasonya. You got something up yo' sleeve. It's gon' come out sooner or later."

She laughed. "I'm not playing no games, Wacco. I just wanted to call and let you see the picture of your daughter. Next time we're in Milwaukee, I'ma let you meet her."

Wacco sat dumbfounded. He wanted to be happy about the possibility of meeting his seed, but he knew Lasonya wasn't being a hunnit. She was up to something. "Okay. That sounds good. Look, I got some shit to do. Text me that picture."

After ending the call, Wacco continued to sit in the chair and think. What was Lasonya up to? Was she trying to set him up for Lucky and Desmond? He had already gotten word that Desmond had been transferred from the county jail, but he didn't know where until Lasonya said a military prison. Was it possible that Desmond was out and knocking his CSG niggas off, trying to get to him? There were too many possibilities. But one thing was for sure: Wacco wasn't going to slip. He had his money right and he was ready for war.

◆◆◆

"I don't think I wanna live in Milwaukee no more," Laronda said as she stared out the passenger window.

Lucky was driving her from April's house to his new house in Brown Deer. "Why you say that?"

"I'm tired of all the drama. I think I just wanna go somewhere where don't nobody know me and start over. Go to school and graduate. Maybe even go to college."

Lucky liked the way she was thinking. "That don't sound like a bad idea."

Laronda turned to look at her father, tears filling her eyes. "So, can we move? I don't wanna be here no more. It don't feel right being in Milwaukee without my mama."

Lucky could feel her pain and hear it in her voice. He wanted to pull over and grab her in his arms and hold her. "I can't leave right now, baby girl. I'm caught up in too much shit."

"But ain't that why you should leave? So, you can get away from it? A couple months ago you was thinking about leaving. Now why you don't want to leave? People keep shooting at us and trying to kill you."

Lucky thought about how to explain his deal to Donny to her. "I made a deal with somebody to do something and I can't leave until it's done."

"Why can't you leave? What good is the deal if you ain't alive to do it?"

"It ain't that easy. I can't just walk away."

"What is the deal?"

"Don't worry about it. I got it."

"What you mean don't worry about it? Everything you do is affecting me too. I got kidnapped and my mama dead. Stop treating me like a kid, like my life ain't on the line too. You supposed to be my daddy. You supposed to protect me. It ain't safe for us here. What kinda deal you made that you can't leave?"

Lucky thought on her words. It was his job to protect her. The woman/child had spoken the truth, and it cut him. "You know what, baby girl? You right. Everything you said was true. It is my job to protect you. I'm so caught up in all this other shit that I lost sight of that. I made a deal with this nigga Donny in Detroit. He took care of Polo for me and I gotta pay him back by starting him a hustling squad in Milwaukee. That's what I'm doing now. That's why I can't leave until I get the Milwaukee-Detroit pipeline up and running."

"And how long is that gonna take?"

"I honestly don't know. I never thought about a timeline."

"So, you gon' sell drugs forever? When we used to go out to eat, you was talking all the legit stuff. Starting a business and writing books. What happened to that?"

"I didn't wanna do this, baby. It just happened. Next thing I know, I looked up and was heavy in the streets. When I was in prison planning my release, I woulda whooped a nigga's ass if they told me a year later I would be hustling and building a team. Sometimes plans don't work out the way we want."

"You know what I liked about you being my daddy, Lucky? You made me feel like I had a real parent. I learned a lot from you and you made me believe in myself. You told me that I could change my life whenever I wanted and that I was young enough that nothing I did would matter ten or twenty years from now. I believed you. Why you can't take yo' own advice and change what you doing? You not that old."

Lucky was speechless. His daughter had fucked him up with his own words. His words inspired her to change and want a better life. He was obligated to give her a chance at that life and make the necessary changes in his life so that he could be there for her as she matured into a young woman.

"You right, Laronda. Anybody can change. And I owe it to you. You all I got. I owe you a better life. I'ma get us up outta this. I promise."

Laronda reached over and hugged him. "Thank you, Daddy."

It was the first time Laronda had ever called him Daddy. The word sounded like music to Lucky's ears. His chest swelled with pride and tears welled up in his eyes. "You just called me Daddy?"

Laronda nodded, tears welling up in her eyes when she seen Lucky's reaction to beings called daddy. "You is my daddy. You did more for me since I knew you than Ricky did my whole life."

The words touched Lucky and he couldn't hold back the tears. "You bet' not tell nobody you seen me cry," he cracked. "I love you, baby girl. I'ma get us up outta here. I promise."

Laronda leaned over and kissed him on the cheek. "I believe you, Daddy. Is Quincy staying at the new house, too?"

"Nah. Them niggas like staying at the old house. Why you asking me about Q? I thought you hated my li'l niggas."

"I, um…was just wondering if I could walk around the house in whatever I wanna wear now," Laronda explained.

Lucky gave her a look. "You sticking with that?"

Laronda rolled her eyes. "Please, Lucky. It ain't even that kind of party."

After dropping Laronda off at the new house, Lucky's phone rang. It was Ryder. "What's good, li'l brah?"

"Wacco here."

Lucky's body tensed, heartbeat speeding up. "Where you at?"

"At the tattoo shop."

"I'm on my way."

◆◆◆

Lucky sat in the back seat of minivan, parked down the street from Hawkstar tattoo shop. Quincy sat in the passenger seat. Ryder drove. All of them were strapped. Lucky had different shooters watching the shop for three days and it finally looked like their patience was about to pay off. They had already watched several CSG members leave the building. There was one more car parked out front, a white Mercedes Benz 750, the same car Lucky had seen parked outside Lasonya's house after he and Melissa had come from seeing his parole officers when he first got out of prison.

"You sure you seen Wacco go in here?" Lucky asked Ryder.

"Yeah. A short light-skinned nigga. He went in with the tall light-skinned nigga that got in the white BMW. A lot of them niggas went in there. All of 'em left except Wacco. It look like they was having a meeting."

"Okay, my nigga. Good shit. Keep y'all eyes open. I been waiting to catch this nigga for a long time and I finally got his bitch ass," Lucky said, hoping to finally get Wacco's ass once and for all. He had taken a lot of losses and was ready to win. Wacco out of the way was one less problem he had to worry about.

"Look. There they go!" Ryder pointed.

The men in the van watched as people began moving from the tattoo shop's front door. There were three of them. They were looking around in all directions as they walked to the car.

"Got yo' bitch ass." Lucky smiled when he recognized Wacco.

"What's good? We runnin' up on these niggas?" Quincy asked, clutching his pistol, ready to put in work.

"Nah," Lucky stayed him. "They looking all around like they expecting something. They gon' see us coming if we go now. Just follow 'em. We gotta do this right the first time."

When the Benz pulled away from the curb, the killers followed in the minivan. Ryder made sure to keep a good distance between the vehicles so they wouldn't be seen. They trailed from the south side of Milwaukee onto the expressway. Twenty minutes later, they exited in Cudahay, an expensive suburb outside Milwaukee. Lucky looked around as they drove. It was late and there wasn't much traffic. If they continued following Wacco, their van might be spotted.

"It look like he finna go home. Ain't too much traffic, so we might have to make our move before he spots us."

"I say we get him at the next stoplight," Quincy suggested.

Lucky took another look around. There were four vehicles on the road. Their van, Wacco's Benz, and two other cars. It was now or never. "Let's get it. Wacco's the driver. Pull alongside," Lucky instructed, opening the sliding door and holding the handle above the door to brace himself.

Quincy got into the middle seat next to Lucky. The stoplight was less than a block away. The Benz pulled to a stop at the light. The van followed a few seconds later and began slowing down. Before Ryder could pull alongside, the passenger door of the Benz opened and a shooter hopped out blazing.

Bullets tore through the windshield, whizzing past the occupants and getting lodged in the interior. Ryder hit the brake, making the van jerk to a stop as he ducked. Quincy flew forward when the van braked, losing his balance and hitting the floor. Lucky was holding the handle above the door, so the van's jerking had no impact on him. When Wacco's shooter jumped out blazing, Lucky lit him up.

Clap, clap, clap, clap, clap, clap, clap!

The shooter fell in the middle of the street, blood gushing from chest wounds. The Benz burned rubber and sped away.

"Get that nigga, Ryder! Go!" Lucky yelled, slapping the back of the driver's seat.

Ryder sat up and jumped into action. He smashed the gas, running over the wounded shooter and chasing the Benz. The European luxury sedan was fast and quickly gained a half block's distance on the minivan. Ryder had the pedal to the floor, but the Japanese four cylinders was no match for the German engineering. The Benz kept a good distance on the van. And just for good measure, a shooter leaned out the window and shot at the van. Bullets thudded into the hood and windshield, making the occupants duck.

"Fuck!" Lucky cursed, knowing he missed an opportunity. "Fuck them niggas, Ryder. You ain't gon' catch that Benz. Get us the fuck outta here."

## Chapter 8

"You think you can take care of this for me?" Lucky asked.

Desmond took his eyes off the road to look over at his brother. "What you talking 'bout?"

"I need to get rid of these bodies. You the Navy SEAL, so I figured you know how to get rid of bodies better than anybody."

"How many bodies you talking about? And where you got 'em at?"

"In the garage. Turn right up here and pull in the alley."

Desmond pulled up behind a black and white garage. Lucky got out of the car and led the way inside. What Desmond saw was like something out of a scary movie. There were bodies piled on top of bodies covering the garage.

"Lucky, what the fuck is this?" Desmond panicked.

Lucky pulled a black .44 from his waist and put it to Desmond's head. "This what I do to snitches, nigga."

Boom!

Desmond snapped awake, happy to be in his living room when he opened his eyes. He had dozed off for a moment only to be greeted by a nightmare. He hadn't had a good night's sleep in a long time. He wanted to talk to someone about the dreams, but he didn't trust anyone enough to let them in his head, so he continued to suffer in silence.

Lasonya's phone ringing on the table got his attention. The ringtone had probably gotten her attention and she might've been on her way back to get it. He wondered if he should answer. Before he found out she had cheated, he would have never even questioned whether or not to answer. He would've called her to let her know it was ringing. They had an unspoken rule that she didn't answer his phone and he didn't answer hers. Now he wasn't so sure about the unspoken rule. What if it was the nigga she cheated with?

Desmond reached for the phone just as it stopped ringing. The missed call showed on the screen. He tried to open the phone, but it was locked. That surprised him. He couldn't remember the last time

Lasonya locked her phone. It made him wonder what she was hiding.

"What are you doing?" Lasonya asked, walking in the living room and seeing him holding her phone.

"Somebody called you. I didn't answer in time," he said, handing her the phone.

Lasonya unlocked the screen and checked. "Oh. It was my cousin, Sylvia. I'ma call her back later."

Desmond watched as she locked the phone and set it on the table, far away from him. "Why don't you call her back right now? It might be important."

Lasonya blew off the call. "Sylvia don't want nothing. Mama done cooking. Want me to make you a plate?"

Desmond stared at her for a moment, trying to recall every lie she ever told and her body language when she told it. She was so good at lying that he wasn't sure when she was telling the truth.

"Why you looking at me like that?"

Desmond wanted to let her know he knew she had cheated, but she would probably wiggle her way out of it. So, he took another angle. "When did you start locking your phone?"

She looked to her phone and then back to Desmond. "You tried to get in my phone?"

"I tried to see who called and noticed it was locked."

Lasonya could see the accusation in his eyes. "You accusing me of something?"

"Are you guilty of something?" he countered.

A flash of anger shone in her eyes. "You lock your phone. I can't lock mine? And since you tryna accuse me of something, what about you staying out all night? I don't question you about it. I didn't say nothing about your 'flat'," she threw up air quotes, "tire that stopped you from coming home. Or about you not telling me you loved me when you hung up the phone. What's up with that?"

"Nah, don't try to flip it on me. You know I always keep it one hunnit with you. All I did was ask a question and you turned it into some other shit. You cold, Lasonya. Deflecting shit onto me while you gettin' busy doing all kinds of bullshit."

Lasonya grabbed the phone from the table and unlocked it. "My password is Marie, Quaysha's middle name. Here. You can look through it. Now gimme yours and tell me your password."

Desmond looked at the phone stretched out in her hand. He wanted to grab it and look through it. He knew he would find some dirt on her. Then he thought about his phone. Pebbles had sent him all kinds of nasty text messages, pictures, and videos. Instead of grabbing Lasonya's phone, he got up and headed for their bedroom.

"I ain't got time to be arguing with you about this bullshit. All I did was ask a simple question and you getting on all kinds of extra shit. Fuck you."

Lasonya was shocked that he had talked to her so strongly. She chased him to the bedroom "Fuck me? Really, Desmond? We going there now? Fuck me?" she yelled, getting in his face.

Desmond got on her level and raised his voice. "Yeah. Fuck you! I'm out here risking my life tryna keep us together and safe while you doing who know what. Then you accusing me of shit. I'm working with the Feds because of yo' ass. I went to jail for you and yo' daughter. I lost my brother because of all this shit. You ain't lose shit. You just sitting back playing all these bitch-ass games and lying. Fuck you, Lasonya. Two times," Desmond spazzed, grabbing his pistol and phone and leaving the house.

Desmond drove aimlessly through the night, thinking about the argument he had with Lasonya. Their relationship was on rocky ground and her being pregnant complicated everything. He wasn't sure if the baby was his. But there was a possibility. And that possibility kept him from making a move. He was stuck until he could catch her red-handed or prove the paternity of the baby.

The ringing of his phone pulled him from the conflicting thoughts. It was Rich Red.

"What's good, li'l brah?"

"We found that bitch, D."

"Evet?" Desmond questioned.

"You know it. Took a li'l bit, but I got that address."

"Okay. Text it to me and I'ma take care of that."

"Already?" Rich chuckled.

◆◆◆

"What's good, Chauncey?" Breed nodded.

Chauncey opened the screen door to let his partner in the house. "What it do, fool? What you on?"

"Shit. Just out here tryna catch a nigga slippin'. I need to get my face dirty."

Chauncey locked the door and the men had seats in the living room. "I got down a li'l bit earlier, but that shit wasn't no flake. You know that nigga Vincent got that diesel. Ronny said he gotta grit from 'em yesterday and that shit was fiya."

Breed's eyes lit up. "Get at that nigga and tell 'em to give us a grit. I'm tryna get my nostrils dirty."

Chauncey shook his head. "That nigga want his shit up front."

"I should take that bitch-ass nigga's shit," Breed snapped. "Where he at?"

"You know Vincent fuck wit' them Trill Niggas. If we hit that nigga, we gon' have to blow all them niggas down."

Breed sulked for a moment. "I hate when these niggas be protecting these soft-ass niggas. Niggas fuckin' up the game."

"What's up wit' Evet? I know her phone full of niggas that got money. Make that bitch give up another nigga."

"Man, that bitch still trippin' off that last move. We didn't rob them niggas and we used her to get him to open the door. She think them soft-ass niggas gon' get at her. She don't even wanna come outside."

"Yeah, that was fucked up," Chauncey laughed

"But fuck that bitch. She ain't shit. Just wanna fuck a nigga car."

Chauncey gave his boy the eye. "Quit actin' like you ain't in love with that bitch, nigga. Know she had you fannin' niggas down over that pussy," he laughed.

Breed mugged his boy. "Fuck you, soft-ass nigga."

After a bout of silence, Chauncey got serious. "Brah, I think you should try to sweet talk the bitch and try to get back good. Since she already hot with the nigga Vel, she might as well let us hit all the niggas she know. We can get on some jack mob shit. Use her to fuck these niggas up. Go to Flint or something and have our way siccin' her on them d-boys."

Breed's eyes grew wide like he just heard a master plan. "Hell yeah, my nigga. Why you ain't been told me this shit? I coulda been made the bitch get down."

"I don't know. I just thought about it. You the one with the stripper bitch. You shoulda been thought about this. But you can't beat the bitch up and try to force her to get down. That shit ain't gon' work. You gotta get on some mack shit. Take her out. Buy her some shit. Tell her you love her. Let her know you tryna build some shit and you need her."

Breed smiled. "Damn. Yo' bitch ass sound like you know what you talking 'bout. I'm on that. But first I need to get right. Who can we hit to get a couple hunnit? I need my medicine and a few dollars to do something nice for her."

Chauncey thought for a moment. Then a light went on in his eyes. "You wanna hit Vincent? If we do, we gotta fuck 'em up."

Breed smiled, murder in his eyes. "Call that nigga."

◆◆◆

Breed pulled the Charger to the curb behind the red Nissan Altima, noticing more than one head in the ride.

"I knew this nigga wasn't gon' be by hisself," Chauncey said, agitated that things weren't going according to plan.

"Fuck them niggas," Breed said as he parked the car. "That just mean we finna get more money. I'm clappin' both them niggas. Let's get it."

After taking a look around to make sure there were no eyewitnesses, the jackers hopped out and approached the Nissan. Breed approached the driver's side window while Chauncey lingered near the trunk on passenger side.

"What's good, Vincent?" Breed greeted as he approached the rolled down window. He noticed the passenger held a pistol on his lap and was watching Chauncey in the side mirror. "I see you got the goons out."

A tall and slim dark-skinned man with dreadlocks sat behind the steering wheel. "It's dangerous out here. What's good, Breed? What you wanted?" Vincent asked.

"Let me get five grits."

Vincent grabbed the scale from the center console, setting it on the dash and pulling out a baggie with twenty grams of heroin. He began scooping the dope onto the scale. Breed waited until the perfect moment to pull his move. When Vincent's hands were occupied getting the drugs ready and the shooter's attention was focused on Chauncey, Breed pulled the .40 from his waist and took aim at the passenger.

Clap, clap, clap, clap, clap, clap!

The shooter never got the opportunity to lift his weapon as bullets tore into his face and chest. He fell against the door and began shaking.

Vincent dropped the drugs in his lap, lifting his hands in the air as bullets whizzed by his face.

Chauncey moved quickly, hopping in the backseat while Breed pointed the pistol at Vincent.

"Give that shit up, nigga!" Breed demanded.

Before Vincent could react, Chauncey grabbed the dope from his lap and began going through his pockets. He took money, drugs, and a gun from Vincent before searching the dead passenger. He also had money and drugs.

"What else in the car, nigga?" Breed asked.

"That's it. Y'all got it," Vincent said, trying to stay calm.

Chauncey checked the center console and glove compartment. When he didn't find anything of value, he climbed from the car. "Let's go, fam."

Vincent looked at Breed to see what his next move would be. When he saw the cold look in the jackboys eyes, he knew he was about to die.

Clap, clap!

"What we get?" Breed asked as he sped away from the scene.

Chauncey sat in the passenger seat counting money. "Look like almost twenty racks and about two zips of food."

"Oooohhh!" Breed yelled, happy with the take. "Put me something together so I can treat my nose, nigga."

◆◆◆

Desmond was dressed in all black with a cap pulled down covering his eyes. He stood on the side of a duplex watching the gray and white one-story house across the street. He had been scoping the spot for a little more than an hour and had already looked in the windows. From what he could tell, Evet was home alone. He'd thought of several ways to enter the house, but none of them seemed logical. A female at home alone might be extra cautious and not open the door for just anyone. He was trying to come up with a way to get inside when a police car turned onto the block, forcing him to duck into the shadows. And that's when he came up with his plan to get inside. After the police car disappeared, Desmond crossed the street, taking off the hat as he knocked on Evet's door.

"Who is it?" she called.

"Detroit police. I'm looking for Evet."

There was silence inside the house. Desmond knocked on the door again.

"Evet, this is Detective Sanders. I need to speak to you. Open the door."

"What do you want? I didn't do nothing," she called.

Desmond could hear the fear in her voice. He was almost in. "I didn't say you did anything. I didn't come to arrest you. Look out the peephole. I'm by myself. I just came to talk." He did a friendly wave and grinned, hoping to disarm her with him smile.

Locks clicked and the door opened. A pretty young brown-skinned woman peeked outside. She looked Desmond over from head to toe. "You don't look like the police. You got a badge?"

"Yeah. I got it," Desmond said, reaching behind him like he was going in his back pocket. Instead of a badge, he came out with a gun and pushed his way inside.

"Help! Somebody help!" she screamed.

"Shut the fuck up and get the fuck in the house!" he yelled, shoving her onto the couch and pointing the gun in her face. "Who all in here?" he asked. He had already looked through the windows, but he wanted to be sure she was home alone.

"Ain't nobody here but me. What you want?"

Desmond lowered the gun and stood up. "I'm not gon' touch you if you don't scream. A'ight?"

She nodded, fear in the whites of her eyes.

He walked over to close the door. "I need you to call Breed."

"I don't got nothing to do with what he do. Please, don't hurt me," she begged, tears spilling down her face.

"I'm not. And I know you don't got nothing to do with him. I just need you to call him. When he comes, I'm taking him with me and you won't see me no more. That's my word."

She stared at him for a moment, trying to gauge if he was telling the truth. Desmond looked sympathetic and nodded. "I'ma leave as soon as he comes. I swear," he said, putting the gun in his waist and sitting on the couch across from her.

"We not talking right now."

"That's okay. Tell him you wanna talk. You know niggas is stupid and gon' fall for anything," he cracked, giving a smile.

Evet grabbed her phone and dialed a number.

"Put it on speaker," he said, making sure she wasn't playing games.

She did and they listened as the phone rang.

"What up, bae? I was just thinking about coming to see you," Breed slurred, sounding high.

"I need to talk to you."

"Okay, okay. I need to talk to you too. I been thinking 'bout how I treat you and I wanna apologize for all the bullshit. I'm sorry, baby."

Evet rolled her eyes. "Thank you for that. Can you come over right now? I really wanna see you."

"Yeah, yeah. I'm on my way right now. I got plans for us, baby. Big plans. Fuck wit'cha boy."

After ending the call, Evet looked at Desmond. "He coming."

"You did good. Thank you," Desmond smiled, standing and pulling the pistol. Fear shone in Evet's eyes when she saw the gun. And the single bullet to her forehead left the fearful look etched on her face forever.

Desmond sat with the corpse, waiting for Breed. Twenty minutes later, there was a knock on the door. Desmond checked the peephole and saw Breed standing on the porch smiling. He unlocked and opened the door, keeping himself hidden. Breed stepped inside and looked around.

"Evet, where you - "Breed stopped talking when he saw his girl laying on the couch bleeding from the forehead.

Desmond appeared from behind the door a moment later, pointing the 9-millimeter in his face. "I heard you was looking for me."

Pop!

J-Blunt

## Chapter 9

Agent Wright sat in the chair inside the debriefing room, staring at the wall. There were pictures of Donny and his crew posted on a drawing board with names and other information written next to the pictures. Because of Desmond, the ATF had everything they needed to bring down Donny and his crew. They had wire taps, drug deals, marked money, pictures, and video, basically a slam dunk in federal court. They could put Donny away for life. But Donny was just a small fish in the ocean of crime syndicates. The Feds wanted the Family. There were whisperings of a multi-state drug ring, but no agency had been able to connect the dots. Agent Wright sat in the chair, hoping that Desmond would bring them one step closer to busting the ring.

"Pictures don't talk back," Agent Johansen cracked, walking into the office and catching her partner in a trance.

"I wish they did," Wright said, spinning in the chair to face her. "That would make this all a lot easier."

"The problem is you expect it to be easy," Johansen said, walking across the room to stand in front of the board. "Anything that comes easy isn't worth having. When you work hard for something, you get more satisfaction when it all works out."

Wright laughed. "You reading another feel good book recommended by Oprah?"

Johansen shot him a look. "As a matter of fact, I am. But that isn't the point. We'll get Donny and everybody connected to him. Desmond is one of the best assets we've ever had. If he can get inside the Family, can you imagine what that would do for our careers?"

"Hell yeah. But first we have to stop the fucking leak. Did you hear anything?"

Johansen shook her head. "No. But there are only five of us on the team. If it's not you or me..." Johansen's words trailed off.

Wright caught her drift. "Who do you think it could be?"

Before Johansen could give an opinion, the door opened and three federal agents walked in, completing the team: Peggy Swain, Larry Hernandez, and Laura Bump.

"Hey, guys," Peggy smiled. The forty-two-year-old blonde woman's teeth were sparkling white like she was in a toothpaste commercial. "Would've been here sooner, but it turns out Larry doesn't like mocha lattes." She laughed.

Wright and Johansen looked to Larry with questioning looks.

The brown-skinned Mexican opened his jacket, revealing a brown coffee stain that covered most of his torso. "I didn't see Benji. Bumped into him. It was an accident."

Everyone in the room shared a laugh.

"Alright, guys. Let's get serious," Agent Wright said, trying to get everyone focused. "Desmond debriefed us and we have a few things we need to discuss, mainly the need for silence and secrecy. This is a big case and somehow Donny knows we're onto him. The only people that know the identity of Desmond are in this room. If Donny finds out Desmond is working for us, he will most certainly be killed. The director and assistant director know of the leak and are conducting their own investigation. This is serious, people. This is a big mission for the Bureau and our team. We're almost at home plate. If you are the leak, we're onto you, so knock it off," Wright admonished, looking around the room and staring everyone in their eyes. When he was satisfied that he got his point across, he nodded to his partner.

"Aright, guys. We've got additional intel that is the closest link that we have to connecting Donny to the Family and we're going to need you guys do some digging," Johansen said as she walked to the drawing board. "Donny recently visited California and we believe that it was to meet with members of the Family. We know this because Desmond confirmed with the dealer in Milwaukee that a new player named Wacco Tony was also in California and may have taken part in the same meeting. What we need is to coordinate with the Bureau in Milwaukee to see if they have anything on Wacco Tony. We need to know who he is and his associates. The faster we move, the quicker we can get to the family and make the bust. I'm going to be emailing all of you assignments after the meeting. Take care of your part."

"And make sure you remember that this is a classified mission," Agent Wright reminded. "Nobody says anything to anybody, no matter who they are. I don't care how long they've been with the federal government. I will do the information sharing with the appropriate people. Am I clear?"

Larry, Peggy, and Laura nodded and agreed with the senior agent.

"Okay. Let's get to work," Wright dismissed them.

Peggy left the meeting quickly, trying to hide the nervous energy that coursed through her body. She made a beeline to her desk and grabbed her cell phone from her purse. She sent a text to Brian Cranston.

*We need to talk.*

He texted back a moment later.

*In a meeting. Might be long. Call u later.*

She texted back.

*Meet me by your place.*

◆◆◆

Brian Cranston loved his job.

Standing 5'7" and 150 pounds on a good day, the blonde-haired, brown-eyed white man was one of the most powerful men on the streets of Detroit. He had been with the ATF for seven years and for seven years, he took advantage of the opportunities being a federal agent presented. When he needed cash, all it took was a phone call and thousands of dollars were available. If he needed drugs, all it took was a phone call. If he needed a new car because a bird took a shit on his window, all it took was a phone call. Everything he needed was literally a phone call away.

"Brian, what's good, my dude?" Boogie smiled, showing off a row of diamond-studded teeth as he stood at the front door.

"Hey, man. Let me in," Brian said.

Boogie didn't move. "TJ don't want no company right now."

Brian mugged the doorman. "If you don't get outta my way, you'll be floating in Lake Michigan when TJ finds out you are the reason he didn't know one of his houses is about to be raided."

Boogie's face went flat as he reached behind him and tapped on the door three times. When it opened, a tall and slim dark-skinned man appeared holding a pistol. His name was Flex.

"What up, Boogie?"

"Brian here. He wanna see TJ."

Flex nodded to Brian. "What's yo' bidness, B?"

"Need to see your boss."

Flex stepped aside. "Come in."

Brian stepped into the living room and saw more money than he knew what to do with spread out on a table that could seat six people. Money machines rattled as two men counted the green backs. He followed Flex to the kitchen, where a short light-skinned man was sitting at a table with kilos of cocaine in front of him. A pretty Columbian woman stood next to him, weighing the drugs on a triple beam scale.

"Brian, what's up, papi?" The light-skinned man smiled, his voice heavy with a thick accent.

"TJ! I see business is good." Brian smiled, eyeing the drugs.

"Thanks to you, my friend. Have a seat. What you need, papi?"

Brian pulled a chair up to the table, eyeing the fine Latin woman. "I came to give you a tip. Your house on the south side is about to be hit."

TJ stopped what he was doing and eyed the Fed. "No shit?"

"No shit. Tomorrow night is D-day."

"Okay." TJ nodded. "How many should I leave inside?"

"Give us two or three guys and a couple of ounces. That should keep them busy for a while. Make sure your boys don't talk."

"You got it, papi. What you need? How much?"

"I'll take my usual five thousand," Brian said, licking his lips at the Columbian woman. "If you could get her to do me a favor, I would really appreciate it."

The woman looked at the federal agent like he stank. "Uh-uh. I don't do favors."

"Yes, you do," TJ said. "If Brian wants a favor, you give Brian what he wants."

"Nuh-uh, TJ. I'm not a little thot," she sassed.

The drug runner looked her from head to toe. "Listen, Tatiana, you gon' be whatever I say and right now you do favors," he told her before turning to Brian. "All the rooms being used. Take her to the bathroom."

Brian smiled at the woman as he stood. "After you."

Tatiana shot the Fed an angry look before walking away. Brian checked out her ass while she led the way. It was perfectly round, bouncing and jiggling in the white cotton shorts as she power walked. When they got to the bathroom, she walked inside, spinning to face him, attitude written all over her face.

"What do you want?"

"For you to lose some of the attitude," Brian said as he locked the door.

"When punk-ass horny mutherfuckers like you think I'm supposed to fuck you like I'm a cheap-ass hoe, that shit gives me an attitude, mutherfucker. I ain't no fuckin' trick-ass bitch. I hustle."

"There wouldn't be a hustle if it wasn't for me. All I want is a little appreciation."

Tatiana rolled her eyes and her neck. "Kiss my ass. Appreciate that."

Brian pulled his pistol and grabbed her by the hair, forcing her to her knees. "I tried to be nice, but you don't want that. Suck my fucking cock, you stupid bitch."

Tatiana mugged him as she unzipped his pants and pulled out his erect penis. She sucked him into her mouth and gave him angry head.

"Yeah, that's it. Suck my white cock, bitch!" Brian groaned, loving the sight of his dick disappearing into her mouth over and over. The aggressive blow job brought him to a quick climax. Tatiana moved her head when the first drop of cum touched her tongue and allowed the rest of his body fluid to spill on the floor.

"There you go, you nasty mutherfucker," she mugged, moving out of the way as semen sputtered from his dick.

"If you didn't have an attitude, I woulda said you did a good job," Brian said, stroking himself over the toilet to get all the nut out. "Next time, I'm going to fuck you in the ass."

Tatiana rolled her eyes and left the bathroom.

♦♦♦

Peggy spent the rest of the day looking over her shoulder, expecting to be cuffed and interrogated at any moment. Thankfully it didn't happen and she was able to make it to the end of her shift. She left the building and drove directly to Brian's house. She hopped out of her Subaru and walked quickly upon the porch and into the house.

"Brian! Where are you?"

"I'm in the kitchen," he called.

Peggy hightailed it to the kitchen and found him popping the top on a beer.

"Who did you talk to about the mission!?" she accused.

Brian looked confused. "What the fuck are you talking about?"

"I told you I was on a team investigating Donny. Now Donny knows. Who the fuck did you talk to?"

Brian sat the beer on the counter. "That wasn't me, baby. I don't know what you're talking about. I've worked on secret missions too. That shit is classified. I know how it works. I wouldn't tell anybody what you told me. It wasn't me, sweetie."

"Somehow Donny found out and now the director is doing an investigation. If it gets back to me, I could lose my job. I might even go to jail!" She panicked.

Brian grabbed her shoulders, looking in her eyes. "Calm down, Peggy. You're going to be okay. You're not going to jail."

She slapped his arms away angrily and began pacing the kitchen. "How do you know? The director of the ATF is investigating! This is serious."

"Don't do this to yourself, baby. The only person you told is me, right?"

She nodded. "Yes."

"Okay. I'm not going to tell anyone that you told me anything. If I'm the only thing connecting you to it, you'll be okay."

She stopped pacing and studied him for a moment. "Really? You'd perjure yourself for me?"

Brian approached her, staring into her eyes lovingly. "I'd give my last breath to protect you, baby. I wouldn't let anybody do anything to you as long as I have breath in my body. I love you."

The words touched Peggy. "You mean that?"

He leaned in and pecked her lips. "Of course. You mean the world to me."

When he backed away, Peggy moved closer, wanting more kisses. Brian gave her what she wanted. When they got hot and heavy, he stopped.

"What?" Peggy asked, wanting more.

"Are you sure you didn't tell anybody else about your mission?"

"Yes. You're the only person I told."

"Okay. What's the agent's name that's working with Donny's people? Just so I can keep my ears and eyes open."

Peggy looked like she was considering telling him. "I can't say. I've already said too much. I don't want to get him killed."

"Okay. That's fine. I get it," Brian said. "You wanna go up to my room and finish this?" he asked, looking down at the bulge that had grown in his pants.

Peggy grabbed his crotch and kissed his lips. "I'm so stressed out. I need help getting away from all my problems."

Brian grabbed her ass. "Go to the room. I'll be there in a minute."

When Peggy left the kitchen, Brian ran a hand over his face. "Fuck!" he cursed, picking up the phone. He dialed a number and waited.

"What's up?" Donny answered.

"I got a problem. She's spooked."

"I don't care. I need to know who the snitch is."

"She's not talking. Her team knows that there's a leak. Whoever you talked to is the snitch or talked to the snitch. They spooked her. She thinks she's going to jail."

"Listen, mutherfucker. I don't care what you have to do to get her to tell you who it is. Just make her tell you. Failure is not an option. I'm going to keep this phone on me. You're the only one with this number. Call me when you figure it out."

## Chapter 10

"I'm thinking 'bout sayin' fuck that jack shit and staying with the hustle. My line's starting to go crazy," Meechy said passing the blunt to Zoe. They were sitting around Rachel's old house, which had become the trap house, kicking it and smoking.

"This shit is sweet. Niggas get free work." Zoe laughed. "Nigga throwing around these twenty-gram packs like it ain't shit."

"And he only want seventy-five a gram. And it's flake."

"I'm stepping on my shit wit' that lactose. Turn that twenty into thirty."

Meechy looked at him like he said something disrespectful. "You only turnin' it to thirty? Shit, nigga, I hit it with that lactose and whip this bitch to fifty every time."

"On what? And they still come back?" Zoe asked, surprised by the stretch.

"I told you it's that flake. I wonder what he holding. Nigga might got them books."

Zoe thought for a moment. "Damn. If I had a book of dog food, I be rich as a bitch."

"You know what? Fuck er'thang I just said. We gotta hit this nigga. I ain't neva seen a whole book."

"You know Lucky ain't one of them sweet-ass niggas so we gotta hit him hard," Zoe said. "I seen the nigga get down. Blew a nigga's face off."

"Where that nigga keep that money and work? You think he got it here or at the new house?" Meechy asked.

"It gotta be at that house in Brown Deer," Zoe said, looking around the living room like he was trying to find a stash spot. "Nigga ain't stupid enough to keep nothing in here. Especially after we turned it into a trap."

Meechy nodded. "Yeah. How you wanna do it? I'm thinking we tell the nigga to bring us a pack and then up on him and make him take us to the safe."

A noise in the kitchen got the jackboys' attention. After sharing a look, they got up and went to investigate. They found Ryder standing near the back door.

"Ryder, fuck you creeping up on niggas like that for?" Meechy snapped.

"I wasn't creeping. The back door was open, nigga. You niggas in here slipping?"

Zoe and Meechy shared a look.

"How long you been in here?" Zoe asked.

Ryder paused for the slightest moment. "Not that long. I was just finna make a move. I'ma holla at you niggas," he said, turning to leave.

"Hold on, Ryder!" Zoe stopped him.

"What's good?"

"Listen, li'l brah. We got some hoes on deck and we need one more person. You showed up just in time."

Ryder stared at them suspiciously. "I'm good. I was on somethin' already."

"C'mon, my nigga," Meechy encouraged. "They bad. Foreign. Come fuck wit' us."

Ryder could see the eagerness in their eyes and knew they wouldn't accept no for any answer. "A'ight. Lemme call Q and let him know what we on," he said, pulling out his phone.

Zoe stopped him from dialing the number. "You don't need that. Q good. You fuckin' wit' us."

Ryder pressed the call button as he slipped the phone into his pocket. "A'ight. We leaving right now?"

"Yeah. We hopping in the box Chevy."

The hustlers left the trap, heading for the old school.

"You got shotgun, Ryder," Meechy said as he climbed in the back seat.

"Where these hoes live?" Ryder asked as he got in the car.

"Over on Fon Du Lac. All of 'em strapped." Zoe nodded as he pulled away from the curb.

"So, me, you, and Meechy going to some hoe's house over on Fon Du Lac, huh, Zoe?" Ryder asked.

Zoe took his eyes off the road and looked at Ryder suspiciously. "I just said that, nigga. You actin' like you got on a wire or somethin'."

Meechy's eyes grew wide when he realized what was going on. He pulled his banger and put it to the back of Ryder's head. "Where the fuck that phone at, nigga?"

"What you on, Meechy? Why you upping on me?" Ryder yelled, lifting his hands.

Meechy slapped him in the back of the head with the pistol. "Shut the fuck up, nigga! Fuck that phone at?" he asked, searching his pockets roughly. When he pulled it out, he checked the screen. The call was open and Quincy's name was on the screen. Meechy showed the phone to Zoe before ending the call.

"Why you do that stupid-ass shit?" Zoe mugged him.

"How you niggas gon' bite the hand that feeds y'all?" Ryder asked, holding his head. "We put you niggas on and y'all gon' turn grimy?"

Meechy slapped him with the pistol again. "Shut the fuck up, nigga! Don't nobody wanna hear that hoe-ass shit."

"Damn, Ryder. You shouldn't have did that shit, fam." Zoe shook his head as he pulled into an alley. "Get out."

"I know y'all finna kill me. I know how this shit go. I ain't gettin' out the car," Ryder refused.

Meechy lifted the gun to the back of Ryder's head and squeezed the trigger.

Ryder's body flew forward, head hitting the dashboard.

"Damn, nigga! Why you didn't wait for him to get out!" Zoe yelled.

"He said he wasn't getting out. Fuck you wanted, for me to negotiate with the nigga? He was gon' die anyway."

"Help me grab this nigga 'fore he bleeds all over my shit," Zoe said, grabbing Ryder and holding him up so blood wouldn't get on the interior.

Meechy got out of the car and opened the passenger door, pulling the dead body from the car. "What you wanna do with this nigga?"

Zoe looked around the alley. It was daylight and they couldn't leave the body in the middle of the alley. "We gotta throw him in the garbage."

After dumping Ryder in a garbage can, Zoe sped out of the alley.

"Go to the car wash so we can clean this bitch," Meechy said, looking around for bloodstains.

"That's where I'm going," Zoe said. "If Quincy heard us, he gon' know we whacked his nigga."

"I know. We can act like we took the nigga to see the hoes. Say he left wit' one and we ain't seen him since."

"That shit might not work if he heard the call."

"Either that or we just go off the nigga. We only need to be around long enough to get Lucky. After that, fuck all these niggas."

"You wanna do it now?"

Meechy shrugged. "Fuck it. Call that nigga and tell him we need another pack."

◆◆◆

"Daddy, I'm finna go shopping with Aunty April and Trina. I need some money," Laronda asked, walking into Lucky and Rachel's room.

"You asking me for some money, or telling me to give you some money?" Lucky asked, giving her a hard time.

"Whatever gon' get you to give me the money."

"Well in that case, I ain't giving you shit."

"C'mon, Daddy! I need some money. They on the way."

"That ain't my problem. I got some money. All you had to do was ask."

"Okay. Can I have some money?"

Lucky shook his head. "It's too late now. I ain't got none to give."

Laronda turned to Rachel. "Can you tell yo' man to give me some money?"

"Give it to her, Lucky. Stop playing. April on the way."

Lucky mugged his girl. "Hold on, baby. Whose side you on?"

Rachel mugged him back. "You ain't know? Girl power, nigga!"

"Hey! I know that's right!" Laronda sang.

Lucky waved them both off. "Whatever. I ain't giving her nothing."

The females shared a look.

"Oh yeah? You ain't giving her nothing?" Rachel asked.

Lucky stood firm. "Nothing. Nada. N to the O."

"Well, we gon' take it then!" Rachel said, diving on top of Lucky. Laronda jumped right in the action and dove on top of Lucky too. The girls jumped him. Rachel put him in a choke hold while Laronda punched him in the body.

"I'm fuckin' y'all up!" Lucky yelled, wrestling from the chokehold and snatching up Laronda in a bear hug. He threw her on the bed and climbed on top of her, pressing his chin into her shoulder. Rachel grabbed a pillow and started hitting him.

"Ouch, Daddy! Okay! I quit!" Laronda screamed.

"Tell Rachel to stop hitting me!"

"Okay! Rachel, stop!"

Rachel didn't stop hitting him. "Let her go, nigga! Let her go!"

Lucky continued digging his chin into Laronda's shoulder.

"Stop, Daddy! You hurting my arm!"

"Busta, tell her to stop!"

Rachel stopped hitting him with the pillow. "Okay. I got yo' ass Lucky," she said, diving on top of him and grabbing his dick.

"Okay! I quit!" Lucky yelled, letting Laronda go and grabbing Rachel's hand. "Let me go, baby. I quit," he whined.

Rachel let him go, smiling proudly at Laronda. "When you want a nigga to stop, all you gotta do is grab that thang between his legs. Bet his ass cooperates."

"That shit was cheating," Lucky sulked.

"Can I have some money now?" Laronda asked.

Lucky looked at her like she was crazy. "Hell nah! Y'all just jumped me."

"Forget him, girl. I got you," Rachel said, going into her purse and pulling out 200 dollars. "Buy you something nice."

"Thank you, Rachel. Bye Daddy." Laronda smiled as she left the room and walked outside to wait for her ride. A few minutes later, the Buick Envoy pulled to a stop in the middle of the street. Laronda sprinted from the porch and jumped in the passenger seat.

"Is we good?" Quincy asked, watching the mirrors as he sped away.

"Yeah. Him and Rachel still in bed. Gimme my kiss," she said, grabbing his face and kissing him aggressively.

"What you tell him?"

"That my aunty was coming to get me. I already talked to my aunty, so we good. You mines and I'm yours. I hope you ready for this."

Quincy leaned over and kissed her again. "Don't worry about if I'm ready for you. I hope you ready for me."

The young couple drove to the mall and did some shopping before hitting a hotel and spending some time getting to know each other intimately. After they finished, they lay in bed smoking a blunt.

"I don't believe you fifteen. Not doing all that. Lemme see that birth certificate," Quincy joked.

"I'm an OG, baby. I told you," Laronda bragged.

"Yeah, a'ight. I hope you don't think we done yet. We got all day," Quincy said, passing her the blunt.

"You the one that needs a break. I'm ready," Laronda sassed.

"Shit, you ain't said nothing!" Quincy said as he rolled on top of her. And that's when his phone rang. "You lucky. Saved by the bell," he said as he grabbed the phone.

"Don't let that be the reason. You know you can't hang," Laronda continued.

"Wait til I get off this phone," he promised as he answered the call on the speaker. "What up, Ryder?"

No one spoke, but Quincy could hear voices.

"I think this nigga pocket dialed me," he laughed. "Ryder? Ryder!"

When he heard Zoe's and Meechy's names, he began listening. He couldn't hear exactly what they were saying. Something about a hoe. Then Ryder screamed and said something about getting up on. Then the call went dead.

"What the fuck was that?" Laronda asked.

"I don't know," Quincy said, worry for his nigga filling his being as he called Ryder back. The call went directly to voicemail. "Damn," Quincy cursed, dialing the number again. The operator answered again. He dialed T.A. next.

"What's good, brah?"

"You heard from Ryder?"

"Not since earlier. I thought he was with you."

"Nah. I had to make a move. He just called and I think he with Zoe and Meechy. I think something just happened. Meet me at the trap."

◆◆◆

"How you feel about leaving Milwaukee?"

Rachel looked up from her phone and saw Lucky watching her. "I mean, I thought about it, but I don't know where to go."

"I was talking to Laronda yesterday and she wanna leave. She said a bunch of shit that got me thinking. We done been through so much. It's my job to protect her. Everybody around us keeps dying and I'm all she got. She wants a better life and I need to give her that opportunity."

Rachel nodded. "You are her only parent. And Milwaukee is a dangerous place for you right now. It might be time to go."

"Will you come with us?"

Rachel got upon from the bed and walked over to Lucky. "I would go anywhere with you, baby," she said, kissing him on the lips. "But what about the deal you made with Donny?"

"I gotta find a way to get out this shit. When I got outta the joint, I didn't have no plans on doing this shit. I was planning to be a square and get married, write books and invest in a business. All this shit just happened. I don't wanna do this. This ain't me."

"Whatever you wanna do, I'm with you. I got your back."

"What about me being on the run? You know I got eight years of parole hanging over my head. Plus, they wanna question me 'bout some murders. You sure you wanna stick with me?"

Rachel stared into his eyes for a moment, letting him see her conviction. "I'm serious about what I said. I love you, Lucky. You my nigga. I'm riding with you. And if you go to prison, I'ma be in that visiting room. My daddy been in jail most of my life. I know how it goes. I got your back."

Lucky bent down and tongued his woman down. "I'm finna call Donny and see if I can get out. How you feel about Atlanta? It's good for black people down there."

Rachel smiled. "I always wanted to see Magic City."

"Me too." Lucky nodded, pulling out his phone. He dialed Royce's number, remembering the last conversation with Donny. He knew there was a rat in his midst and he had switched the phones of everyone in his inner circle to burner phones.

"What's up, Mil?" Royce answered, using Lucky's nickname.

"You with him?"

"Yeah. Hold on."

There was a brief pause before Donny got on the phone. "What's up? Everything good?"

"Yeah. Yeah. We good these ways. I wanted to talk to you about my exit. I'm thinking about retiring."

There was a change in Donny's tone. "Wait a minute, brotha. We had a deal. I took care of that situation for you and you owe me. This wasn't part of our plans."

"I know. But I didn't wanna play ball forever. You know I did the pad and pen. Things is crazy around my way and I got a lot on my plate. I already got a sentence hanging over my head. I need to make an exit before shit gets worse for me."

"C'mon now, Mil. You can't change the rules in the middle of the game, baby boy."

"I didn't even know what game we was playing until I got the ball. You forced this on me. I didn't want this. I'm not tryna be at the top of nobody's food chain."

Donny let out a hot breath. "Listen, my nigga. You signed that deal. You owe me."

"I know that. But how long you expect me to keep paying you? I don't wanna play this game forever."

Donny went silent for a moment. "There is a fracture in the Family and a spot might be opening soon. This is a big deal. Power players are in this. You can have a seat at the table and experience real juice. Real power. The kind of power where that little sentence that's hanging over your head won't mean shit. The kind of power that will make things like that go away. Stay the course. Trust me. Big things are on the horizon."

Lucky thought about Desmond and knew those big horizons may never come to fruition. "That sounds like a good thing, man. But it's not for me. I can't do this forever. I need to retire one day."

"Okay, Mil. It sounds like you got your mind made up. I can't force you to do something that you don't want to do. I'm going to look over the contract and get back to you. I'll let you know something soon."

Rachel watched lucky expectantly as he hung up the phone. "What did he say?"

"He knows I don't want to do this forever. Said he gon' let me know something soon. If I got to, I'll say fuck that nigga and do me. My family matters more than anything."

Rachel smiled. "I love when you show yo' gangsta. That shit is sexy."

Lucky bent down to kiss her. "You know what I think is sexy?"

Rachel kissed him again, excitement lighting her eyes. "What?"

"You with no clothes on."

"Come take 'em off then."

Lucky reached down and grabbed her shirt, lifting it over her head. She wasn't wearing a bra and her nipples were pointing at him like two little fingers. He bent down and hooked his thumbs inside her shorts, pulling them down. She wasn't wearing any panties. He kissed the V between her legs.

"Mmmhhh," Rachel moaned, rubbing the back of his head.

When she lay back on the bed, Lucky spread her legs and dove in face first. He attacked her pearl tongue like it was his favorite piece of candy, licking and sucking the sensitive ball of flesh.

"Yeah, baby! Oh my God! Ssss! Mmmhhh!" Rachel moaned, gripping the back of his head and pulling his face into her womb.

Lucky continued to please his woman, sticking two fingers inside her pussy and curling them against the front of her womb like he was telling someone to come, stroking her G-spot.

"Oh, Lucky! That feel so good, baby. Oh shit! Oh shit!" Rachel screamed as her orgasm built up.

"Oh, baby! I'm finna cum, Lucky! Oh, God! Oh God! Oooh!"

Lucky continued delivering pleasure as Rachel's body locked up and juice gushed from her womb, covering his face and hand. He stood over Rachel, looking in her eyes as he slipped the cum-coated fingers in his mouth and sucked them.

"They shit look so sexy," Rachel moaned, loving the sight of him sucking her juices.

Lucky had just started taking off his clothes when his phone rang. He wanted to ignore it, but now that he was hustling, every call meant more money in the bank. "Let me get this real quick."

Rachel mugged him. "Seriously, Lucky!"

Lucky pulled out the phone and checked the screen. "I'ma just see what he wants, baby. Zoe, what's good, my nigga?"

"I need to see you, boss. Me and Meechy."

Lucky looked at Rachel. She was mugging him, daring him to leave in the middle of having sex. "Um, okay. I'm in the middle of something right now. Let me get with you later."

"C'mon, Lucky. My line dumping, my nigga. I need that."

Lucky looked at Rachel again. She was still watching him. "Okay. I'ma get that to y'all ASAP." After ending the call with Zoe, Lucky hit Quincy.

"What's good, Lucky?"

"I need you to get up with Zoe and Meechy for me. You got enough?"

"Yeah. I just need his number. But listen, I just got a crazy ass call from Ryder. I guess he wit' them niggas and he was saying something about some hoe's house and somebody upping on him. I tried to hit him back, but he didn't answer."

Lucky was so worried about fucking his girl and busting a nut that he didn't give Quincy's concern much thought. "Don't trip on that shit. They might've got up with some hoes and now he ain't answering. You know how that shit be. I gotta go. I'ma fuck with you later. Zoe's number is 555-1385." After ending the call, Lucky turned his attention back to Rachel. "Now, where was we?"

◆◆◆

"What he say?" T.A. asked.

Quincy dropped the phone in his lap and shook his head. "He rushed me off the phone like he was on somethin'. You tried to call Ryder again?"

"Yeah. Nigga still ain't answering. You sure you heard him say they upped on him?"

"That's what it sounded like. And I heard Meechy say somethin' about his phone. Somethin' ain't right about them niggas. I know some snakes when I see 'em. And them niggas is cobras."

"What you wanna do?"

"We finna get up wit' these niggas and see where Ryder at. Lucky wants me to drop 'em off some packs. If them niggas look like they on something, I'm bangin' they asses," Quincy said before picking up the phone again and calling Zoe.

"What's good, Q?"

"You got it. Lucky wanted me to get up wit'chu. Where you at?"

There was a pause on Zoe's end. "Uh, I'm in traffic. What happened to Lucky? I needed to holla at him."

"He busy. He wanted me to get up with you."

"Okay. A'ight. Bet. Where you at?"

"I'm swerving. I'ma meet you at the trap in like twenty minutes."

"Okay. In a minute, fam."

"Yep."

"Why you ain't ask him about Ryder?" T.A. asked.

"'Cause I wanna see that nigga's face. Nigga's eyes don't lie."

Quincy and T.A. got to the house first. They were standing in the living room when Zoe and Meechy walked in.

"What's good, family?" Zoe nodded, eyeing the Detroit hustlers for a sign of hostility.

Quincy eyed the Milwaukee jackboys and nodded. "What's good?"

Both duos picked up on the other's negative energy and the room became charged with the threat of violence.

"You got that?" Meechy asked, ready to pull his strap and clear the room.

Quincy nodded towards the table near the couch. Two baggies with twenty grams of heroin were on it. "There it is."

Meechy and Zoe looked at the drugs, but neither made a move to pick it up.

"What y'all on, fam?" Zoe asked.

"Same shit y'all on," Quincy said, hoping one of them made a move so he could have a reason to kick it off.

The men stared at each other for a few beats.

"What y'all do with Ryder?" T.A. asked.

"We dropped that nigga off wit' some hoes over on Fon Du Lac," Zoe said.

Quincy watched every word leave Zoe's lips. "Gimme they number so I can get up wit' 'em. Ryder ain't answering his phone."

Zoe looked to Meechy. "You got them hoes' number?"

"Yeah. I got it," he said, reaching for his pocket.

Quincy and T.A. went for their bangers and pointed them at Zoe and Meechy.

"What you niggas on, brah?" Zoe yelled, pissed that the young gunners had got the drop on him.

"Where Ryder at, nigga? I heard that call," Quincy mugged.

"C'mon, brah. You niggas trippin'. He with the bitch, Shacoya. I'm finna give you the number," Meechy said, going in his pocket slowly and pulling out his phone. He searched it for a moment before showing the Detroit goons. "Here go the number. Call her."

Quincy nodded to his nigga. T.A. pulled out his phone and called the number. "Ain't nobody answering."

"He prolly in that pussy, nigga. Y'all bogus for pulling them swords. That shit ain't a hunnit at all, family," Zoe mugged.

Quincy knew they were lying and thought about laying both of them down. But Lucky would be pissed if he killed them and didn't have proof that they did something to Ryder. So instead of shooting them, he gave a warning. "If my nigga don't get back at me, y'all gon' see me again. Grab y'all shit. We locking up."

The Milwaukee killers mugged the out-of-towners as they grabbed their work from the table.

"That's a violation, my nigga. We gon' see y'all later." Meechy mugged him as he and Zoe left the trap.

J-Blunt

# Chapter 11

Lasonya lay in bed rubbing her stomach while thinking about Desmond. He was acting different. She remembered when he used to worship the ground she walked on. Tell her that he loved her for no reason. Give her kisses and say that he missed her lips. Now he was acting cold. Didn't even want to say he loved her. It was like he knew she cheated with Lucky. But if he knew, why was he still coming home and why hadn't he confronted her? Was he holding it to his chest and waiting for the right time to confront her? And how would he decide when the time was right?

"Damn," she mumbled, wishing she had never crossed the line with Lucky. It made her wonder if Desmond was cheating. A week ago, she didn't think he was capable of cheating. He had an honest heart. He was genuine and real, the best boyfriend she'd ever had. He had risked his life and freedom for her. Now he barely mumbled a full sentence when they spoke. Something was going on with him and she needed to find out what was creating the space between them. She needed advice, so she went to find her mother.

Marcy was in the kitchen cooking dinner. "Hey, baby. Why you looking sad? You don't feel good?" Marcy asked.

"I think Desmond is cheating on me," Lasonya said, fighting to hold back tears.

Marcy looked up from the pork chops she was cooking. "Why would you say that? Desmond is a good man. Y'all about to have a baby."

"He stopped telling me he loved me and all we been doing is arguing lately. He been staying out all night. Had the nerve to say he got a flat."

"Well, you know he working with the police, baby. He involved on some serious shit. I don't know if he is that kind of man, but we do got that intuition. Is that what you feel, or is yo' hormones going crazy from being pregnant?"

"He cheating, Momma. I feel it."

"You know they got them apps that track people's phones. Hook his up and see where he at."

"I already did it. But I don't know my way around Detroit, so I can't tell if he where he say he at."

"Only one way to find out, baby. Betta hop in an Uber and track his ass. It might be expensive, but at least you gon' know if he cheating on you."

◆◆◆

Cully's was considered one of the best restaurants in Detroit. The five-star diner was frequented by Michigan's upper class, making it the place to be on a Saturday night. Seats were in such high demand that customers made reservations weeks in advance to get a seat. Desmond was able to score reservations from Donny.

"Oh my God, Desmond! You are so crazy!" Pebbles said, busting out laughing.

"You think I'm playing? I seen this midget porn star take all ten inches of this nigga. I couldn't believe what I was seeing because midgets so fucking little. Shit, I thought the nigga's dick was finna come out the bitch's mouth."

Pebbles busted out laughing again. "That shit sound too crazy. I'ma have to look for that video. I gotta see this li'l bitch take all that. I'm regular-sized and I don't like them big-ass dicks busting my guts open. Especially if they don't know what they doing."

"Glad I don't got that problem." Desmond smiled, raising his eyebrows. "I got that mean left stroke."

"What-ever, nigga." Pebbles blushed.

"You know you like that stroke. Be having yo' face twisted like this," he cracked, twisting his face into an ugly sex face.

"Fuck you, nigga!" She laughed, throwing a breadstick at him.

"Girl, you betta stop throwing shit up in here. You know these stuffy mu'fuckas would love to kick us out."

"I'm done eating anyway. All of these bourgeois muthafuckas can kiss my ass," Pebbles sassed.

"Can't take yo' ass nowhere," Desmond laughed.

"Yes, you can. I'm classy and nasty. When I'm supposed to be classy, I do that. When it's time to get nasty, I do that too. You know all about that gag reflex," she said, taking a breadstick and deep throating it.

Desmond's eyes popped. "You betta chill before I leave without getting my dessert."

Pebbles licked her lips. "I got some edible panties and some chocolate and strawberry sauce at home. You can turn me into a dessert and eat me."

Desmond looked around for the waiter. "Check please!"

When the couple left the restaurant, they hopped in Desmond's Tahoe and dipped. Desmond and Pebbles were so wrapped up in each other that they didn't notice the Toyota Highlander tailing them.

"I'm looking for that video right now. Where you see it at?" Pebbles asked, searching her phone.

"Type in Mighty Mouse takes it all."

Pebbles typed the words into her phone. Seconds later, the video popped up. Her eyes grew wide and her mouth dropped open. "Oh my God!"

"Didn't I tell you?"

Pebbles stared at the phone transfixed. A midget lay on her back, holding her toes, legs in the air. And a man with a huge dick was long stroking her. "Oh my God! She is taking all of it."

"That's a brave young lady," Desmond cracked.

Pebbles continued to watch the clip. "Damn. This shit is starting to get my pussy wet."

Pebbles wore a tight Moschino dress with no panties. Desmond reached a hand between her legs and felt her pussy. "Damn. You wet as hell," he said, bringing the finger to his lips and sucking her juice off.

"Gimme some," Pebbles said, grabbing his hand and sucking on it. "This ain't big enough," she said, setting her phone down and unbuttoning his pants.

"Get it then, baby!" Desmond encouraged, leaning back and giving her room to get down.

Pebbles freed his dick and then slurped it in her mouth like she was hungry. Her head bobbed rapidly as she sucked him.

"Aw, shit! Suck that muthafucka!" Desmond moaned, gripping the steering wheel with one hand and the back of her head with the other.

Pebbles moved a hand between her legs and began fingering herself while chewing on Desmond.

"Damn, baby. I'm finna bust. Swallow it all," Desmond groaned.

Pebbles sucked him harder and faster.

"Aw shiiiiiitt!" Desmond moaned as he erupted.

Pebbles continued sucking him, swallowing every drop of semen that squirted into her mouth.

"Damn, that shit was fiya!" Desmond breathed, sounding out of breath.

"I told you about my gag reflex." Pebbles grinned, adjusting his pants.

"Wait til we get to yo' house. I'ma fuck the shit out of you," Desmond promised.

When he pulled up to her house, they hopped out of the Tahoe, moving quickly to her front door to kick off a freaky fuck session. Pebbles was sticking her key in the lock when the Toyota Highlander pulled up. An angry Lasonya jumped from the passenger seat.

"Desmond! Desmond, what the fuck you doing?"

When Desmond heard her voice, he thought he was tripping. He looked up and saw Lasonya storming towards him angrily. "Shit!" he cursed.

"Who is that bitch?" Pebbles asked, copping an attitude.

"No, bitch! Who the fuck is you?" Lasonya yelled, walking up on the porch.

Desmond stepped between the women. "Lasonya, what the fuck is you doing?"

"What am I doing?" she asked incredulously. "What the fuck is you doing, nigga? Taking this bitch out on dates to restaurants while I'm stuck in the fucking house pregnant with yo' baby. I wanna go out to eat too. I don't wanna be stuck in the house waiting on you every night while you out fucking with the next bitch."

"She pregnant?" Pebbles asked

"Ain't nobody talking to you, bitch! Me and my man talking," Lasonya snapped, reaching around Desmond and snatching Pebbles by the hair.

"Lasonya, chill!" Desmond yelled, pushing his baby mama away from Pebbles. "Don't come out here tryna make no scene about me and what I'm doing when you was doing the same thing."

Lasonya was momentarily stunned by the accusation. "I ain't the one out here cheating! You the one that got caught, so don't try to switch it up on me, nigga. Was she sucking yo' dick while you was driving? Because I seen the raggedy-ass bitch's lace front disappear?"

"Sure did, bitch," Pebbles taunted. "Ask him 'bout my mouth. Swallowed every drop."

Lasonya punched Desmond in the chest and tried to attack Pebbles.

"Come say it to my face, bitch!"

Desmond shoved Lasonya backwards. "Chill, Lasonya! Fuck is wrong with you? Ain't nobody finna be out here fighting you. If yo' ass woulda kept yo' fucking legs closed, this shit wouldn't even be happening. This ain't her fault. It's yo' fault. You did this shit. You stepped out first. I know what happened while I was locked up."

Lasonya looked crestfallen. All her anger dissipated, her eye turning sorrowful. "It wasn't like that, baby."

Desmond's anger was turned up by her admission. "Oh, now I'm yo' baby? At first I was a fucking cheater, but now that yo' sins done came out, I'm yo' baby again? Fuck you, Lasonya. I'm doing me," Desmond said, spinning and walking towards Pebbles.

Lasonya grabbed his arm. "Desmond, wait!"

He spun around angrily. "What, Lasonya? Ain't nothing else to say. You played me. Is that even my baby, or is it his?"

Tears began rolling down Lasonya's face. "It was an accident, baby. Me and Lucky was drunk. It only happened one time. I'm sorry."

Hearing Lucky's name knocked the wind out of Desmond, making him stumble a little. It took a few seconds for her words to register. The sting of betrayal hit him in the heart, spreading through his body as fast as lightening. When he spoke again, he didn't even recognize his own voice. "You cheated with Lucky?"

Lasonya hung her head, letting the tears do the talking.

Desmond staggered again, feeling lightheaded. He sat down and just stared at Lasonya in shock. "You fucked Lucky?"

Lasonya went to him and wrapped him in a hug. "It was an accident, baby. I'm sorry. Please, come home and let's talk about it."

Desmond remained sitting, visions of his brother and Lasonya's sex faces flooding his brain. When the scenes became too much, he shot to his feet and pushed Lasonya away. "Get the fuck away from me before I fuck you up!"

"Desmond, please!" Lasonya cried, taking a step towards him.

"GET THE FUCK AWAY FROM ME!" he screamed, eyes wild and the force behind his words making both of the women jump. No one dared approach him.

Silence filled the air, the only noise being Lasonya's sniffles.

When Desmond spoke again, his voice was filled with the agony of betrayal and heartbreak. "Leave me alone, Lasonya. Don't come looking for me. Don't call me. Don't text me. Don't have nobody else call me or text me. I'm done," he said, spinning and walking towards Pebbles's house.

"Desmond?" Lasonya called. "Desmond, please don't do this. Desmond?"

He didn't respond. There was nothing left to say. He followed Pebbles into the house and closed the door, leaving Lasonya on the sidewalk crying and calling his name. He flopped down on the couch and just sat there staring at the wall. He couldn't believe Lucky had betrayed him like that. Their whole lives, it was just them. They were each other's keepers. Their bond was supposed to be unbreakable. He supported Lucky the entire fourteen years he was in prison, and Lucky had stabbed him in the heart.

"Can we talk?" Pebbles asked.

Desmond spun towards the sound of her voice and saw her sitting on the sofa across from him. He tried to talk, but no words came out. He shook his head no. Pebbles respected his wish and left the room. She came back a few moments later with a bottle of Hennessey and a half-filled glass, giving them both to Desmond. He began to drink silently. Pebbles sat on the couch across from him, waiting. It took ten minutes and a glass of Henny for him to find his voice.

"I can't believe she fucked my brother."

"Do you think the baby is yours?" Pebbles asked.

Desmond shrugged his shoulders. "I don't even know. I just can't believe my own brother did this to me. I never thought it was him."

"They say the people that you love hurt you the worst," Pebbles said.

The words packed so much truth that Desmond had to swallow them with a shot of Hennessey.

"I know I just met you, D, but if you need my help, I got you. If you need somewhere to stay, you can stay here."

He nodded, sitting the bottle of Hennessey and the glass on the table as he stood. "I need to get some air."

Pebbles stood with him. "You want me to come with you?"

He shook his head and walked towards the door. "Nah. I just need to clear my head. I'll be back."

He walked outside, hopped in the Tahoe, and drove around aimlessly. Lucky's and Lasonya's faces played continuously in his head. How could they? He picked up the phone and called Lucky.

"What's up, Des?"

"It was you all this time?"

Lucky could hear the pain in Desmond's voice and knew immediately what he was talking about. "Brah, I'm sorry, man. It was an accident. I wanted to tell you, but I didn't know how."

"We Harrisons, my nigga. Just me and you. I woulda did anything for you. I was there for you when nobody else was. I did that time with you and this how you do me?"

Lucky's end of the line went silent. He stayed on the phone, but didn't speak.

"I woulda never did nothing like this to you, Lucky. Dog, you cut me deep with this one."

"Listen, Des, I'm sorry, brah. You my nigga and I didn't mean to do you like that. I love you, brah. For real. It was an accident."

"I'm good, Lucky. I see how it is. I just wanted to hear you say you fucked her. I don't need nothing else."

"Desmond, I'm——"

Desmond ended the call. He'd heard enough. The pain was too much. From this moment forward, he promised that he would do everything in his power to never feel this kind of pain again.

Lasonya was heartbroken.

It was true. Desmond was cheating. And he ended their relationship. Everything that she tried to prevent from happening had happened. And to make the situation worse, she couldn't say for sure whose baby she was pregnant with. She felt like shit. Like Desmond said, it was all her fault. She destroyed her family before it could even start.

When she walked into the house, Marcy looked up expectantly. When she saw the tears streaming down Lasonya's face, she stood to greet her with open arms.

"No, baby. Don't tell me you was right."

Lasonya went to her mother and lay her head on her bosom and cried. "He broke up with me, Mama. It's over."

"Come sit down. Tell me what happened. Was he cheating?"

Lasonya sat down on the couch, laying her head on Marcy's shoulder. "Yeah. I think he left me for her."

Marcy got mad. "What! Tell me where he at and I'ma go put his ass in the hospital."

"No, Mama. It's my fault. I did it. I'm the reason he left."

"Don't blame yourself, baby. You not the reason he cheated. You did everything you was s'posed to do. He just another no good-ass nigga. And if I see him again, I'ma pop a cap in his ass."

"No, Mama. It really is my fault."

Marcy tilted her head to the side so she could look in Lasonya's face. "What do you mean it's your fault? What did you do?"

Lasonya closed her eyes so she wouldn't see her mother's face when she told what she did. "I slept with Lucky."

Marcy's eyes got so big that they almost popped out of their sockets. "You did what?"

Lasonya kept her eyes closed and continued crying.

"Lasonya, how could you do something like that? Why would you sleep with his brother?"

"I don't know, Mama. It was an accident. We was drinking."

"But that ain't no excuse for you to sleep with his brother! Dammit, Lasonya."

The mom and daughter became silent for a moment. "Do you know which one of them is the father of the baby?"

Lasonya shook her head.

"Oh, Lord!" Marcy cried out, continuing to hold her heartbroken daughter.

"I'ma go lay down," Lasonya said weakly, pulling herself from her mother's embrace.

She went to her bedroom and lay on Desmond's side of the bed, hugging his pillow and continuing to cry. Visions of the life she wished they had flashed in her mind. Now it was all gone. And it was Lucky's fault. He came onto her first. If he would've never kissed her in Annie's kitchen, she wouldn't be in this shit. She couldn't let him get away without feeling her pain. It was all his fault. She picked up the phone and dialed a number.

"So, that's why you called me? So, you can have yo' nigga's brother get at me?" Wacco accused.

"I don't know what you talking about. This is me. Lasonya."

"I know who the fuck this is. Last time I talked to you, niggas tried to get down on me soon as I hung up the phone. I knew yo' snake ass was on some bullshit."

"That wasn't me, Tony. I swear to God I didn't have nothing to do with that."

"Yeah, a'ight. I think you need to stay the fuck away from me 'cause if I catch you, I'm fuckin' you up. I don't care that we got a baby. I'm killin' yo' bitch ass."

"Tony, wait! Just listen to me for a minute."

"Say what you gotta say, Lasonya, 'cause I got shit to do."

"I swear to God I didn't have nothing to do with what happened to you. I'm calling because I know where Lucky is."

There was a brief pause on Wacco's end. "What the fuck kinda games you playin', Lasonya?"

"I'm not playing. Fuck Lucky. That nigga ruined my life."

Wacco chuckled. "Okay. I'ma play yo' game. And if some bullshit pop off, I'ma start fucking up everybody you know until I can get to you. Where is Lucky?"

"He staying with a girl named Rachel. Last time I heard, she lived..."

## Chapter 12

Lucky hung his head and threw the phone on the bed. Hearing the pain in Desmond's voice opened up a wound in his heart. Even though he was mad at Desmond for becoming a rat, he didn't want to cause him pain. He knew him fucking Lasonya had crushed his brother, especially since they had been crushing on each other since they were kids. And the fact that Lucky was the one who slept with her was extra betrayal.

"What happened with you and Desmond?" Rachel asked. She had been lying in bed while he was on the phone but didn't know what they were talking about.

"I fucked up, baby. I did some fuck nigga shit," Lucky breathed.

In Rachel's eyes, fuck nigga shit and Lucky's name didn't belong in the same sentence. "What did you do, baby? Is it that bad?"

Lucky took a moment to spill the beans. "Me and his girl fucked while he was locked up."

Rachel's jaw dropped. "You had sex with Lasonya? Isn't she pregnant?"

Lucky nodded.

Rachel cocked her head to the side, looking at Lucky crazy. "Is it yours?"

"I really don't know. I guess it's a possibility. The shit happened so fast. I didn't wear a rubber. It was over in like two minutes."

Rachel's mind looked blown. "Damn, Lucky. That's fucked up."

"I already know. I really didn't mean to do that shit. Even though me and Desmond wasn't seeing eye to eye about that snitch shit, I never wanted to hurt my nigga like that. We all each other had all our life. And while I was locked up, that nigga rode out the whole fourteen years with me. I feel like shit right now."

Rachel kissed him on the shoulder. "I love you, baby, but you should feel like shit. You did some grimy shit."

Lucky mugged her.

"I'm not gonna lie to you, baby. What you did was wrong," Rachel said.

Lucky let out a long breath. "I know. I just wish it was something I could do to make it right."

"I think you just have to give it time. It's only y'all two. He needs you and you need him. He will see that."

Lucky's phone began ringing. "I hope you right, baby," he mumbled before checking the screen. "What's good, Q?"

"They found Ryder," he said, a hint of sadness in his voice.

"Okay. Where that nigga at?"

"He dead, Lucky. They found him in a garbage can with one to the head."

"Damn, li'l brah. That's fucked up."

"I know. You heard from Zoe or Meechy's bitch asses?"

Lucky looked to Rachel. "You heard from yo' cousin?"

"No. Did they find Ryder?"

"Yeah. In a garbage can with a bullet in his head."

"Oh my God!" Rachel cried out.

"Nah, she ain't heard from her cousin," Lucky told Quincy. "But we gon' find them niggas. One thing about a snake is they think they can't be caught. They gon' show back up sooner or later."

"And I'ma be waiting on them niggas. When you come outside, get at me. Me and T.A. at the trap."

"A'ight. I'ma get up with y'all in a minute," Lucky said before ending the call. "If it ain't one thing, it's another."

"I'm sorry for even hooking you up with my cousin. I feel like this shit is my fault," Rachel apologized.

"You good, baby. You didn't know that nigga was gon' do this shit. What I don't understand is why. We was all eating together. They was on the team. I can't believe they did all that for forty grams."

Rachel thought for a moment. "Wasn't Zoe tryna get you to come meet him that day? What if he really wanted you?"

Lucky's eyes grew wide with the realization. "You right! That was the day we was fucking. Instead of going, I sent Q. Damn. That nigga was tryna get to me, wasn't he?"

Rachel looked upset. "I'm sorry, baby. I didn't know."

Lucky nodded. "I know. It's all good, baby. Just know that if I catch yo' cousin, I'm fuckin' him up."

Rachel accepted his words. "I know. He deserves it."

◆◆◆

"Damn, I need some more diesel," Meechy lamented after hanging up his phone. "My line's going crazy and I gotta keep tellin' my heads I ain't got shit. Fuck."

Zoe looked towards his burner that sat on the table. Ever since he ran out of boy, he didn't even bother turning it on. "You see I don't even turn my shit on. Them dope boy dreams gone, my nigga. We gotta get back to gettin' it the ski mask way."

"Ryder's bitch ass fucked up the lick. Damn, we almost had that nigga," Meechy said regretfully.

"It might still be a way to get that nigga. Them niggas still using cuz's old house. We might be able to lamp on the niggas and catch 'em like that."

Meechy thought for a moment. "Them bitch-ass Detroit niggas trained to go. First we gotta figure out a way to get them niggas out the way. Shit, why not use Rachel? Blood thicker than water."

Zoe shook his head. "Nah. She already told the fam that I'm shiesty. She picked that nigga over me. Ain't that some shit?"

"Not really. Know a bitch gon' choose that nigga that's puttin' dick to her over er'body. Turn on the fam for that sweet meat."

Zoe nodded. "Yeah. That's how them hoes be. But what if we use somebody else to get at that nigga? All we gotta do is get the nigga away from them Detroit niggas for one minute."

Meechy nodded. "Yeah. Have somebody that we introduced to him get up wit' 'em. Tell 'em we gon' give 'em a cut to make the call, then knock they ass off and him too."

The plan got Zoe geeked. "Hell yeah. Who you wanna use?"

Meechy thought for a moment. "What about Lil Dave? I know that nigga be down to pull a caper."

"Yeah. I know that nigga down. Call Lil Dave. Let's get this nigga, fam."

Meechy picked up the phone and dialed a number.

"What's good, Big Meech?" Lil Dave answered.

"You got it, li'l nigga. I got a move that I wanna holla at you about. You ready to get some real money in yo' pockets?"

"You know I am, nigga. What's the move?"

"Lucky."

"Lucky?" Lil Dave asked. "Ain't that the nigga y'all fuckin' wit'?"

"Change of plans, my dude. The nigga got at least a book of food. Is you in?"

"Hell yeah! Come get me right now!"

"We 'bout to mob through. First I need you to call him and let him know you wanna cop. Me and Zoe got the rest."

"Nah, fuck that. I want in. I'll call the nigga on a three-way right now if you put me in."

"Okay. I got you. Call him."

The line went blank for a moment. When the call merged, Lucky's phone began ringing. "You still there?" Dave asked.

"Yep. Do yo' thang, boy."

"Hello?" Lucky answered.

"Lucky, what's good. This Lil Dave. You good?"

"Yeah. Come ride down on me. I'm at the spot."

"In a minute, brah," Lil Dave said, disconnecting the call. "You heard him. Come get me right now. I'm at my baby mama house on Burleigh."

"We on the way."

◆◆◆

Wacco sat in the passenger seat, staring out of the Buick's tinted windows. He kept his eyes on the SUV ahead of him. It was loaded with four of his killers. They were headed for Lucky's trap. According to Lasonya, this was the spot where Lucky spent the most time. She also wanted him dead, which surprised Wacco. He knew his baby mama wasn't all the way one hunnit, but he never imagined she would turn on her people. And if something went wrong or the information wasn't what it was supposed to be, he was to going to start fucking up everybody Lasonya knew.

"Park at the corner so we can watch Emmy n'em get down," Wacco told Cyco.

"I hope yo' baby mama ain't on no bullshit," Cyco commented.

"If she is, that just mean we got more people to fuck up. Get our niggas target practice."

When they got to Lucky's block, Cyco parked the Buick at the corner while the Suburban kept on going. It pulled over and parked a few houses down. Wacco sat on the edge of his seat, waiting with bated breath for the fireworks to fly.

◆◆◆

When Lucky got the text from Lil Dave, he looked to Quincy and T.A. "He outside. I know them niggas sent him at me. They out there somewhere, so be on point. Let's fuck these niggas up."

Q grabbed the AR-15 from the couch and walked towards the back door. "You know I'm ready."

T.A. didn't speak. He just grabbed the Draco and followed Quincy.

Lucky adjusted the pistol in his waist before walking out the front door. He immediately noticed the grey Dodge Magnum parked out front. The windows on the back were tinted so he couldn't see who was in the back seat, only Lil Dave in the driver's seat. The next thing he noticed was the Suburban parked across the street. The SUV didn't have tints and the windows were rolled down, so Lucky was able to see all four of the faces that watched him walking down the walkway. The niggas in the Suburban didn't try to hide their hostile looks. In fact, when they saw Lucky, they began talking and moving around. Lucky realized that the biggest threat to him wasn't Dave or whoever was hiding in the Magnum, but the niggas in the Suburban. He stopped walking and went for the pistol in his waist as the front and rear doors on the driver's side opened and two niggas hopped out with choppers.

"Oh shit!" Lucky screamed, letting the pistol ride at the niggas as he took off running for cover.

Pop, pop, pop, pop, pop, pop, pop, pop!

The semiautomatic rifles joined the fire fight as the CSGs shot back. The block was turned into a warzone.

Brrrrreaaaaatttt! Brrrrreaaaaatttt! Brrrrreaaaaatttt!

Bullets could be heard smacking houses, cars, and smashing windows as two more CSGs hopped out of the truck and joined the gun battle. The Dodge Magnum peeled out as Lil Dave fled the scene. Lucky dove behind the neighbor's porch and took cover. Bullets tore into the wood, sending wood splinters flying. When it seemed like it was too late, the Detroit gunners came from behind the trap with their guns blazing.

Two CSGs folded to the ground, caught off guard. T.A. and Quincy gunned them down. The remaining CSGs spun around with their guns sparking, moving towards their suburban. The Detroit shooters ducked for cover on the side of the house. The SUV's engine revved and tires squealed as the CSGs burned rubber. Quincy and T.A. came from the side of the house, letting their choppers ride at the fleeing vehicle. When the smoke cleared, two CSGs lay in the streets bleeding.

◆◆◆

King couldn't get enough of Carla.

He was so infatuated with her that he was willing to risk everything. His five-year relationship with the mother of his twins. Defying Wacco's order. Even his brotherhood with her husband Cyco, his day one and CSG nigga. None of the people above crossed his mind when he pulled the white BMW into the parking lot of McGovern Park.

When Carla saw the headlights of her boo thang's BMW, she hopped out of her pink Maserati to greet him. "Hey, my King!" She smiled, wrapping her arms around his neck and tonguing him down.

King gripped her phatty, lifting her off the ground and onto the hood of her car as they made out like horny teenagers. When they came up for air, they began giggling.

"How much time you got?" King asked, staring into her pretty blue eyes under the moonlight. That's what had gotten to him ten years ago. Carla and her brother were the only people in the hood with blue eyes. Back then, obligations and situations kept them apart. But now they were grown and realized they could have their cake and eat it too.

"An hour. Maybe a little more. Cyco with Wacco. My son is with my sister. What about you?" Carla asked, staring into her side nigga's handsome face. King was 6'5", light-skinned with curly hair, and had a good sex game. Carla had resisted the pretty boy for ten years until the temptation became too much.

"You know I got all night. Nicole knows how it is out here. She don't question nothing I do."

"Well in that case, let me get the bag out my car. I got a surprise," Carla said, hopping off the car. When she bent over to reach in the window, King began grinding on her ass. "Stop! Lemme get the bag!" Carla giggled, wiggling her ass against him. When she turned around, she was holding a plastic bag.

"What's that?" He asked.

"Some goodies. C'mon. Let's go!" Carla said, grabbing his hand and leading him through the park. It was after ten p.m. and the park was closed. She led him down a lamp-lit path to a grassy area in the open. "I been thinking about fucking you under the moon and stars for a long time," Carla admitted when they got to the spot she wanted.

King pulled her close. "This is perfect, baby. Now you gon' tell me what's in the bag?"

Carla handed it to him. King looked inside and saw a sheet, whipped cream, and cherries. "Oh! I like the way you think, baby." He smiled, taking the sheet out and laying it on the grass.

The part time lovers stripped naked and lay on the sheet. Carla grabbed the bottle of whipped cream in one hand and King's dick in the other. She squirted some on the head and then sucked him in her mouth.

"Oh shit!" King groaned.

Carla continued spraying his dick with whipped cream and sucking it off. Then she sprayed some on his balls and sucked it off as well. She continued teasing him with her mouth and the whipped cream until King couldn't take it no more.

"I'm finna nut, girl! Here it come!"

The couple was so lost in their own world that they didn't notice the four killers dressed in red approaching from different directions until it was too late.

"That head game look official." Flacco grinned as he approached holding a chrome .44 caliber Desert Eagle.

"What the fuck!" Carla screamed, trying to cover herself with the sheet.

King went for the pistol wrapped in his pants.

"I wouldn't do that," Flacco said.

King stopped moving when the infrared beam moved over his body. He looked over and saw another Blood standing near his feet holding a Glock. "Who the fuck is y'all niggas?" King mugged them.

Flacco walked over and kneeled beside the lovers, grabbing the box of cherries and eating one. "I think you asking the wrong question. You need to ask what we want."

"Man, y'all know who the fuck I am? Y'all need to ride out 'fore shit get ugly."

Flacco and the Bloods laughed. "Y'all hear this nigga? Talking 'bout do we know who you is? Yeah, I know who you is, King. Yo' CSG niggas ain't all built up to hold they tongue. You apply pressure and niggas break. Pistol told me you second in command behind Wacco. Now I'ma answer yo' first question. I'm Flacco. I'm from East Saint Louis. In my city they call me a nightmare because I made a whole family eat a baby. I came all the way here to see yo' leader. Which one of y'all gon' tell me where he at?"

"What you want with my brother?" Carla asked.

Flacco's eyes grew wide and he looked at her like she was the answer to all his problems. "Damn. Two for the price of one. I don't got that much time, so I'ma make a deal. The first one that takes me to Wacco, I won't kill."

Carla got defiant. "Fuck you, nigga. I ain't tellin' you shit."

Flacco lifted the .44 to Carla's face and squeezed the trigger. A chunk of Carla's cheekbone landed on King as his lover's face was blown apart.

"Ahh shit! What the fuck!" King screamed looking to Carla as she lay in the grass twitching.

"I gave her the opportunity to take the deal. She said fuck me. Now I'm giving you a chance. Where is Wacco?" Flacco asked, pointing the hand cannon in CSG lieutenant's face.

King looked to all the Bloods, knowing he was about to die. He figured out all the missing CSG members had died at their hands and he was destined for the same fate unless he made the deal.

Flacco waved the .44 in King's face. "What's it gon' be, blood?"

"Wait! I'ma tell you! Please don't kill me, man," King begged.

Wacco listened patiently as the terrified drug dealer spilled his guts. King was so good at telling that he even told the Bloods where one of their safe houses was. After pumping all the information from King and eating the entire box of cherries, Flacco stood.

"As promised, I won't shoot you. Go on, get dressed and get outta here."

King looked relieved as he grabbed his clothes.

"B-dog. This one on you." Flacco smiled, turning to his youngest shooter.

King looked horrified as the infrared beam cut through the dark and landed on his forehead.

Pop!

J-Blunt

## Chapter 13

Desmond pulled the Tahoe into the parking lot of the McDonald's and parked. He entered the fast food restaurant and spotted Agents Wright and Johansen in a booth near the back.

"What's up?" He nodded, sitting down in the empty seat across from them.

"What's going on at home? You staying somewhere else?" Wright asked.

"Yeah. Having problems at home," he answered vaguely.

"Care to elaborate?" Johansen asked.

Desmond looked the woman in her eyes, allowing her to see a glimpse of his anger. "She cheated on me while I was locked up. We're done. I'm staying with Pebbles."

"I know that situation is rocky at home, but that is a federal safe house. We need you there. That's how we protect you."

"I don't need y'all to protect me. But Lasonya and her family might. Just keep watching them until you get what you need to bring down the family. She's pregnant, and if she goes back to Milwaukee right now, it could be dangerous."

"That isn't how this works, Desmond. You're the asset," Wright cut in.

"Okay. Change the rules. While I'm working with y'all, I need you to protect my family. You've seen what I can do. I'll protect myself. And I'll continue to give regular updates. Nothing is changing but my location. I have to get ready to drive to Milwaukee. I gotta make a drop."

"Dammit, Desmond, you're changing the rules and my boss isn't going to like this. We need to be able to monitor you."

"You will. I'll still meet regularly. Y'all don't trust me now?"

"C'mon, Desmond," Johansen breathed. "We have protocols. Rules. We can't just break them whenever we want."

"I'm not going back to that house," Desmond said with finality.

Wright let out frustrated breath. "Shit, Desmond. Why do you have to be so goddamn stubborn?"

"That's what makes me good," he cracked. "If we're done here, I gotta hit the road."

"We're good," Johansen nodded. "Get us a picture of Quincy so we can give it to our Wisconsin Bureau. And be safe."

After leaving the restaurant, Desmond hopped in the Tahoe and went to pick up a kilo of heroin. From the pickup spot, he jumped on the highway and began the long trek to Milwaukee.

About twenty minutes into the drive, his phone rang. He looked at the screen, but didn't recognize the number.

"Hello?"

"Desmond, what's going on, brother?"

The voice sounded familiar, but Desmond couldn't place it. "Who is this?"

"Damn, brother, it's been a while, but I didn't think you would forget who I am. This is Alpha 6."

Kim Lee's face immediately jumped into Desmond's head. "Kim, what's going on, brotha? Damn, it's good to hear from you. Shit is so crazy in my world right now."

"I heard. First Mate Amber told me a little bit. And tracking down a number on you was like trying to find a tier one asset. If it wasn't for Colonel Jones being our CO, I might've never found you."

"Yeah, brother. I'm in pretty deep. How is Amber? I haven't talked to her in a while."

"That's an understatement. More like you broke up. But she's a tough girl. She's not letting it affect her. So, you're really working with the Feds?"

"Yeah. I tried to help my brother out and got caught up. I'm working with the ATF to get my life back. But forget me. How are you? How is the leg?"

"It's better. It didn't get amputated, so that was good. Lots of muscle damage. Tore my knee up. I completed rehab with the Warrior Transition Unit. I put in my papers to be reinstated with the SEAL's. Right now, I'm waiting for my file to be reviewed by the Physical Evaluation Board. Hopefully I'll know something soon."

"Sounds like you're on your way."

"What about you? Are you trying to get back in?"

Desmond let out a long breath. "Man, I don't know what the hell I'm doing. Lately it seems like all the plans I've been making are being shredded. I stopped making plans. I'm just seeing where I end up I guess. Focused on trying to complete this shit with the Feds."

"Damn, Des. Sounds like you're going through a lot, brother. But don't give up just because it's hard. We're never out of the fight. You should work your way back into the Navy. Amber told me they're tracking Slayer's backstabbing ass. I want to be a part of the team that makes the capture and I want you with me. You have what it takes to lead your own team. Don't lose sight of your goals and talents. You're a good man. Don't let what's happening around you taint your vision."

"Yeah. I hear you, Kim. I want to get back active and I would love to be the one to get Slayer. As soon as I put this behind me, I'm reaching out to Colonel Jones to be reinstated."

"That's my guy!" Kim celebrated. "And hey, if you ever need help, I'm just a call away. I relocated to Minnesota so I'm not that far."

After ending the call, Desmond thought about Kim and being reinstated in the Navy. His plans to be a father and husband appeared to be ruined. It was only right that he should be focusing his attention on the military.

Five hours later he pulled into Milwaukee and sent Lucky a text.

*I'm here. Tell Quincy to meet me at Olympic bowling alley.*

Lucky replied back: *He on the way.*

Twenty minutes later, Quincy pulled into the parking lot and parked next to the Tahoe.

"What's good, D-Money?" he asked, sliding into the passenger seat.

"You got it, li'l brah. What's up with you?"

"Tryna stay alive out here. I didn't know Milwaukee was this live. Er'time a nigga turn around, I gotta blow something down."

Desmond looked over. "Y'all good?"

"Yeah. Some fuck shit happened yesterday. Them CSG niggas came to the trap and tried to fuck us up. Got the spot hot. And some shiesty niggas we was fuckin' wit' got down on Ryder. All this shit gettin' the city hot."

That got Desmond's attention. "How the fuck CSG find the spot?"

"That's what we tryna figure out."

"Damn. It sound like y'all got a lot of shit going on."

"We do. We could probably use you out here with us."

Desmond laughed. "Nah. I'ma sit this one out. Lucky should be able to figure it out for y'all."

Quincy gave him a look. "What's up with you and Lucky?"

"Nothing. Why you say that?"

"When we first came to the Mil, you acted like you didn't know him. Then the nigga showed me a picture of you he had in his phone. What y'all on?"

Desmond wondered how much the young gunner knew. "Me and Lucky got history. That's it."

"That shit just seems weird, family," he mumbled, eyeing Desmond suspiciously. "He called you a fuck nigga after that shit with them Bloods and now he sent me to meet you. It seem like y'all got some bad blood."

Thoughts of killing Quincy flashed into Desmond's head for a moment. If Donny found out that he and Lucky knew each other before he came to Milwaukee, that could raise suspicion. And the fact that Donny had everybody on high alert because of the leak at the federal building might paint an even bigger target on Desmond's back. He needed to make Quincy stop asking questions.

"Don't worry 'bout that shit, my nigga. Just focus on gettin' this money and staying alive," Desmond countered.

Quincy nodded. He realized Desmond wasn't going to give him an answer and the conversation was over. "Fa sho'. Take it easy on them highways," Quincy said before climbing out of the truck.

◆◆◆

Adrian couldn't believe that Pebbles wasn't fucking with him anymore after everything they had been through. For an entire year he spent countless hours, thousands of dollars, and unlimited energy proving his love. Then she turned around and shitted on him. When he found out she let another nigga move in two months after they broke up, he started seeing red. And the fact that the nigga put his hands on him in front of Pebbles was enough to make Adrian want to commit murder.

"C'mon, Adrian. I need the keys to my car so I can get to work!" Na-Na yelled, holding her humongous J-cup titties down as she chased Adrian outside.

"Tell Connie to come pick you up again. I gotta make another move," Adrian refused, hopping in the white Dodge Neon.

Na-Na caught up to him and grabbed the driver's door before he could close it. "Nah, nigga. Gimme my muthafuckin' keys! You ain't finna keep taking my car."

"Move around, bitch! I gotta make a move!" Adrian yelled as they began a tug of war with the door. Na-Na was a big girl, standing 5'11"and 240 pounds. When she began pulling on the door with both hands, there was no way she was going to lose to Adrian's skinny ass. When Adrian realized he wasn't going to get the door closed, he jumped from the car and pushed Na-Na as hard as he could.

"Move the fuck around, bitch!"

The Amazon stumbled backwards a few steps, but didn't fall. The only thing the shove did was piss her off. She was already mad that he was using and abusing her and she wasn't going to put up with it anymore. She bull rushed Adrian like a defensive end trying to get through an offensive lineman to tackle the quarterback. She forced him back, smashing him into the side of the car. Her shoulder dug into his solar plexus, knocking the wind from his body. Instant pain gripped his torso as he began gasping for air like he was having an asthma attack.

"Gimme my muthafuckin' keys, nigga!" Na-Na yelled, tackling him to the ground and snatching the keys from his hand. After taking the keys, she walked back towards the apartment.

Adrian lay on the concrete gasping for air and watching helplessly as his sugar mama flipped the script. Not only did he feel like he was about to die, he also felt humiliated that a woman had gotten the best of him. He couldn't let her get away with it. He dug into the waist of his pants, gripping the butt of the .380 Smith & Wesson. He aimed it at Na-Na's back and squeezed the trigger twice.

Pop, pop!

"Aaahh!" Na-Na screamed, grabbing her ass and falling to the ground as a bullet pierced her right buttock.

Adrian stood weakly as the air crept back into his lungs.

"Muthafucka, you shot me! Help! This muthafucka shot me!" Na-Na screamed.

Adrian limped over and stood over the injured woman. "I should kill yo' bitch ass!" he threatened, pointing the gun in her face.

When Na-Na saw the anger in his eyes and gun in her face, she cowered. "I'm sorry, Adrian. I didn't mean it, baby. You can take the car. Please don't shoot me. I'm sorry."

Adrian thought about killing her. He was tired of being fucked over by women.

"What happened, Na-Na? You okay?" a neighbor called.

"Help! Call the ambulance! He just shot me!"

Adrian reached down and snatched the keys from her hand before racing to the Neon and speeding away.

"Stupid-ass shit!" he cursed, banging his fist against the steering wheel. He had fucked up and shot Na-Na. She was probably telling the police all she knew. And he took her car. That was another charge. Jail was certain and Adrian hated being locked up. That shit was worse than dying. And all this was Pebbles's fault. He would've never even fucked with Na-Na if Pebbles hadn't kicked him to the curb.

"Fuck jail," he told himself as he drove directly to Pebbles's house. When the police caught up to him, he was holding court in the streets, and Pebbles's bitch ass and her new nigga were coming with him.

◆◆◆

Desmond pulled up to Pebbles's house with his eyelids feeling like they had weights hanging from them. He was beyond tired and it took everything in him to keep his eyes open during the drive back to Detroit. He'd outdone himself by making the trip to Wisconsin and back in one day and his body was letting him know. After parking, he lurched from the Tahoe, hit the alarm, and staggered up the walkway towards Pebbles's house. He'd sent a text to let her know he was close, so the door was already unlocked. He walked inside, locking the door behind him and collapsing on the couch. It only took a few seconds for sleep to grip him.

"Desmond, get up. Come to bed," Pebbles said, grabbing his arm.

"I'm good right here, baby," he mumbled.

"No. Come to bed. Get up," Pebbles tugged his arm, refusing to let him sleep.

"Damn, girl," he fussed, struggling to get up.

Pebbles helped him up and tried carrying him. "Shit, D! You heavy as hell," she complained, as they went to the room.

Once inside, Desmond fell into the bed still fully dressed.

"Stop acting crazy and take off your clothes," Pebbles scolded.

"I'm good," he mumbled.

Pebbles stared at him angrily for a few moments before bending down and untying his shoes. She had taken off most of his clothes and set his pistol on the dresser when the doorbell rang.

"Who the fuck is coming by my house this late?" she mumbled, leaving the room and heading for the front door. "Who is it?" she called, looking out the peephole. When she didn't see anybody standing on the porch, a strange feeling overcame her. She was about to turn around and head back to the room when the alarm on Desmond's truck began blaring.

"What the fuck?" she questioned, looking out the window. She didn't see anyone near the truck. She went back to the room to get the alarm key.

"Who was at the door?" Desmond mumbled.

"Nobody. Probably some kids playing. Where yo' keys? Yo' alarm going off."

Desmond knew something was wrong with the situation. Somebody rang the doorbell and disappeared. Now his truck alarm was going off. He wanted to go see what was going on, but was too tired. Maybe it was some bad-ass kids.

"They in my pocket," he mumbled.

Pebbles picked his pants up from the floor and took the keys from his pocket before walking to the living room. She pulled the curtain back on the window and pointed the key at the truck as she hit alarm button. The Tahoe's alarm continued to sound. After pressing the button a few times, Pebbles got frustrated and opened the front door. She stepped onto the front porch, pointing the key at the truck and hitting the button. The alarm stopped. She turned to walk back inside when she saw someone running towards her from the side of the house.

"Ahhhh!" she screamed.

"Shut the fuck up, bitch!" Adrian yelled, slapping her in the face with the gun. Pebbles crashed into the door, grabbing the side of her face.

"Get'cho ass up!" Adrian yelled, snatching her up and shoving her into the house. "Thought you ass was gon' play me, bitch? Where the fuck that nigga at?" he asked, looking around for Desmond.

"Get the fuck outta my house, nigga!" Pebbles screamed.

"Oh, you wanna protect that nigga? You wanna choose him over me?" Adrian yelled, a jealous rage lighting his eyes.

Desmond thought he was dreaming when he heard Pebbles scream. Then he heard a man's voice and Pebbles telling him to leave the house. That's when he realized he wasn't dreaming. He shot out of bed, looking around for his pistol. He spotted it on the dresser. No sooner had he grabbed it than a single gunshot echoed through the house.

"Shit!" he cursed, scrambling from the room. He had just stepped into the hall when the feeling of danger came over him. He looked up as Adrian pointed the gun at him and fired.

Pop, pop, pop!

Desmond ducked back into the bedroom as the bullets thudded into the walls a few feet from where he had been standing. If Adrian had better aim, Desmond would've been dead. Thinking fast and not wanting to make himself a target, he grabbed his cell phone and used it to peek down the hall to see where Adrian was.

The jealous ex-boyfriend was creeping down the hall when he saw the tip of the cell phone poke out of the bedroom. He took aim and began shooting again.

Pop, pop, pop, pop!

Desmond pulled his hand back when Adrian started shooting, but he'd seen enough to get him. He pointed the gun into the hallway without looking and fired three shots.

Pop, pop, pop!

"Ah shit!" Adrian yelped.

Desmond lifted the cell phone again to peep into the hallway and saw Adrian laying on the floor, the pistol lying next to him. He stepped into the hallway, keeping the gun pointed at Adrian. "Where is Pebbles?" Desmond asked.

"Okay, man. I give up," Adrian groaned, clutching his chest.

Desmond moved closer, kicking the gun away. "Where the fuck is Pebbles?" he asked again, pointing his gun at Adrian's head.

"She is the living room," Adrian groaned. "Call an ambulance. I think I'm dying."

Desmond ignored him and walked into the living room. Pebbles lay on the floor by the front door. There was a bullet hole in her forehead and blood pooling around her body. The sight pissed Desmond off.

"Stupid-ass nigga, what the fuck wrong with you?" Desmond yelled, pointing the gun at Adrian again.

"I didn't mean to do it, brah. Call an ambulance for me, my nigga. I think I'm dying," he moaned.

"Nah, nigga. You already dead," Desmond said before putting his brains on the floor.

"Stupid-ass nigga," Desmond cursed, trying to decide his next move. The police were probably on the way and there was no way he could be seen or caught. Explaining two dead bodies would blow his cover. He went to get dressed and called Agent Wright.

"What's up, Desmond? Why you calling so late? Are you okay?" he answered groggily.

"Hell nah. Pebbles's jealous-ass ex-boyfriend just came and painted her brains on the floor."

All the sleep disappeared from Wright's voice. "Where are you now?"

"I'm in the house getting dressed."

"Where is he?"

"In the hallway." Desmond paused. "Dead."

"Dammit, Desmond! This is why we didn't want you to leave the house. This is why we have the fucking rules!" Wright snapped.

"A'ight. But the rules ain't the problem right now. The police are probably on the way and there is evidence of me all over this house. This shit could blow my cover."

"Get outta there right now. There is a safehouse about ten minutes away. I'm going to text you the address. I'm on my way. I'll clean it up when I get there. Just make sure you get to the safehouse and stay put. And most importantly, don't get caught!"

# Chapter 14

Quincy's nose was wide open and he knew it.

Despite all the drama and dead bodies surrounding him, the only thing he wanted to think about was spending time with Laronda. In the little time they had been creeping around, Quincy was starting to develop real feelings. He wanted to come out of the closet and reveal his relationship so they could be together out in the open. But they both agreed now wasn't the right time. Things were too complicated. So, they continued to creep, stealing whatever time they could and drowning themselves in the moments they were together.

When he pulled the Buick up to April's house, Laronda leapt from the porch and ran to the CUV.

"Hey, baby!" She smiled, climbing in the passenger seat. The balloons and big-ass bear in the back seat got her attention. "What is that?"

"Hey, baby girl. That's for you," Quincy smiled.

Laronda's eyes grew wild with surprise. Then she sprinted from the truck and ran into her aunt's house. The reaction caught Quincy off guard. He didn't know what to do so he reached into the backseat, grabbing the big-ass bear with the balloon, and walked upon the porch. April and her daughter, Trina, were walking outside.

"What up, April? Hey Trina," he greeted the women.

When April saw Quincy and the gifts, she laughed. "So that's why she came runnin' in the house like she was crazy," she laughed. "C'mon in here, Q. She in the room."

Quincy walked inside and found Laronda in the bedroom hiding her face in a pillow. "What's up, Laronda? You good?"

"Yeah," she mumbled, keeping her face hidden.

"Can you look at me? Why you actin' crazy?"

When Laronda showed her face, there were tears in her eyes. "Because ain't nobody ever did nothing like that for me. I didn't know how to react. I'm sorry."

Quincy kissed her forehead. "It's all good. I was driving past one of those gift tents and when I seen it, I thought about you. Now I'ma have to start buying you shit all the time so you can get used to it," he laughed.

"Fuck you." She laughed with him, wiping her tears. Then she looked at the bear and balloons. "Thank you. The bear is cute."

"You're welcome. I just got one more thing," he said, going into his pocket and pulling out a tennis bracelet.

Laronda's eyes got watery again. "You keep on making me cry," she whined.

"This is the last one. I promise. Let me put it on you," he said before hooking it around her ankle. "Do you like it?"

Laronda moved her leg from side to side, staring at the jewelry. "I love it," she said before tackling him onto the bed and sticking her tongue down his throat.

The young lovers allowed their hormones to take over, striping off their clothes and making the bedsprings squeak. When they were done, they lay in bed smoking a blunt.

"When you told me about the shootout yesterday, I was worried about you," Laronda confessed. "I'm getting tired of all the drama."

"That's how it is in the streets, baby. Niggas ain't playin'. Gotta get down or get laid down."

"You ever thought about doing something else?"

"Nah, not really. But with all this drama around us, I might have to find something else to do. Niggas can't get no money, always having to put in work. Niggas keep being snakes or ending up dead."

"I don't want you to die," she mumbled.

Quincy turned her face towards his so they could look in each other's eyes. "I'm not gon' die, baby. You hear me. I'ma always be here with you. Always."

Laronda kissed him. "You better be. I wish my uncle Desmond would help y'all. My daddy told me stories about how he be fucking shit up. If him and my Daddy wasn't——"

"What happened? Why you stop?" Quincy asked.

Lucky's words about not telling Quincy that he and Desmond were brothers played in her head. "Uh, nothing. I wasn't saying nothing. I just want you to be safe."

Quincy frowned. "Who is yo' Uncle Desmond?"

"Uh, nobody," Laronda stuttered, trying to think of an excuse. "He on my mother's side. Forget him."

Quincy connected the dots in his head. He remembered the argument between Lucky and D-Money after he shootout with the Bloods. He remembered how D-Money didn't want to meet Lucky the first time they came to Milwaukee. And he remembered Lucky having a picture of D-Money in his phone when he thought D-Money was in jail.

"D-Money is yo' uncle?" he asked.

Laronda's eyes grew wide as a deer caught in a pair of headlights. "No! What? Hell nah."

Her overreaction was all Quincy needed. "C'mon, Laronda. I ain't stupid. We ain't gotta do the lyin' and shit. We better than that, baby girl. I ain't never lied to you. Why you feel like you gotta lie to me?"

Laronda looked away, unable to meet his eyes.

Quincy tried to figure out why D-Money being her uncle was being kept a secret. They were all playing for the same team. "This ain't making no sense, Laronda. We all on the same squad. Why you didn't want me to know D-Money is yo' uncle?"

"I can't say. Can you just leave it alone?"

Quincy thought about it some more. "Why wouldn't Lucky tell us that one of the most savage niggas alive is his brother?"

"Just leave it alone. Please. I wasn't supposed to say nothing. Can you just forget about it?"

Quincy was silent for a moment. Thinking. "I wanna leave it alone but now that I know, I got a lot more questions. You can trust me, Laronda. I been one hunnit with you all this time. You know how I feel about you. You my baby girl. I want everybody to know that me and you doing our thang. I trust you. Why can't you trust me the same way? Whatever you say ain't gon' change nothing between us. But you keeping secrets is gon' fuck with me. Lucky is my big homie and I respect him to the fullest. Just tell me why nobody won't tell us they was brothers?"

"My daddy didn't want nobody to know," she mumbled.

"I get that. But I don't understand why."

Laronda became silent.

"C'mon, baby. You can trust me."

"Because Desmond working with the Feds."

The revelation rocked Quincy. His eyes grew wide and jaw dropped. "What? You bullshitting, Laronda. On what, you serious?"

Laronda didn't say another word.

Quincy was beyond shocked. Hearing D-Money was working with the Feds was like being told your mother is a man. Except it was true. He knew Desmond was trained to go. Had seen him put in work. Shit, D-Money had even seen him put in work. Then it hit him. D-Money had seen him kill people and had given him a kilo of heroin!

"Shit! D-Money the police!" he yelled, jumping out of bed and grabbing his clothes.

"What you doing? Where you going?" Laronda asked.

"D-Money is the police! He seen me get down on niggas. He just gave me a brick of dog food."

"Calm down, Quincy. You can't tell nobody I told you. You promised," Laronda whined.

"But that was before you told me he is the police. He working with the Feds, baby. The Feds gon' come get all of us. They don't fuck around," he panicked, throwing on his clothes quickly.

"What if I can talk to him? What if he leaves you out of it?"

Quincy shook his head. "You don't get it, Laronda. These the Feds. Ain't no talking to them. I gotta go."

Quincy hopped in the Buick truck, trying to figure his next move. D-Money was the fucking police and Lucky knew it all along. That's why they got into it after the shootout with the Bloods. That was the fuck nigga shit that Lucky accused him of. That's why Lucky thought he was in jail. D-Money must've made the deal to get out and now he was in Detroit, probably working to bring down everybody.

"Damn," Quincy cursed, unsure of his next move. If Desmond was working to bring down everyone in Detroit, what did that mean for them in Milwaukee? He grabbed the phone and was about to call Donny when he thought about Laronda. If Donny found out D-Money was the Feds and Lucky knew, he would order him and T.A. to kill everybody. Even Laronda. Quincy didn't want to be the one to hurt Laronda or her people. But he also didn't want to sit back while everybody got brought up on federal charges and sent to the pen.

"Why this shit had to happen to me?" he questioned aloud, trying to think of the right move to make. He settled on making a call to Lucky.

"What's good, li'l brah?"

Quincy wanted to tell him what he knew, wanted to go in on him for lying. But he decided that a face to face was better. "I need to holla at you. It's important."

"A'ight. Say no more. I'm at the crib. Come through."

Lucky sat the phone on the table after ending the call with Quincy. The young gunner sounded stressed about something and Lucky was hoping he didn't have to deal with another problem. He had too many of them. Every time he turned around, something else went wrong. Right now, he was dealing with his shortage of drug dealers. Since he lost Zoe, Meechy, and Ryder, their sales had slowed down. Now he was trying to figure out how three people were going to move a kilo and expand the business. It seemed next impossible.

"Baby, can you look at my car? It's making funny noises," Rachel asked when she walked into the living room.

"You know I ain't no mechanic, right?"

"But you a man and you probably know more about it than me. I just wanna know if you think it's serious."

"A'ight. I got you, baby. Where the car?"

"In the garage. Here go the key."

After taking the key, Lucky grabbed his pistol and went to the garage to check in the car. These days he kept a gun in every part of the house. He made sure that a weapon was always in arm's reach, even in the bathroom. He wasn't about to get caught slipping. He went to the garage and started Rachel's car. A clicking sound came from the engine. He popped the hood to check. He was listening to the engine when Quincy walked into the garage.

"What's good, Q?"

"You got it, Lucky," Quincy said, looking Lucky up and down. "I'm tryna figure out why you had me meet with D-Money yesterday."

Lucky glanced over and noticed Quincy's body language. He looked serious and was staring at Lucky intently, like he was looking for something. "'Cause I was busy. That's why I asked you to take care of it for me. Why?"

"So, what did he do that made y'all fall out? You said y'all had an issue when you called him a fuck nigga. What did he do?"

Lucky stood up and eyed Quincy. Something was up. The young gunner knew something. "You got something you wanna say, my nigga?"

"Yeah. When we first came to Milwaukee, D-Money acted like he didn't know you. Then you turned around and showed us a picture of him in yo' phone. I wanna know what's going you with you and D-Money."

Lucky knew that Quincy had figured out they were brothers. His next questions were how he found out and how much he knew. "It seem like you already know. Say what you gotta say."

"Is yo' brother working with the Feds?"

Lucky remained calm on the outside but on the inside he panicked. The cat was out of the bag! Shit was about to hit the fan! "Who told you all that?"

"C'mon, Lucky. Don't bullshit me, my nigga. This shit serious, brah. My life and my freedom on the line."

Lucky could see the seriousness of the situation in the young gunner's eyes. Everything had unraveled. The heroin operation was over. The question was how much Quincy had told Donny and T.A.

"I don't know where you got yo' information from, but they lying."

Quincy stared at him, wondering if he should reveal his source. Since the situation was serious, he had to keep it real in hopes that Lucky would do the same. "Laronda told me."

Lucky chuckled. "Yeah, right."

Quincy remained serious. "I'm not playing, Lucky. Laronda told me. We been kicking it for a li'l while. We wanted to tell you, but it never seemed like the right time."

Lucky mugged Quincy. "You fuckin' my daughter?"

Quincy shrugged. "Yeah. But I don't think that's the biggest issue right now. I trusted you and D-Money. I put in work for you niggas. My niggas died for you niggas. And now y'all gon' get us all knocked? What kinda fuck shit is that?"

Lucky got mad. "Check this out, li'l nigga. I ain't with that fuck shit. Don't even try to put that on my name. I don't get down like that. Get that shit right."

"So, D-Money is working with the Feds?"

Lucky just stared at him, unable to say the words.

"So, what's supposed to happen, my nigga? We all finna go down because of this nigga? If you sayin' you ain't with that fuck shit, then how we gon' handle this? I got love for you brah, and I got love for yo' daughter. But I ain't finna go to jail for no fuck nigga."

Lucky was beyond pissed off. Desmond's snitch ways had caught up to him and put the entire family's life in danger. There was only one thing to do. "It's really only one thing to do if niggas ain't tryna go to jail. He my brother, but I can't condone that rat shit. I'm mad at the nigga, but I can't bring myself to do nothing. If you think you can do him, do it."

Quincy and Lucky shared a long look and he searched Lucky's eyes to see if his words were true. "I got it, brah. I'ma take care of that."

Lucky nodded in agreement. "Did you tell Donny?"

"Nah. I wanted to holla at you first. I got respect for you. Plus, yo' daughter and me is…you know. If I told Donny, he would probably try to kill all y'all."

Lucky nodded again. "A'ight. Good looking out. I'ma try to figure us a way out of this shit. If push come to shove, I'ma just take my daughter and leave."

When he mentioned leaving with Laronda, Quincy looked sad. "I guess I understand. I gotta make a move. I'ma get with you in a minute," Quincy said, turning to leave.

Lucky pulled his pistol and ran up behind Quincy, pointing the gun at his head.

Pop!

Quincy's body collapsed like all the bones had been snatched out of his body. Lucky stood over him, watching his li'l nigga die.

"Lucky, you okay?" Rachel yelled, running into the garage. When she saw Quincy laying on the floor, she looked to Lucky. "What happened?"

"Laronda told him about Desmond. He was gon' try to kill my brother."

Rachel looked confused. "Why would Laronda do that?"

"They fucking," Lucky breathed. "I'ma get rid of this body. We can't tell Laronda what happened or that we know she told him. We gotta keep this between us."

◆◆◆

Flacco sat in the Suburban watching the big white colonial house that sat upon an acre of land. It was night. Cars filled the driveway and lined the street. Wacco's family was having a get-together after Carla's funeral. There were at least twenty people in the house, all mourning the loss. Flacco and his killers had been watching Wacco for a week. He lived in a condominium in Cudahy. The building had round the clock security and Wacco hadn't left the house much the last couple of days. When he did move, it was only during the day and he was surrounded by security like he was the president. But tonight was different. He was still surrounded by six goons. Three sat in a car in the driveway and three went into the house with him. But it was night, and the nighttime belonged to the East Saint Louis Nightmare. And he had something Wacco and his niggas didn't have: the element of surprise. Seated in the Suburban with Flacco were three Bloods. Parked down the street was a car with four more Bloods in it. Everyone was heavily armed and ready to go to war.

"Call Jordan. Tell him to set it off," Flacco told his passenger.

B-Dog pulled out a phone and made the call.

"What's good, blood?" Jordan answered.

"Kick it off," the young gunner spoke.

"Watch the fireworks. We finna set this bitch off." Jordan laughed and ended the call.

Flacco watched in the rearview mirror as one of the Bloods hopped out of the black Dodge Intrepid and sprinted towards the back of the colonial house, making sure to keep to the shadows so he wouldn't be seen. In his hands was a pistol and a half gallon milk container filled with gasoline. While the Blood got busy lighting a fire behind the house, the Dodge crept down the block with the lights off. It pulled alongside the Blazer that held Wacco's security.

Brrrrreaaaaatttt! Brrrrreaaaaatttt! Brrrrreaaaaatttt!

Pop, pop, pop, pop, pop, pop, pop!

Blocka, blocka, blocka, blocka, blocka!

Gunfire from several weapons lit up the night as the Bloods hit Wacco's niggas hard. Two of them died instantly. One nigga was able to escape the barrage of bullets. He hopped out of the Blazer and ran towards the house, firing a pistol blindly behind him. Jordan hopped out the passenger seat with an AK-47 and let it ride.

Brrrrreaaaaatttt!

Fire sparked from the barrel as the high-powered rounds tore into the back of the escapee. When he fell to the ground, Jordan walked up and stood over him, letting the gun talk.

Brrrrreaaaaatttt!

"That's how you do it." Flacco smiled, excited by the bloody murder.

Two more Bloods hopped out of the Intrepid and rushed towards the house. Before they could get to the porch, the front door opened and Wacco's niggas came out sparking.

Tat-tat-tat-tat-tat-tat! Tat-tat-tat-tat-tat-tat!

Two Bloods went down and Jordan had to hide behind a parked car.

"Let's get it," Flacco said, gripping the AR-15 and hopping out of the Suburban. The other three Bloods followed. They walked towards Wacco's defenders, letting their war machines act up. One CSG nigga went down while the other two took cover. One hid behind the house, the other behind a car. The shooting continued as Flacco's Bloods gained ground on the two remaining CSGs. Then the Blood that had set fire to the back of the house crept up behind the unsuspecting CSG nigga that hid on the side of the house.

Pop!

The CSG nigga collapsed from a bullet to the back of the head. The Blood was so busy smiling at his handiwork that he didn't see the final CSG nigga taking aim at him from behind the car.

Boom, boom!

The Blood folded as his life was taken. But his death was quickly avenged by Flacco. He trained the AK-47 on the CSG and lit him up. When the shooting stopped, there were six dead CSGs and four dead Bloods.

Flacco took a look at his niggas. They were waiting for him to make a move.

"Let's get 'em!" Flacco yelled.

The Bloods rushed the house. Chello was the first one through the front door followed by B-Dog. Wacco's family members were standing in the living room with shock upon their faces. Others were on the phone with the police. The young Bloods took aim and started shooting whoever was standing in front of them. Screams of panic filled the house and people ran in all directions, tripping over one another. The young Bloods chased them, continuing to add to their body count.

When Flacco stepped into the house, he had one mission in mind: kill the nigga with the blue eyes. He walked past bodies lying on the floor, putting bullets in the heads of those that hadn't died. When he got to a flight of stairs, he looked up and saw Wacco. The blue-eyed man was looking over the balcony holding a pistol. He pointed it at Flacco and fired.

Clap, clap, clap!

Flacco dodged the bullets, ducking behind a wall. He held the assault rifle around the corner and fired blindly at the top of the stairs. When he looked out again, Wacco was gone. The thrill of the kill made Flacco smile as he took the stairs two at a time. When he got to the top, he paused to listen. Screams and gunshots filled his ears as his niggas continued to run through the house terrorizing everything. There was a short hallway before him with two rooms on each side. He started creeping towards the first door when he heard a noise come from a room across the hall. His heart began pounding as he switched directions and moved towards the room the noise came from. The door was closed. He thought about kicking it open and running in, but thought better.

Wacco was strapped, so Flacco kept his back against the wall and reached down to turn the knob. When he pushed the door open, gunshots rang out

Clap, clap, clap, clap!

Bullets exploded through the door where Flacco would've been had he not hidden behind the wall. A female screamed in the room across the hall.

"I know you in there, Wacco. I can smell yo' fear and hear yo' heart beating," Flacco called.

"Well bring yo' ass in here and come get me then," Wacco called back.

Flacco laughed. "So, you gon' hide in there like a bitch-ass coward while yo' whole family dies?"

Wacco answered with more bullets.

Flacco knew he couldn't get in the room and time was running out. The police were on the way and he had to go. That's when he got an idea. He crept to the room across the hall, opening the door slowly. When bullets didn't rip through the door, he took a peek inside. Nobody was visible, so he took a look around and found a teenage girl hiding in the closet.

"Come here," he ordered.

The girl didn't move. She was too scared. Flacco snatched her by the hair. "Bring yo' ass here!" He led her out of the room, holding her hair in his fist and keeping her in front as a shield. When he got to the room Wacco was holed up in, he stopped.

"Don't shoot, Wacco. I got a surprise for you," he said, moving the girl slowly into the doorway.

When Wacco saw his little cousin, he didn't shoot. "Let her go, nigga!"

Flacco moved behind the girl, using her as a shield to get a look into the room. Wacco was standing in the corner across the room, pointing his gun towards the door.

"You know the difference between me and you, Wacco? Survival is far more important than having sympathy. You don't––"

Clap, clap, clap, clap!

Wacco's pistol sounded and the girl's body jerked from bullets to the chest. Flacco ducked out of the way and released the body. She fell to the floor and began shaking.

"Damn. You killed the li'l bitch. Boy, you's a savage," Flacco laughed.

Chello came running up the stairs a few moments later. "We gotta go, Blood."

"Come here. We got one more in here." Flacco waved him over.

Chello stood next to his leader, glancing at the girl that lay bleeding on the floor.

"When I say go, we running in. You ready?"

Chello nodded.

"Go!"

Chello rushed into the room blindly and right into Wacco's line of sight.

Clap, clap, clap, clap!

The young Blood's body was filled with bullets. Flacco followed right behind Chello, using him as a shield and letting his chopper ride.

Brrrrreaaaaatttt!

Wacco's body folded to the ground, riddled with bullets from the chopper. Flacco walked over to where Wacco lay and pointed the chopper in his face.

"This for Mariah, nigga. Tell the devil Flacco sent you."

Boom!

J-Blunt

## Chapter 15

"Where are we on the investigation of the Family?" the director of the ATF, Richard Stimson, asked his assistant.

"The team has been able to track them as far as Wisconsin. We need more time to get a bigger fish. But we've got a good asset. He's getting close."

"Ah, the Navy SEAL!" Richard smiled. "How is he doing? Still tearing up the city and dropping bodies?"

"As a matter of fact, he is." Mark laughed. "Seems this guy is a magnet for bad guys. And he kills them all. Fucker doesn't miss. It's starting to get a little messy, but it's worth it if we can bring down the Family."

Richard stared at his second in command for a moment. "Where are we on the leak?"

"Haven't found it yet. Still looking."

"This case is starting to get messy with the leaks and all the bodies our SEAL is leaving around. Do we have enough evidence to break up and bring charges on the ring in Detroit?"

"We have more than enough. Wire taps. Pictures. Video. Audio. We might even be able to charge Donny under the RICO Act."

Richard went quiet for a moment, contemplating.

"What are you thinking?" Mark asked.

"I'm thinking about mailing it in on the investigation of the Family and just bringing in the guys we have. If we can get enough charges on them, somebody will roll over and save us time and manpower."

"I thought of that several times, but Johansen and Wright think they're close to getting the entire kit and caboodle. I was going to give them a little more time before coming to you. The SEAL did more work in the short time we've had him than we could've imagined. Cut our investigation time in half."

"What the hell? Let's make the move and start bringing them in. If we can hit a guy with the RICO, that's good enough for me. If we can get the Family, even better."

Mark paused. "Our lead agents won't like this."

"So? We're the bosses. If you like, you can get other agents to lead the arrests. Special Agent Martinez's team is a good one. Send them."

◆◆◆

Rich Red loved being the center of attention. It was in his nature to shine and he did a damn good job at it. He pulled the Audi truck up to the Gucci store with all the windows down, blasting "Whoa" by Lil Baby. In the passenger seat was a thick caramel-skinned woman with a low haircut dyed blonde. She wore a teal blue summer dress and heels. Her name was Gayle.

"C'mon, baby. Lemme show you how a nigga wit' real money shops. Ain't no price limit. If you want it, get it," Rich bragged as he climbed from the truck. He walked around to the passenger side and opened the door for his cutie with a big booty.

"Thank you, baby." Gayle smiled, loving the display of chivalry.

"I'll do anything for you, baby." Rich smiled, helping her from the SUV.

They were walking towards the front door when a Gucci store employee came outside. "Sir, this is not a parking spot."

"I know," Rich said, tossing him the keys. "Go park it for me."

The worker looked at the keys and then back to Rich, confusion upon his face. "We don't have a valet."

Rich turned and walked back to the worker. "Everythang I do is VIP, my nigga. As of right now, you don't work for Gucci no more. You work for me. Go park my truck and when you come back in, show me the 2021 summer collection." While he was speaking, Rich Red pulled out a stack of 100 dollar bills and gave the worker five. After a wink, the baller grabbed Gayle's hand and led her into the store.

"Mr. Red!" a woman called.

Red turned to see a short middle-aged white woman smiling at him like he was Denzel Washington. "Susie! What's up, baby!"

"You are, Richy! What can I do for you today?" She beamed, opening her arms for a hug.

"Me and my friend wanna get fly. What you got?"

Glee lit her eyes. "I just got a new shipment from Paris!" Then she turned to look at Gayle. "Wait until you see the dresses for next spring! They are to die for."

As Susie was walking away, the valet was walking back in the store. "Michael, get Mr. Red a bottle of champagne! Hurry up!"

Rich Red and Gayle sipped champagne while trying on the newest Gucci threads. He ended up spending $12,000 and tipped Susie a band for treating him like the king he was. When they walked out with the shopping bags, Gayle was looking at him like she wanted to eat him alive.

"Damn, Rich. I never experienced nothing like that."

"Get used to it, baby. This how I live. Fuck with me and I'ma fuckin' with you." He winked as they threw the bags in the backseat and drove away from the store.

Gayle leaned over and kissed him on the ear. "Thanks for everything. Shopping and spending money got my kitty so wet," she purred.

"Feed me some so I can taste it."

Gayle slipped a hand under her dress and stuck two fingers in her pussy. Then she fed them to Rich. He sucked on her digits like she had stuck them in a sweet-tasting sauce.

"Mmmm! That was good."

"Now let me taste you," Gayle whispered, kissing his neck while going for the button on his pants. After freeing his dick, she leaned down and sucked him into her mouth.

"Oh yeah, baby!" Rich moaned, loving the warmth of her mouth.

Gayle tried to show appreciation with her mouth for him spending seven thousand dollars on her new clothes. She deep throated until she gagged, giving him the best head, she could muster.

"Aw shit!" Rich groaned, bringing the truck to a stop.

Gayle knew her head game was fire and she was encouraged by his moans and the truck stopping. She kept on sucking until Rich stopped her.

"Ay, chill! Sit up."

When she heard the fear in his voice, she sat up. That's when she saw what had made him stop the truck. Unmarked black sedans had the truck surrounded. Several federal agents had their guns trained on the truck. Then one of the agents grabbed a bullhorn.

"Richard Benson! Cut off the vehicle and get out with your hands up!"

"What's going on?" Gayle panicked.

"I don't know. But don't say shit," Rich coached as he shut off the truck and hopped out with his hands up. "What's going on? What I do?"

Several federal agents approached him with their guns drawn. "You're being arrested for breaking federal drug laws. You have the right to remain silent. Everything you say..."

◆◆◆

Rich Red paced the holding cell, mind running a hundred miles an hour. What did the Feds want? What did they know? How much time would he be facing? Did his uncle know he was locked up yet? They hadn't given him a phone call, but he knew to call a lawyer as soon as he got one.

The door on the cell opened and two federal agents appeared, one a Latino man, the other a black man.

"Richard, I'm Special Agent Martinez and this is my partner, Special Agent Williams. We want to have a couple of words with you. Can we talk?"

Rich Red knew the code and he was sticking to it. "Hell nah. I wanna call my lawyer."

"You'll get your call," Agent Williams spoke up. "We just want to have a couple words with you before you make the call."

"I'm good. I ain't got nothing to say," Red refused.

"You sure about that?" Martinez asked, looking at Red like he might regret not having the conversation. "We have lots of evidence on you and your people. We're going to gather up everyone, but we picked you first for a reason. We're offering you the first deal. Cooperate with us and tell us about your uncle and the Family and we'll make sure you don't spend a day in prison. Otherwise, you'll be charged with the RICO Act and get life in a federal prison."

The thought of life in the Feds hit Rich in the chest like a sledgehammer. But he knew the rules when he signed up: shut the fuck up and take your weight.

"When can I get my phone call?"

◆◆◆

Donny sat behind the desk in his office, snapping the pocket watch open and closed while going over paperwork for a possible business venture. A wealthy group of investors wanted him to join their latest investment into a condominium. He was looking over the numbers when his phone rang. It was his lawyer.

"What's up, Matt?"

"Donny, this is not a social call. I just left the jail and the Feds are indicting your nephew."

Donny dropped the contract and pocket watch, his eyes growing wide with alarm. "What the fuck is going on? What do you know?"

"Feds ain't saying much, yet. But it's the Feds. You know they don't move until they got your ass nailed to the cross. Hurry up and set your affairs in order, because they're asking about you and the Family."

"Shit!" Donny panicked, shooting to his feet. "Do what you can to get my nephew out. And be on standby because I might need you."

"What are you going to do?"

"I'm going to find the rat that got us in this shit." After ending the call with his lawyer, Donny raced from the office and found Royce.

"What's good, boss man?"

"Load up the cars. The Feds just arrested Richy and they coming for me next. I gotta find out who this snitch is!"

Donny and two SUVs of hitters left the cleaning service and drove over to his mole inside the federal building. When they were outside, Donny called him.

"What's going on, D?"

"Where are you?"

"I'm in bed. What's up?"

"Open the door. I'm coming in."

"Wait. You can't come to my house. Where are you?"

Donny hopped out of the truck with his hitters. "I just said open the door."

By the time Donny got to the front porch, Brian Cranston was opening the door. He was half-dressed, wearing only a pair of sweatpants. "You can't just show up to my house. How the hell did you find out where I live?"

Donny pushed past him and walked in the house followed by his four of goons. "Your people just arrested my nephew and are asking about me and the Family. What do you know?"

Brian looked confused. "What? Your nephew got picked up? When?"

"Not that long ago. Tell me something, Brian. What's going on? What do they know?"

"I'm not sure. I'll have to make some calls or go to the fed building."

Donny wondered why he wasn't picking up the phone. "Well, why aren't you on the phone or getting dressed?"

"C'mon, Donny. You can't just show up at 8:30 in the evening on a Sunday and expect me to find answers to all of your questions. This shit takes time. And I don't appreciate you showing up at my house like this. How the hell did you find out where I lived?"

"Fuck that! My freedom is on the line and I pay you to keep me free. Now I need you to tell me something. Tell me what's going on. Who the fuck is the snitch in my clique?"

"Brian, is everything okay?" a blonde-haired woman asked, appearing in the bedroom doorway. When she saw the living room

170

filled with black men, a frightened look crossed her face. Then she recognized Donny. "What is he doing here?"

"I'm okay, Peggy. Go back in the room."

Donny spun to look at the woman. "Is that who I think it is?"

"No, Donny. Leave her alone!" Brian said forcefully, going to stand in front of his girl.

Donny nodded to Royce. "Get her."

One of the goons grabbed Brian and removed him from in front of the woman while Royce grabbed her and brought her into the living room.

"You're investigating me, right?" Donny asked.

"I don't know what you're talking about."

Donny chuckled. "Listen, Peggy. I know you just lied to me, so I'ma ask you this one more time. If you lie to me again, I'm going to kill Brian," he said, pointing the gun at Brian. "Are you investigating me?"

Peggy looked at Brian.

"Tell him or he'll kill me!" Brian shrieked.

"Yes," she nodded.

"That's good. Since you're investigating me, that means you know who the rat is in my organization, right?"

The woman looked to Brian again. "I can't say."

Donny lowered the pistol and shot Brian in the leg.

"Ahh!" Brian screamed. "Tell him, Peggy! You're going to get us killed."

Donny lifted the gun to Brian's chest. "Who is the rat, Peggy? Who is it?"

Tears began spilling down the woman's face. "If I tell you, I'll go to jail."

Donny shot Brian in the chest.

"If you don't tell me, you won't live long enough to be charged. Who the fuck is the snitch, bitch?"

"Just tell him, Peggy! Tell him!" Brian screamed, clutching his wounds.

"It's Desmond. His name is Desmond," she confessed.

Donny looked to Royce. "Who the fuck is Desmond?"

The goon shrugged. "Never heard of him."

Donny turned the gun on Peggy. "Who the fuck is the snitch? And if you lie to me again, I'm going to blow your brains out."

Peggy closed her eyes, bracing herself to be shot in the head. "His name is Desmond. He is the Navy SEAL. D-Money."

Donny looked stuck for a moment. His eyes growing wide in disbelief. "D-Money is a snitch? My army man?"

Peggy nodded.

Donny looked to Royce, still wearing the look of disbelief. "You hear this shit?"

"Yeah." Royce shook his head. "You never know who it is until it comes out."

The pistol coughed, sending a bullet into Peggy's head. She fell on the ground dead. Royce turned his pistol to Brian.

"Wait, Donny. Don't——"

Pop!

"Set this bitch on fire so they don't have no evidence," Donny said as he headed for the door.

"Where we going?" Royce asked.

"You take some people to D-Money's house. I'm going to find my truck. It has a GPS. I'm calling OnStar. We're going to make sure his bitch ass don't show up to court to testify."

◆◆◆

"Rich, this D-Money. Fuck you at, nigga? Call me when you get this message," Desmond said before hanging up the phone. He called Rich Red four times, surprised that he hadn't heard from him all day. It wasn't like the young stunna not to answer his phone, especially for Desmond. After throwing the phone on the passenger seat, he continued driving to Rich Red's house. When he turned onto Rich Red's block, he got the shock of his life. Several unmarked cars were parked on the block and the house was taped off with yellow tape.

"What the fuck?" Desmond questioned aloud, pulling over to watch the scene. Several agents came out of the house with evidence bags and put them in their car before going back in the house.

Desmond picked up the phone and called Agent Wright.

"Hey, Desmond, I was just about to call you. You okay?"

"Yeah. I'm good. I'm down the street from Rich Red's house and your people are all over it. What the fuck happened?"

"That's what I was about to call you about, man. It's over. The higher-ups ended the investigation and are rounding up Donny and his people. We need to pick you up."

Desmond was surprised. "The investigation is over? What?"

"Yeah. They moved without even telling us. Martinez is leading the detains. You may have also been compromised, so we need to get you safe."

Desmond was even more confused. "I've been compromised? How? You telling me that Donny knows who I am?"

"It's possible. Two agents were found dead a little while ago. One of them was Peggy. We think Donny did it. She was the leak."

"Shit!" Desmond cursed, sitting back and allowing all the information to sink in.

"Yeah. We didn't want it to go like this, but you did your job. It's over. You can come to me, or I can come to you."

"Okay. I'm coming - shit!" Desmond cursed, slamming the truck in drive and speeding away.

"You okay, Desmond?" Agent Wright asked, sounding worried.

"Hell nah! Donny knows where the house is. Lasonya and her daughter are in there. If Donny knows I'm the informant, he's going to the house!"

"We just left the meeting and already dispatched agents to the house. They're on the way right now."

"They might not get there in time. I'm on the way there."

◆◆◆

Lasonya sat on the front porch staring at the sky, lost in a daydream. In the dream, she and Desmond were married. The baby was born. It was Christmas. She was recording Desmond playing with his son. Everyone was happy and smiling. She longed for a happily ever after like Christians longed for the return of Jesus. But because of desperation, she had ruined her chance. Now she had to sit around and hope that Desmond would forgive her. The one thing she had going in her favor was him not kicking her family out of the house. That gave her hope that one day he would return. The question was, when?

"Lasonya, come on in this house, girl," Marcy said, standing in the doorway behind her. "It's dark outside. Desmond gon' come back when he ready."

Lasonya let out a long sigh. "I wanna call him so bad."

"You gotta let him work it out on his own. It's gon' be hard for him to accept something like that. Staying on the porch in the dark ain't gon' make him come back no faster. Get on in here."

Lasonya got up slowly just as a black SUV turned onto their street and sped towards the house. It came to a screeching stop in the middle of the street.

"Who is that?" Lasonya asked, hoping Desmond was about to get out of the truck.

Instead of Desmond, four niggas with guns began piling out, heading for the house.

"Get'cho ass in this house! Hurry up!" Marcy yelled, snatching Lasonya in the house and locking the door. "Get the baby and y'all hide!"

Lasonya ran for her daughter while Marcy ran for her purse. The 'bout it 'bout it matriarch pulled out a big black .357 and pointed it at the door. There were two loud bangs on the door before it came crashing open. Two men rushed in with machine guns. What they didn't expect to see was an armed grandmother that knew how to shoot.

Boom, boom, boom, boom, boom, boom!

The hand cannon roared, sending hot metal into the chest and face of the first two intruders. They went down in a heap, never to breathe again. Knowing the gun was empty, Marcy ran towards the back of the house to get one of Desmond's guns and check on her family.

"Oh no, bitch!" Royce said, entering the house as the grandmother made a run for it. He lined the .45 sights to her back and began blazing.

Boom, boom, boom!

The slugs tore into Marcy's back, knocking her to the ground face first. Royce and another shooter crept through the living room, keeping their guns ready in case Desmond or someone else came out shooting. Marcy wasn't dead and tried to crawl away. Royce walked up behind her, pointing the gun at the back of her head.

"Where is D-Money, bitch?"

Marcy turned to look over her shoulder at Royce. "You gon' find out soon. My son-in-law is going to fuck y'all up." She smiled, attempting a laugh and coughing up blood.

"If you don't tell me where he at, I'ma blow yo' head off, you old bitch!" Royce threatened.

Marcy attempted to laugh and coughed up more blood. "I'm not scared to die, nigga. That just means I don't get to see yo' ugly-ass face no more."

Royce was about to kill her when tires screeching outside got his attention. "Who the fuck is that?"

Marcy smiled. "I told you my son was gon' fuck——"

Boom!

Royce's .45 barked one last time, sending a bullet into Marcy's head. He turned just in time to see Desmond running up on the porch pointing a pistol.

Pop, pop, pop, pop, pop, pop, pop, pop, pop, pop!

Royce was able to dodge the fuselage of rounds, ducking behind the wall. His partner wasn't so lucky. Six rounds of hot led laced him from his forehead to ball sack. He fell next to Marcy, dead.

Desmond rushed into the house, the adrenaline boosting his speed, quickness, and reflexes. When Royce came around the corner shooting, the Navy SEAL dove out of his line of fire, continuing to advance until he was on the opposite side of the wall as Donny's hired gun. When Royce peeked from behind the wall to see where Desmond was, he was surprised that the trained assassin was a few inches from his face. He tried to lift the gun but was too slow. Desmond punched him in the throat, making him stumble backwards and grab his neck. When he realized he was still holding the gun, he tried to point it at Desmond again. Again, he was too slow. Desmond took the gun with one hand and pistol whipped him with the gun in his other hand. Royce stumbled backward and tripped over the dead bodies in the hallway. Desmond jumped on top of him and began beating him in the face with the pistols. Royce's lips busted open, his nose cracked, and eye sockets shattered. Desmond continued smashing Royce's face with the guns until his forehead began caving in.

"Desmond, stop!" Agent Johansen yelled as she and another federal agent entered the house with their guns drawn.

Desmond didn't stop. He continued to smash Royce's face until most of it was caved in. Johansen grabbed Desmond's shoulders and tried to stop him. He shrugged her arms off him and continued the beating.

"DESMOND, STOP!" Agent Johansen screamed again.

Her words finally cut through the madness and Desmond stopped. His hands, arms, and shirt were covered with blood. Royce was dead, his entire face caved in. Desmond looked at Marcy's body lying next to him and was instantly gripped by sadness. There was a hole in the side of her head and a couple more in her back. Blood pooled around her body.

"No, Marcy!" he groaned, laying a hand on her back.

"Check the rest of the house," Agent Johansen told her partner.

When Desmond heard those words, he jumped to his feet and ran toward the back of the house. "Lasonya! Lasonya, where you at!"

"I'm in here!" she called from their bedroom closet.

Desmond snatched open the door and found her huddled up on the floor with Quaysha. He knelt down and wrapped them in his bloody embrace. "I thought y'all..." He couldn't even finish the words.

"Where is my mother?" Lasonya asked, happy to see Desmond but needing to see her mom.

Desmond looked her in the eyes, sadness playing on his face.

Lasonya read the look. "No! No, no, no!" she screamed, leaving Quaysha with Desmond and running to find her mother. She found Marcy in the hallway amongst the dead intruders. "MAMA! NOOOOO!"

Desmond remained in the closet with Quaysha, not wanting her to see the carnage in the hallway.

"I want my granny, Desmond," she whined.

"She had to leave. But she'll be back. Right now, I need you to put this jacket over your head so I can take you outside, okay. It's some stuff out here that you can't see. Okay?"

Quaysha nodded. Desmond grabbed a jacket from the hanger and put it over her head, leading the child past the bodies. When they were outside, he put her in the unmarked car. Then he went back inside to get Lasonya.

"No, no, no!" she wailed as she knelt next to her dead mother.

"C'mon, Lasonya. She gone. You don't need to see her like this."

Lasonya didn't acknowledge him. Just continued crying. Desmond picked her up and carried her away from Marcy's dead body. When they were outside, he put her in the car with Quaysha.

Agent Johansen approaches him a few moments later. "I'm sorry, Desmond. What the hell happened?"

"I don't know. They got here before I did and killed her mother."

"We have to get you and these girls into protection. Get in the car."

"I'm good," Desmond refused. "Take Lasonya and her daughter."

"What are you going to do?" Johansen asked.

Desmond walked toward the Tahoe. "What I do best. Destroy shit."

J-Blunt

## Chapter 16

T.A. sat on the couch smoking a blunt and staring at the wall. He was zoned out, thinking about his niggas and trying to accept the fact that all of them were dead. Scooby, Demon, Ryder, and now Q. Even though they hadn't found Quincy's body, T.A. knew he was gone. No one had heard from him since yesterday and it wasn't like Q to go missing. Being the sole survivor was a hard pill to swallow. And it made him realize the truth behind the saying "here today, gone tomorrow".

"What's up, my nigga?" Lucky asked, walking into the living room and seeing the young gunner staring at the wall.

"I'm just thinking about my niggas," he mourned.

When Lucky saw the pain in his li'l nigga's eyes, he felt bad. "Fucked up what we been through, my nigga. But look at it like this. We warriors, my nigga. Savage. We survived shit that a lot of niggas didn't. We bagged a lot of niggas to stay alive. That means something."

T.A. thought on Lucky's words. "That's real shit. I just never pictured that I would be the last one alive. I'm eighteen, the youngest of all those niggas. I thought we was finna come here and fuck the city up and run up a check. But this city is wild. Murda Mil for real. Now, I don't know what the fuck to do."

"You do the only thing you can do and keep it moving. Keep grinding. Keep living."

T.A. let out a long breath. "Yeah, I hear you. I just wish I knew what happened to Q. You think it was Zoe and Meechy?"

Lucky nodded. "I wouldn't put it past those niggas. But don't trip. We gon' fuck them niggas up. That's my word."

The front door opening made the men look up. Laronda walked into the house.

"What's up, baby girl?" Lucky nodded.

"Nothing. I'm good," she said, pausing like she wanted to say more.

"You good?" Lucky asked.

"Uh, yeah. Have y'all heard from Quincy?"

Lucky raised an eyebrow. "Not since yesterday. Why?"

Laronda crossed her legs and began wiggling like she had to pee. "I was just wondering. I didn't see his truck outside. Um, I'ma go to my room."

Lucky and T.A. watched her walk towards the back of the house.

"What was that about?" Lucky asked T.A.

The youngster shrugged. "I don't know. I thought she didn't like us."

Lucky looked at T.A. suspiciously. "Is that li'l nigga fuckin' my daughter?"

T.A shrugged again. "I don't think so."

Lucky was still staring at T.A. when his phone rang. Donny's name showed on the screen. "What's good, boss?"

"Shut it down. It's over with. D-Money is a rat!"

Lucky's eyes grew wide as the sun and his heart began beating twice as fast. "What you just say?"

"It's over with, Mil. Feds doing a sweep. Clean your hands. You ain't gon' hear from me no more. Take care of yourself. You a good nigga."

When Donny ended the call, Lucky sat with a stunned look upon his face. Desmond's cover was blown. Donny wasn't in jail, so that meant his brother's life could be in danger.

T.A. noticed the look on Lucky's face. "What happened?"

"It's over, li'l brah. Donny on the run from the Feds. He said they sweeping."

T.A.'s eyes got so big it looked like they might pop out of the sockets. "What?"

Lucky nodded, devastation written on his face. "He said it's over."

"What happened? How it go down?"

Lucky couldn't tell him Desmond was working with the Feds. "He said somebody was a rat. It's over."

T.A.'s young world was rocked. "Damn!"

Lucky got up from the couch and headed for his bedroom. He dialed Desmond's number on the way. When he walked in the room, Rachel was sitting on the bed going through her phone.

"You okay?" she asked when she saw his face.

He closed the door and began whispering. "Donny know Desmond is working with the Feds."

Rachel's eyes popped and she sat up in bed. "Oh shit! Is he okay?"

"I don't know. I'm calling him right now, but he ain't answering the phone."

When Desmond's phone went to the operator, Lucky called again. This time Desmond answered.

"Yeah."

"You good, brah? Donny just called me and said he knows you working."

There was a pause on Desmond's end of the line. "I know. He came at me last night."

"Where you at, brah? You good?"

"Yeah. Marcy's dead."

Lucky's mind was blown by the news. "Damn, brah. That's fucked up. What happened?"

"Donny's people came to the house. Listen, Lucky. I really don't got too much holla for you, man. I'm good and I'ma take care of Donny. You won't owe him nothing else."

"C'mon, Des. I know I was bogus, but we gotta move past this shit. Plus, you in danger, my nigga. You want me to come to Detroit?"

Desmond laughed. "For what? To get in my way? Stay at home. I got this. And I'ma ask you not to call me no more if it ain't no emergency, or life or death. I ain't feeling you right now, brah. You snaked me. We supposed to be better than that. I ain't tryna fuck with you right now."

Lucky was silent for a moment, allowing the words to sink in. The bond with Desmond was broken and it hurt. "You got it, brah. Be safe."

"Yep," Desmond mumbled before ending the call.

"What he say?" Rachel asked.

"That he good. They killed Lasonya's mama and he probably finna hit back."

Rachel put a hand over her mouth. "Oh my God!"

Lucky continued to look hurt. Rachel searched his face. "What he say about you and him? He still mad?"

Lucky dropped the phone and sat on the bed. "Yeah. Said he don't wanna fuck with me. Only call if it's an emergency."

Rachel crawled over to him and wrapped him in a hug. "I'm sorry, baby."

"It's all good. We ain't kids no more. Niggas is grown. He gon' do his own thang and I'ma do mine. One thing I'm not about to do is kiss a nigga's ass. Especially a nigga that's a rat. Fuck 'im."

◆◆◆

Meechy sat in front of the TV in a pair of boxers and a tank top watching *Black Ink Crew* while smoking a blunt. Although he liked the tattoo show, he really wasn't paying it that much attention. He was thinking about Lucky. He had never wanted to jack and kill a nigga so badly in his life. He hated Lucky and his Detroit niggas with a passion. And he almost had him until those bitch-ass CSG niggas got in the way. He needed to figure out a way to score that bag. He knew Lucky was holding and he wanted to hit that safe.

Footsteps from behind made him look over his shoulder. A tall and thick white woman was strutting into the living room wearing a black panther mask, a skintight leather catsuit with the crotch missing, and stiletto high heels. In her hand was a whip. She walked in front of Meechy and posed, blocking the TV.

"C'mon, girl. Move. I was watching that."

She ignored him. "Did I tell you that you could smoke weed in my house, mutherfucker?"

Meechy looked up at her like she lost her mind. "You betta get the fuck out the way. Fuck you think you talkin' to like that?"

The woman slapped the blunt out of his hand and grabbed him by the face. "Who the fuck do you think you talking to like that, bitch-ass nigga?"

Meechy didn't respond, just stared into her eyes angrily.

"Oh, you think you tough? Huh?" she asked, bringing her heel between his legs and shoving the tip into his crotch. "You don't like me callin' you nigga?"

"Grrrrrr!" Meechy growled.

Excitement lit the woman's eyes. "You like when I step on your balls? Huh? Is that what you like?" she asked, pressing her foot harder into his crotch.

"Grrrrrr," Meechy growled again.

She slapped him across the face and removed her foot from his balls. "You like it because you're a nasty mutherfucker, Meechy. Get on your knees, you nasty mutherfucker."

Meechy got up from the couch and got on his hands and knees.

"Since you wanna act like a dog, I'm going to treat you like a dog. Bark, doggy. Bark."

Meechy ignored the command.

"Oh, you can't hear, mutherfucker?" the woman said, raising the whip high in the air and smacking him on the ass. "I said bark mutherfucker! Bark!"

"Roof-roof! Roof-roof-roof!"

"Bark like a little dog. I didn't say you could be a big dog," she ordered, whipping him again.

"Arf-arf-arf!"

She patted him in the head. "Good dog. Now lick my feet, little doggy. Lick my feet."

Meechy leaned his head down and began licking her toes.

"Yeah, little doggy. That feels good. That's a good little doggy. Now go find that blunt for me, little doggy," she said, sitting on the couch and opening her legs, revealing a hairy pussy.

Meechy crawled over to find the blunt and brought it back to her.

She patted him on the head. "Now get me a lighter, little doggy. I want to get high."

Meechy crawled into the bedroom to grab a lighter and crawled back.

"Good boy," she said before lighting the blunt and taking a long puff.

Meechy remained on his hands and knees, watching her smoke. The woman blew a cloud of smoke in his face, continuing to smoke. Then she reached a hand down and began stroking her hairy pussy. "You want to lick my pussy, little doggy? You want to lick it?"

"Arf, arf!" Meechy barked.

"Come here, little doggy. Come lick my pussy."

Meechy crawled between her legs and began licking her pussy like a dog lapped up water.

"Yeah, little doggy! That feels good," she purred, slapping him on the ass with the whip. "Mama wants some of the little doggy's dick. Let me see your dick, little doggy."

Meechy lifted up, remaining on his knees as he slid his boxers down revealing his hard dick.

"Stand up and bring it to Mama," she ordered.

Meechy stood and moved his dick to her face. The woman grabbed him by the balls and began squeezing.

"Grrrrr!" he growled.

"You like when I squeeze your balls, little doggy? You like that?" she asked, squeezing harder.

She got her answer when nut began shooting from his dick onto her face and chest.

"Bad doggy!" she yelled, slapping him with the whip. "I didn't say you could cum, little doggy. Get on your knees!"

Meechy got on his knees and the woman began whipping his bare ass with the whip.

"Grrrrr! Arf, arf! Arf, arf, arf!" Meechy barked and growled while getting his ass whipped.

Their fun was interrupted when Tee Grizzly's "Sweet Thang" began playing on Meechy's phone. It was Zoe's ring tone.

"AK-47," Meechy said, saying their safe word.

The woman frowned. "C'mon, Meechy. I was just starting to have fun," she whined.

Meechy stood and went to his phone. "This might be important. Hold on. What's good, Zoe?"

"What it do, family. I just thought of how we can get this nigga."

Meechy's eyes lit up. "Okay. I'm listening."

"I just talked to my cousin, Mya, and found out Rachel still working at the club, my nigga. We follow her home, run in, and take it all!"

Meechy nodded, a smile creeping onto his face. "Hell yeah! It's on, my nigga. Let's get on that tonight."

"You already know. You at the crib?"

Meechy looked to his snow bunny. "Nah. I'm laid up with something new right now. I'ma hit the crib in 'bout an hour or two."

"Already. I'ma fuck with you later. Hit me when you get to the crib."

Meechy couldn't wipe the smile from his face after hanging up the phone.

"Look like somebody got some good news." The dominatrix smiled.

"Hell yeah," he grinned, walking over to the woman and wrapping a hand around her throat. "Gimme that mu'fuckin' whip! It's my turn to run this shit."

◆◆◆

"Hey, Duke," Rachel greeted the muscular bouncer as she walked up the steps of the strip club, Exotica.

"Sup, Black Barbie?" He nodded. "You hittin that main stage tonight, girl?"

"You know I got something special planned. I need these niggas to make it rain," She laughed, stepping past the security and into the club. After greeting a few regular customers and some dancers, Rachel went to the back room to change.

"Hey, girl," a light-skinned stripper greeted Rachel.

"Hey, Candy. What you doing here on a Monday night?"

"I need some extra coins. My man got locked up and I gotta come up with some money to help him get a lawyer," the woman answered as she slid into her heels.

Surprise shone on Rachel's face. "AJ got locked up?"

Candy nodded. "Yeah. He took the police on a high-speed chase and everything. He said he almost got away, but he crashed."

"That's fucked up, girl. Hopefully they don't keep him too long."

"Yeah. I hope so too," Candy sighed. "You heard about Wacco?"

Hearing the name sent a chill up Rachel's spine. "Nah. What happened?"

"Girl, he dead."

Rachel's eyes bucked. "Yeah, right? Somebody killed Wacco?"

"Yep. That shit was all over Facebook. Killed him and a lot of his family members. The news said it was one of the worst murder scenes in Wisconsin."

Even though it sounded like a bunch of innocent people died, Rachel was happy that Wacco was dead. That was one less problem for Lucky to worry about. "Did they say who did it?"

"Ain't nobody heard nothing yet," Candy said as she walked over to the mirror to check her appearance. "But it's gon' come out. You know can't nobody keep they mouth closed. I'ma get out on this floor and get this money."

"Okay, girl. I'ma be out there in a minute," Rachel said, pulling out her phone and calling Lucky.

"What up, baby?" he answered.

"Wacco dead!"

There was a pause on Lucky's end. "For real?"

"Yeah. Candy just told me. She said it's all over Facebook."

"Wow!" Lucky mumbled. "Did they say who did it?"

"Nope. I gotta change and get out on this floor. I just wanted to let you know."

"Okay. I'm finna get on Facebook right now."

186

## Chapter 17

After hanging up with Lucky, Rachel got dressed and hit the floor to make some money. She spotted a regular customer watching her when she walked out of the back room. Carl was a forty-three-year-old machine operator that liked to get lap dances from Rachel while telling her everything that was wrong with his marriage.

"Hey, Carl!" Rachel beamed, smiling at the trick like he was an A-list celebrity.

"Hey, Black Barbie. I was waiting for you to come in." He grinned.

"I'm here now. Do you like my outfit?" she asked, spinning so he could get a 360° view of her body in the green bikini top and white boy shorts.

Carl ogled her body as she spun. "I love it," he nodded.

"What you want me to do?"

He pulled out a wad of cash. "I want a lap dance."

Rachel spun around, sitting down on his lap and grinding. "How have you been doing?"

"Working hard. Me and my wife are thinking about a divorce. We both know it's not working out."

"Aw, that's so sad," Rachel said, looking towards the door as two niggas dressed in all red walked in.

"Not really. Neither one of us are happy. We just——"

Rachel stopped listening to Carl as she watched the niggas in red sit down and begin scoping the club. Something in her gut told her these were the Bloods that were trying to kill Lucky. Candy approached them and they had a couple of words. One of them handed her some money before she walked away.

"Carl, I need to go check on something real quick. I'ma be right back," Rachel said quickly before going to track down Candy. She was at the bar.

"Who is them niggas in red?"

"The one who gave me the money is Jordan. I don't know the young one's name. They wanted me to get them two bottles of Ace of Spades. They got money, so I'm finna milk them pockets."

Rachel took another look at the newcomers. One looked to be in his late twenties or early thirties. The other was younger, late teens or early twenties. Both had light brown skin. They looked like brothers. "I'm going back with you. I need some of that new money."

"What about Carl? You know he only want you to dance for him."

Rachel looked at Carl. He was watching her, expecting her to come back. "He gon' be okay. These niggas bought Aces. I can't let them get away. I got the younger one."

After getting the bottles of top shelf, the women sauntered to the table, ready to entertain.

"Oh, shit! You see she brought a friend for you, my nigga!" the older one said to the younger one.

"Hey!" Rachel waved, staring at the younger nigga. "I'm Black Barbie. You want a lap dance?"

The young nigga looked intimidated.

"Hell yeah, he want a lap dance!" the older one spoke for him.

Rachel sat down next to him and put a hand on his thigh. "You good?"

He nodded and popped the top on the bottle of liquor. "Yeah, I'm straight."

"What's yo' name?"

He took a long drink from the bottle. "B-Dog."

Rachel peered at him like she was trying to read him. "How old are you, B-Dog?"

"I'm twenty-one."

Rachel continued to give him the look. "No, you ain't. But I'm not trippin'. I like poppin' li'l niggas' cherries," she flirted, moving her hand higher up his thigh. He tensed up, so she leaned over and whispered in his ear. "I won't bite you, baby boy. Unless you want me to. Can I dance for you?"

He nodded and grinned. "Yeah."

Rachel stood and twerked for him before sitting on his lap and grinding. She could feel his tool growing in his pants as her eyes roamed the club and locked onto Carl's. He shook his head before getting up and leaving. A part of Rachel felt bad for doing her regular like that, but she was on a mission. He would have to get over it.

"I never seen you around here before. Where you from?" Rachel asked, leaning back and laying her head on B-Dog's chest while continuing to grind on his lap.

"I'm not from Milwaukee."

Rachel grabbed his hands and put them on her titties. "Where you from?"

"East Saint Louis. We just up here taking care of some bidness."

She spun around to straddle his lap and look him in his eyes. "What kinda business?"

"Ay, we tryna get up outta here, shawty," the older one spoke. "Only reason we came in here was because we heard y'all had the baddest bitches in the city. We ain't tryna be in here all night. Y'all tryna make some extras?"

Rachel and Candy shared a look, speaking with their eyes.

"What y'all talking 'bout?" Rachel asked.

"Grab a couple more girls and come back to our spot. We got five hunnit a head."

"I'm down," Candy nodded.

"I'ma go grab Sherry and Tweetie," Rachel said as she got up.

The four dancers left the club with the Bloods and hopped in the back of the black Suburban. Twenty minutes later, they pulled up to a townhouse on 53$^{rd}$ and Center. Jordan led the women into the house, where Flacco was chilling in the living room.

"We back wit' some bad bitches!" Jordan announced.

Flacco got up to greet the dancers. "What's good? What's good? I'm Flacco. Come sit down. Lemme see what y'all got goin' on," he said, eyeing the women so he could make his selection.

When Rachel walked by, she locked eyes with the Saint Louis Nightmare. His eyes were black as midnight and soulless. A chill went through her body.

Flacco noticed her reaction and smiled. "What's yo' name?"

"Black Barbie."

"Stand up and spin around for me."

Rachel stood and did a twirl in the tight black dress, allowing Flacco to get a good look at the goodies.

The Blood licked his lips. "I want you. Come with me."

His voice carried so much authority that Rachel didn't even question whether or not she should go with him. When he walked towards the bedroom, she followed. When they were inside, he closed the door.

"You a dancer, right?" he asked, plopping down on the bed and licking his lips while checking out her body.

Rachel nodded. "Yeah."

"You got paid already, right?"

She nodded again.

"Dance for me," he commanded.

Rachel set her purse on the bed and started with a slow wind, gyrating to a song playing in her head. A few moments later, she pulled the dress over her head and threw it at Flacco. He allowed it to land on his chest, continuing to watch the show. Rachel did the splits and twerked. She simulated several sex acts, rubbing all of her body parts and turning Flacco on.

"Take the rest off," he commanded. "Leave on the heels."

Rachel stripped from the boy shorts and bikini top, continuing to dance sexy.

"Come here."

When she closed the distance between them, Flacco reached a handout and stroked it across her pussy. His touch sent a shiver through her body.

"Do I scare you?" he asked, rubbing her pussy again.

She shook her head. "No."

He chuckled. "Good. Give me some head."

Rachel shook her head. "I don't turn tricks."

Flacco laughed and began unbuttoning his pants. "You got paid five hundred dollars. You gon' do what I tell you to do."

Rachel held her ground. "I don't do tricks. I just dance."

Flacco pulled out his hard dick. "Give me some head or gimme my money back."

Rachel grabbed her purse, pulled out five hundred dollars and laid it on the bed.

Flacco just stared at her, piercing her with his cold eyes. "Get out of my house."

Rachel bent down to gather her clothes.

"Leave those clothes on the floor and put the purse back on the bed."

Rachel looked at him like he was crazy. "This is my stuff. I'm not leaving naked."

Flacco pulled a gun from his waist. "Either you leave naked or you don't leave at all."

The look in his eyes told Rachel to leave while she could, even if that meant leaving naked. She walked out of the bedroom door and past her girls.

"What you doing?" Candy asked.

"She leaving," Flacco answered, following her to the door. "And anybody else that ain't fucking can give that money back and leave with her."

None of the other women budged or said a word. Rachel stepped out into the night alone and naked. She did her best to cover her body as she walked off the porch, about to go the neighbor's house to use the phone and maybe get some clothes. She had just walked up on the porch next door when a car pulled up.

"Rachel!"

She looked and saw Zoe hanging out the window of his Chevy. Meechy was in the passenger seat. She didn't know if she should be relieved or scared. True, he was her cousin. But he was also beefing with her man. She didn't want to get involved.

"What the fuck wrong with you, girl? You gon' just stand there? Get in. Fuck yo' clothes at?"

Deciding that getting in the car with her cousin was safer than knocking on a stranger's door with no clothes on, she ran and climbed in the back seat.

"Fuck yo' clothes at?" Zoe asked as he drove away.

"Bitch-ass nigga just took 'em 'cause I didn't wanna fuck him. Gimme a shirt to put on," Rachel explained.

"I got you," Meechy said, taking off his shirt and handing it to her. "Who is the nigga that took yo' shit? You want us to fuck him up?"

Rachel's eyes lit up. "Some Blood niggas from Saint Louis. They got my clothes and my phone. Would y'all fuck 'em up for me?"

The cutthroats shared a look.

"Them Bloods in that house you was just at?" Meechy asked.

"Yeah. You know them?"

"Hell nah. And I don't want to either. Them the niggas that killed Wacco's whole family," Zoe said.

Rachel wore the shock on her face. "Are you serious?"

"Hell yeah," Meechy nodded. "Them niggas been fucking them CSGs up. You might have to charge that shit they took to the game. Them niggas is certified."

Rachel didn't know what to think or say, so she stayed quiet.

"Where you live at?" Zoe asked. "Lemme take you to the crib."

That question got Rachel talking again. "Oh, hell nah. Lucky told me what you did. I'm not gettin' in that. Take me to Aunty Jean's house. What the hell you niggas doing out here anyway?"

"We ain't on shit. Just grabbed some loud. And I don't know what the fuck Lucky on. We didn't do shit."

"Yeah right, Zoe. Why you ain't come around no more? Y'all ran off with his dope and killed Ryder. Y'all bogus for that. Lucky put y'all on and y'all got on some snake shit. You made me look bad. I the one that hooked y'all up. That was foul, cuz," Rachel vented.

The car went silent for a moment. Then Meechy spoke.

"You want me to take it from here?" he asked Zoe.

"Do you."

A sinking feeling entered Rachel's stomach. "Uh uh. Stop the car. Let me out right now, Zoe," she said, grabbing the door handle.

Meechy spun around in the seat and busted her in her shit. A white light flashed behind Rachel's eyes and she could taste the blood in her mouth.

"Ain't nobody playin' with you, bitch! Tell us where the fuck you live!"

It took a few moments for Rachel to get her senses back. When the stars went away, she saw Meechy kneeling in the front seat, facing her direction, his fists clenched.

"Where the fuck you live, bitch?" he yelled again.

Rachel knew she couldn't take them home or they would fuck up Lucky. But she didn't think they would hurt her that badly, so she lifted her feet and started kicking. "Get away from me! Leave me alone!"

Meechy caught a heel to the chin before grabbing ahold of her legs. "Punk-ass bitch!" he yelled, throwing her leg down and diving in the back seat. He was a big nigga, six feet tall and every bit of 240 pounds. He landed on top of Rachel and started beating her ass. His fists rained down on her face and head like lightning and thunder. All Rachel could do was ball up and scream.

"Zoe, help me! Help me, cousin! Please help!"

Zoe continued driving. "We need that address, Rachel."

Meechy continued to deliver blows to Rachel's head, hands, and arms. When his knuckles started to hurt, he began choking her. "Where the fuck you live, bitch? Where the fuck you live?"

Rachel tried to pry his hands from her throat, but couldn't. He was too big and too strong. She foamed at the mouth and began turning blue in the face. When she felt her consciousness fading, she gave in. "Okay," she whispered weakly.

Meechy let her go and Rachel began choking as the air rushed into her lungs. He gave her a few moments to catch her breath.

"What's the address, bitch?"

◆◆◆

Lucky lay in bed thinking about his current situation. Wacco was dead. Polo was dead. The heroin operation was over. For the first time in a long time he felt like things were getting better. Like he might be able to leave the street life behind and get back to the plans he made upon his release from prison.

"Daddy, can I lay in bed with you?" Laronda asked, walking in the room and hopping in bed with Lucky before he could consent.

"I guess I don't got no say in this," he laughed. "You a li'l too big to be getting in bed with me, ain't you?"

Laronda curled up next to him, laying her head on his chest. "We never got the chance to do this when I was little. We making up for it now."

Lucky wrapped his arms around her, kissing her atop the head. Truth was, he liked being cuddled up with his daughter. And he loved the bond they were creating. "No matter how old you is, you gon' always be my baby."

"Aw! Thanks, Daddy," she gushed.

They lay in silence for a few moments before Laronda spoke again. "Can I ask you a question?"

"Yeah. What's on yo' mind, baby girl?"

"Do you know what happened to Quincy?"

Lucky thought about how to respond. Laronda wanted to talk land she was probably about to tell him about her and Q creeping. He needed to play this right. "Not for sure, no. I think I know what happened. Why?"

"You think he dead?" she whispered.

"I hate to say so, but yeah. It ain't like that li'l nigga to go missing."

Lucky could feel Laronda's warm tears staining his T-shirt. "What's going on, baby girl? You okay?"

Laronda was silent for a moment. Lucky gave her time to work it out.

"I gotta tell you somethin', but I don't want you to be mad at me."

"Okay. I'm listening."

Laronda looked up to see his face. "Promise you won't be mad?"

"I promise I won't be mad. Why you cryin'? What's goin' on, baby girl?"

"Me and Quincy was messing around."

Lucky kept a poker face, not showing any reaction. "Okay. I figured something like that was going on by how you reacting."

"You not mad?" she sniffled, wiping away tears.

Lucky shook his head. "Nah, I'm not mad. I just wish you woulda told me sooner. How long y'all been messing around?"

"A couple of weeks. Like right after Mama died. He came over Aunty April's house to check up on me. He was real nice. Even though it wasn't that long, I really liked him. He made me feel special and didn't judge me. We wanted to tell you, but it didn't seem like the right time with all the drama going on."

"Well, at least you got to get to know him and he made you happy. If he don't come back, you gon' always have those memories," Lucky said, trying to be supportive and kissing her atop the head again. Truthfully, he wanted to lecture her ass about telling Quincy that Desmond was his brother and working with the police, but that might open another can of worms and lead to her asking more questions, so he left well enough alone.

The sound of a car pulling into the garage got his attention. He checked the time on his phone.

"She back early," Lucky commented. "It's only 11:30."

"Maybe Rachel got tired of those thirsty niggas and quit," Laronda laughed.

When he heard the front door open and close, Lucky called out to his girl. "Rachel, Laronda talking shit! She said you got tired of dancing on those bunions!"

"Daddy!" Laronda yelled, slapping him in the chest and jumping out of bed. "I didn't say that, Rachel. He lying," she called, heading for the living room. Then she screamed. "Ahh!"

Lucky sat up, becoming alert. "Laronda, you good?"

When she didn't answer, he got out of bed and called her again. "Laronda?"

Still no answer.

He grabbed the pistol from the bedside table and was walking towards the door when he heard a voice that sent a chill up his spine.

"Come out here, Lucky. We gotta holla," Zoe called.

Lucky crept towards the living room with his pistol ready. He didn't know how Zoe got in the house, but he was about to make him wish he never came over. When he got to the living room, what he saw took his breath away. T.A. was kneeling on the floor. Laronda was next to him. Zoe stood behind them, pointing a pistol at both of their heads. A few feet away was Rachel. She wore a T-shirt, her face battered and bruised. Meechy stood behind her with a pistol to her head, using her as a shield.

"Unless you want yo' people filled with holes, betta put that gun down," Meechy snarled.

Lucky set the gun on the floor. "What y'all on? It's like that, for real?"

Meechy shoved Rachel on the floor and pointed the pistol at Lucky. "We need that work, my nigga. Let us get that."

Lucky put his hands in the air. "Okay. You got that. Just let them go."

"Nah, nigga. It don't work like that," Zoe spoke up. "I'ma watch them while you take my nigga to that stash. You try some bullshit, I'm shooting yo' daughter first."

"C'mon, brah. I know how this go. Y'all got me, my nigga. Let them go," Lucky tried to negotiate.

"Quit stalling, nigga. Let's go 'fore I pop yo' bitch ass," Meechy said, waving the gun in Lucky's face.

While they were going back and forth with Lucky, no one noticed Rachel slip her hand under the couch. Lucky planted guns all over the house and there was a shotgun under the sofa.

"I'ma give y'all the shit. Just——" Meechy slapped Lucky with the pistol.

Lucky stumbled into the wall, but didn't fall. During the commotion, Rachel pulled the shotgun from under the couch and pointed it at her cousin.

Kaboom!

The shotgun's kick scared the shit out of Rachel and the gun leapt from her hand. Zoe's body folded in half and flew across the room as the 12-gauge slug tore into his ribcage.

The blast scared Meechy, making him flinch. He turned and saw Zoe laying on the floor and the shotgun next to Rachel. "Bitch!" he cursed, turning his gun towards Rachel.

Lucky dove at Meechy's knees as the pistol fired.

Pop!

The bullet barely missed Rachel as Meechy fell to the floor. Lucky climbed on top of him and tried wrestling the gun from his grip. Laronda got up and began stomping Meechy in the face until he let go of the gun. T.A. grabbed the shotgun.

Chh-chh!

The sound of the shotgun cocking made everyone pause. T.A. pointed the gun at Meechy's face and squeezed the trigger.

Kaboom!

The jackboy's face disappeared as blood, bones, and brains spattered everyone.

"Ahhhh!" Laronda screamed, wiping pieces of skull from her pants.

Lucky sprang into action and prepped Rachel. "Listen, baby. We gotta go. The neighbors gon' call the police and me and T.A. can't be here when they get here. Say it was self-defense."

J-Blunt

## Chapter 18

Lucky was unable to sit still as he waited in the car. He looked towards the hospital doors expectantly, wishing the next person to walk out would be Rachel. Meechy had fucked his girl up, broken her nose and left knots all over her face and bruising around her neck. It had Lucky so mad that he wished he could put the dead nigga's face back together and blow it apart again.

"She good, Lucky," T.A. said from the passenger seat. "She a fighter, my nigga. You see how she got down on her own cousin. You got a real one, my nigga."

"I know," Lucky breathed. "I just wish I could be in there with her. Everybody handle that first body differently. I just wanna make sure her head in the right spot. Her first one was her cousin. Somebody she loved. I don't know if that is easy to digest."

T.A. pointed to the hospital doors. "Well, you about to find out right now. Here they come."

Lucky looked up as Rachel and Laronda walked out of the hospital. He blew the horn and flicked the lights to get their attention, then jumped out of the car and opened the back door. When Rachel walked up, he saw the face mask that she wore to protect her nose. Her left eye was swollen shut and her lips were fat.

"Damn, baby," he groaned, wrapping her in his arms.

"I'm okay," she mumbled into his shoulder.

He let her go and helped her into the car before getting in the driver's seat. "What the police say? You good?"

"I told them I shot both of them. They didn't believe me at first, but Laronda backed me up."

"They was some bitch-ass police," Laronda added. "I think they was going on what the one of the neighbors said about her having a boyfriend. They wanted to know if you did it and she took the rap."

"Y'all did good," Lucky nodded. "Is both of y'all good? Seeing that shit for the first time or killing somebody can fuck with yo' head."

"I'm good," Laronda said. "That's what they snake asses get. You tried to get money with them niggas and they tried to rob you. That was bogus."

Rachel was quiet, staring out the window.

"You good, baby?" Lucky asked, watching her through the rearview mirror.

She continued looking out the window. "I don't know how I feel. I'm high on these pills so I can't really think or feel nothing. That was my cousin. But I don't regret it. He let Meechy do this to my face. I just——" She stopped talking, her eyes growing wide as she met Lucky's eyes in the rearview mirror. "I seen those Bloods and I know where they live!"

It took Lucky a moment to follow what she said. "You talkin' 'bout the niggas that came by my house?"

Rachel nodded. "Yeah. They came to the club and got some of us. They took my clothes and kicked me out the house because I wouldn't fuck they leader. That's how I ran into Zoe."

"Them the niggas murked Demon," T.A. spoke up. "We gotta get down on them niggas."

"We is. Fo sho'," Lucky promised. "Tell me where they live so I can check it out."

When Rachel told him where the house was, Lucky parked down the street and watched. It was three in morning, so there wasn't any movement.

"How many of 'em is it in there?"

"I seen three in the house. But they leader is a beast, baby. I never been scared of a nigga, but he almost made me piss on myself. His name is Flacco. You gotta be careful with him."

"I will," Lucky said, continuing to watch the house.

"Let's get them niggas now," T.A. said, pulling his pistol, ready to move.

"We gon' get them niggas, li'l brah. But not tonight. My daughter in the car and my girl is fucked up. She said the nigga a beast, so we gotta do our homework."

"I think you should do it as soon as possible, baby," Rachel spoke up.

"Me too, Daddy," Laronda cut in. "We need to put all this behind us."

"Not tonight," Lucky said, pulling away from the curb. "We gon' get 'em, but not now."

When they got home, Lucky put Rachel in bed and laid with her until she fell asleep. It didn't take long because of the drugs. After tucking her in, he went to clean Meechy's blood out of the carpet and off the walls. While cleaning, he thought about what to do with his life after he killed Flacco and the Bloods. It seemed like a good time to move away and start over. He could turn himself in and put the legal troubles to rest. As far as he knew, the police couldn't connect him to any new crimes. He was wanted from running from his P.O. and the police wanted to talk about Melissa and her family being killed and Tyler and Trev. If there were no new charges, he could turn himself in and do whatever time the P.O. suggested. His guess was anywhere from one to two years, as long as there weren't any new charges. He could get his mind right and come up with a new plan while he was down, get back to writing. The more he thought about it, the more sense it made. He was going to call the lawyer, Brandon Williams, when he got up to have him look into his situation to make sure he didn't have any new charges.

After he finished cleaning up the blood and brains, he jumped in the bed with Rachel. He fell asleep thinking about starting a new life.

◆◆◆

A black crow sat high in the tree, watching the soldiers move quickly through the brush towards the cabin. A raised fist from the squad leader made the team pause. Hand signals were given and the six-man team broke into two groups. Three flanked the left side of the cabin, hiding in the grass and training their rifles in the front door. The other three moved towards the back of the house, hiding behind trees and bushes, training their guns on the back door. Communication devices in the soldiers' ears began to chatter.

"Alpha 3 and Alpha 4, you are a go. I repeat, Alpha 3 and Alpha 4, you are a go!"

Desmond sprinted from his hiding spot at the front of the cabin and ran to the front door at the same time Slayer made his move from the squad at back of the cabin, running to the back door. They reached the cabin at the same time and lobbed stun grenades through the windows before taking cover. Seconds later, there were two loud explosions. The blasts were signals for the rest of the teams to go. Kim rushed towards the front door with a shotgun and blew the locks off. Country kicked the door open and the team rushed inside. The same thing was happening at the back door.

"What the fuck?" Desmond cursed, staring in horror at the scene before him. The living room floor was covered with dead bodies, at least fifty of them.

"Duke, we got a problem," Kim spoke into the com. "Something isn't right."

Static filled the com's followed by a high-pitched deafening beep.

"Ahh!" Desmond screamed, snatching the communication device from his ear.

"What the fuck was that?" Country asked as he and Kim ripped the coms from their ears.

"I don't know," Desmond said before calling out to his team leader on the other side of the wall. "Duke! You guys good back there?"

There was no answer. Desmond wanted to get to the kitchen to check on the rest of the team, but dead bodies covered every inch of the floor. And then they began moving.

"What the fuck?" Country yelled, raising his rifle and shooting the moving dead closest to him.

Tat-tat-tat-tat!

The bodies continued to rise, standing up and grabbing at the soldiers. The trained killers let the rifles talk while backing out of the house.

Brrrrreaaaaatttt! Brrrrreaaaaatttt! Brrrrreaaaaatttt!

The dead bodies fell down only to rise again.

"Ahhhh!" Country screamed as one of the dead grabbed him and bit him on the neck.

Desmond and Kim continued shooting their guns as they backed out onto the porch. A noise from behind made Desmond look to his right. More zombies were coming from the trees surrounding the cabin. There were hundreds of them. When Desmond's rifle ran out of bullets, he dropped it and grabbed the sidearm. He fired at the dead closest to him, giving them all dome calls. And then one caught his eye. It was Marcy. Half of her face was blown off. She was standing directly in front of his gun, but he didn't shoot. And that's when he felt the hands of the zombies grabbing at his clothes and teeth sinking into his flesh.

"Ahhhh!" Desmond yelled, screaming himself awake. He shot up in bed, grabbing the pistol that lay next to him, and searching the dark room for zombies. That's when he realized it was only a bad dream.

"Shit," he cursed, wiping the sweat from his forehead. After throwing the gun on the bed, he grabbed his phone to check the time. It was almost noon. Checkout time. He climbed from the bed and went to the bathroom. After freshening up, he grabbed the overnight bag from the table and left the room. He dropped the room key off at the front desk before hopping in the Tahoe and getting on the highway. He was driving from Detroit to Minnesota. Not wanting to have a repeat of the fatigue he'd experienced when he drove from Detroit to Milwaukee and back to Detroit, he stopped at a hotel.

Five hours later, he pulled into Minneapolis and used the GPS to find Kim's house. It was a small white cottage on the south side of the city. He knocked on the door and waited. The curtain on the door moved and Desmond was staring into a pair of brown slanted eyes. When the door opened, Kim Lee was all smiles.

"Desmond! What's up, brother?"

"Kim! What's good, brother!?" Desmond grinned as the men hugged.

"C'mon in, man. How was the drive?"

"Long as hell." Desmond laughed as he stepped into the house.

"You want something to eat or drink? I got some beer or juice."

"I'll take a beer," Desmond said as he followed Kim to the kitchen.

After grabbing two brews, the men sat at the table.

"So, you fucked up Detroit, huh?" Kim laughed.

"Not yet. That's what I wanted to talk to you about. I need help. And some firepower."

Kim gave him a look. "What you got going on, brotha?"

"I'ma spare you the long version. When we talked a little while ago, I was on a mission. I was working with the Feds to bring down some drug dealers in Detroit. My family was in protective custody while I worked. Well, my cover got blown and they went to the house looking for me, but I wasn't there. They killed my girl's mother and I want payback. The problem is, he's gone underground, and he's probably got a small army protecting him since he's wanted by me and the Feds."

Kim looked surprised. "This sounds like some Mission Impossible shit."

"Will you help?"

"Dammit, Des. I'm waiting for my decision from the Physical Evaluation Board. I really want to get back to the naval base and get reinstated. I want to go after Slayer and look that traitor in the eyes when he tells me why he betrayed us."

"I want that same thing. Trust me. And as soon as I get this punk mutherfucker Donny, I'm calling Colonel Jones and getting reinstated. But I can't leave without taking care of this."

Kim took a sip of the beer and thought for a moment. "I want to help, Des, but I don't want to ruin my shot at getting back my frog suit back. If we blow up these guys and get caught, we can kiss the Navy goodbye."

Desmond nodded. "I understand. I'm not going to ask you to do something you don't want. What do you have for firepower? I need the good shit."

Kim smiled. "Wait til you see this shit!"

They left the kitchen and went to a locked shed behind the house. Inside was a cache of weapons and explosives. Desmond grinned like a kid in a candy store.

"Damn, Kim! Where the fuck you get all this shit?"

The Japanese man smiled. "I'm a collector. Take what you need."

Desmond stuffed a duffle bag with enough weapons to start a small war. When he felt he had enough firepower, he turned to Kim. "Thanks for this, man. I just have one question. I remember you being good with riddles and I got one. How do you find a man that doesn't want to be found?"

Kim thought for a moment. "Take something he loves and make him come to you."

Desmond thought about the answer to the riddle. He needed to find something Donny loved. And then it hit him. "Thanks for everything, man. I gotta get going."

Kim wrapped Desmond in a hug. "Be safe. And get your ass back to the base. I want you with me when I find Slayer."

Desmond nodded. "I wouldn't miss it for the world."

After heading to the truck, Desmond loaded the guns in the back seat and hopped in the driver's seat. He had just started the truck when Kim walked out the front door with a duffel bag. Desmond let down the window. "What's going on, brotha?"

Kim walked to the passenger side. "Unlock the door. I can't let you go at this alone. Plus, I need some practice."

Desmond smiled as he unlocked the door. "I knew you wanted in when I first walked in the house."

Kim laughed as he sat the duffle bag in the backseat. "What can I say? I love shooting bad guys. You have any way to find him?"

Desmond pulled out the phone as he drove away from Kim's house. "I'm going to takes something he loves," he said before dialing a number.

"What's going on Desmond?" Agent Wright answered.

"You find him yet?"

"No. He probably fled the state. We're going through traffic cam footage."

"What if I told you I might know how to find him? Would you help me?"

"I'm listening."

"Check the evidence from all the places you searched and let me know if you find a gold pocket watch."

♦♦♦

Donny sat in the chair staring out the window at the high afternoon sun. He couldn't believe that his run was over. All the plans he made, all the moves he busted, all the sacrifices were for nothing. The Feds were chasing and all he could do was hide. Yesterday he was the King of Detroit. Today he was the king of a cabin hidden in Michigan's Upper Peninsula surrounded by eight bodyguards. Oh, how the mighty fall. And he traced it back to one man: D-Money. He should've known that a soldier with enough skills to kill the way D-Money did was too good to be true. But Donny had made a fatal mistake, and now it was about to cost him his freedoms. Damn.

A car driving down the dirt road got the security's attention. They pulled assault rifles and flanked both sides of the road as a blue Land Rover drove up to the house. Donny marched out of the house to greet the driver as he climbed from the truck.

"Where is it? Did you find it?"

The man shook his head. "No. I searched the office, but it wasn't there."

"What do you mean you couldn't find it? I left it on the desk at the cleaning service. How hard is it to find?"

Chase cowered under the boss's fury. "I looked all around, but couldn't find it. The place was ransacked. I think the Feds came in. Maybe they have it."

Donny looked devastated. "That don't make sense. What would the Feds want with my watch? That watch has been in my family for four generations. I want my watch! Call every pawn shop and jewelry store in all of Michigan and find my muthafuckin' watch!"

♦♦♦

Desmond sat inside the Tahoe, looking out the windshield intently. Agent Wright sat in the passenger seat. Kim Lee was in the back. They were all watching the pawn shop up the street. Agent Wright had given Desmond the watch. He had pawned it and instructed the shop owner to call him if anyone contacted him about the watch. Less than twenty-four hours had gone by when there was a hit. And the three of them were waiting for the caller to make the pickup. He said he would been there at 5:00 the next day. The clock in Desmond's dash read 4:52.

"I think that's him!" Agent Wright pointed.

The man was tall, dark-skinned, with a fluffy beard covering most of his face. He climbed from a blue Land Rover and took a cautionary look around before entering the shop.

"I'm going to take a look," Kim said as he climbed from the back seat and trotted quickly towards the shop.

"If this is him, I want you to tail him," Wright explained. "We're going to find out where Donny is before we call it in. I'm not letting Martinez take this one from me. We worked too hard to let someone else get credit for our collar."

Desmond nodded. "I agree."

A few moments later, Kim walked out the pawn shop and hopped in the truck. "That's him. He's bargaining about the price. He should be out in a minute."

A minute turned out to be five. When the tall man jumped back in the Rover, Desmond began to follow. They expected a short drive, but instead took a long drive to the northernmost part of Michigan. After several hours on the highway, the Rover turned onto a side road. Desmond kept a good distance and pulled over on the side of the highway. The area was heavily wooded, so he and the crew climbed out to follow on foot. A quarter mile from the highway was a log cabin surrounded by trees. Desmond got an eerie feeling when he saw the house. It reminded him of the one in his dream.

"You okay, Desmond?" Kim asked, noticing his startled look.

"Yeah. I'm good," he said, shaking off the bad juju.

"Let's get back to the truck so I can call it in," Agent Wright said. "We're a long fucking way from Detroit."

When they got back to the vehicle, Desmond and Kim grabbed duffle bags from the trunk and began putting on tactical gear.

"What are you guys doing?" Wright asked, watching them strap up.

"We're saving the taxpayers some money," Desmond said.

"No, Desmond! This wasn't what we agreed to."

"We didn't agree to nothing. I told you I knew how to find him and you agreed to help. Now me and Kim are about to take him down. You coming?"

"No! No! That's not how this works. This is a federal investigation. Donny is a fugitive of the federal government. You are hampering our investigation!" Agent Wright yelled.

Desmond and Kim continued strapping on gear and weapons.

"We're about to make a citizen's arrest. You coming?" Desmond asked, slinging an AR-33 over his shoulder.

Agent Wright realized he wasn't going to be able to talk the men down and got with the program. "Give me one of those rifles and a vest."

"We'll do a quick recon to see how many of them are on the property," Kim said.

"I'll take the back. You got the front. Wright, you take a flank. Let's do a com test," Desmond said before clicking the communications device in his ear.

"Loud and clear," Kim nodded.

Agent Wright stuffed a com link into his ear. "Am I good?"

Desmond nodded. "Let's get it!"

The trio crept up to the cabin, spreading to cover it from all angles. Desmond crept around to the back, staying about a hundred yards away so he wouldn't be detected. He lay in the brush and looked through the scope. Two men guarded the rear. One on the porch looked bored. Another was a few feet away with his face his in a cell phone.

"I'm out back. Two guarding the door. What you got, Kim?" Desmond whispered into the com.

"I got two guarding the door. Windows are covered. Can't see inside," Kim radioed.

"Wright, you got anything?" Desmond asked.

"Looks like we got one patrolling the property. Windows are covered. Don't know how many inside," Wright whispered.

"Okay. We go in hot on my signal," Desmond said, lining his scope up with the man's head that was on the porch. "Lock onto the targets."

"Target one locked," Kim radioed.

"I got him," Wright said.

Desmond did a count down. "3. 2. 1. Execute."

The assault rifles fired at almost the same time and their targets went down. "Go!" Desmond yelled into the com as he jumped up and rushed the cabin. He pulled a stun grenade from his pocket, snatched out the pin, and lobbed it in the window. There was a small explosion inside. He kicked the door open and rushed in with the rifle ready. The kitchen was empty.

While Desmond was rushing the house from the rear, Kim was lobbing a stun grenade through the front window. After it exploded, he kicked open the front door and ran inside. Unlike the kitchen, the front room was occupied by two guards, but they were disoriented from the blasts. Kim cut them down easily. Desmond and Agent Wright got into the living room at the same time. When the smoke cleared, two bodies lay on the ground. The men looked around and noticed a hallway with three closed doors. Desmond signaled with his hands for them to check the rooms. The trio kept their rifles high as they crept to the doors. When they got to the first door, Desmond made more hand signals. It was for Kim to take high, he would take low, and Agent Wright to open the door. After a silent three count, the Fed yanked he door open.

Brrrrreaaaaatttt!

Agent Wright stumbled into the wall as chopper bullets hit him in the chest and shoulder. Desmond and Kim returned fire, cutting down the man that had bought the watch from the pawn shop. They did a quick check of the room, noticing the open window.

"Wright, you good?" Desmond called, running to the federal agent's side.

"Yeah, ah, shit! Sonofabitch hit me in the shoulder and my vest."

"Get him, Des. I'll take care of Wright," Kim said.

Desmond jumped out the window, pausing for a moment to listen. Leaves rustling about fifty yards away got his attention. He looked in that direction and saw Donny running through the woods. The chase was on! Desmond broke into a sprint, pulling the pistol from the side holster. Donny turned to see Desmond chasing and began shooting.

Pop, pop, pop!

Desmond ducked behind a tree and took aim at Donny's back.

Clap, clap!

"Ahh!" Donny screamed as he face planted in the dirt.

Desmond crept up to him, keeping his gun ready.

"Okay, D-Money. You got me, my nigga," Donny grunted, rolling into his back. "I'm done. Help me get outta here and I'ma forget all about this and make sure you get straight. I got a half mil for you, baby boy. Just get me outta here."

"I don't want yo' money." Desmond mugged him, moving closer and keeping the pistol pointed in Donny's face.

"Tell me what you want, D. Whatever you want, I got it for you."

A picture of Marcy popped into Desmond's head. "I want yo' life."

Pop!

# Chapter 19

"I think I'ma turn myself in after I take care of Flacco," Lucky said.

Rachel turned to look at him through her good eye. "Are you sure you wanna go back to jail?"

"Shit, what other choice do I got? I'ma call the lawyer that helped me with that battery case and have him check to see if I got some shit hanging over me that I don't know about. If all I got is this absconding from parole, I'ma get it over with."

"Okay. Whatever you wanna do, I'm with you. Did you tell Laronda?"

"Nah, not yet. But I will. And when I turn myself in, I want y'all to leave. Go find a house somewhere. Atlanta or something. I wanna come out to a new city and have a new start."

"I like the sound of that. The sooner the better. When you gon' take care of Flacco?"

"I don't know. I need to figure a way to get in that house. I don't wanna shootout in the middle of the street. I wanna run in there and fuck them niggas up."

"I could probably helped you get in," Rachel suggested.

Lucky blew her off. "Nah, baby. You been through enough. You need to focus on getting better. It's only been a couple days since you got out the hospital. I don't wanna put you in no more danger."

Rachel sat up in bed. "You don't gotta protect me, Lucky. I can handle it. He took my phone. I could knock on the door and get them to open it. You and T.A. can wait on the side of the house until the door open. Then run in. They probably wouldn't even be expecting it."

Lucky had to admit that the plan wasn't bad. But he didn't want Rachel to get hurt. "It don't sound like a bad plan, baby. But I keep thinking about you getting hurt. You just got fucked up by Meechy and that shit got me wanting to protect you as much as I can."

Rachel leaned forward to kiss him, looking in his eyes. "Thank you for wanting to protect me, baby. You my man, and I think that's what you supposed to do. But I'm also not as fragile as you think.

And I'm all the way down for you. I love you, and I would do anything for you, just like I know you would do for me. It's us against the world. Let me help you. I want to put this behind us so we can get on with our new life."

Lucky stared into his woman's good eye, seeing the love and loyalty in her brown iris. "Okay. We moving tomorrow night."

◆◆◆

Lucky and T.A. crept through the dark, keeping low and remaining quiet. They ran down the alley and crept behind the blood's house. They tried to look in the windows, but all the blinds and curtains were closed.

"You take the right side," Lucky told T.A.

The men crept around to the front of the house, making sure the coast was clear. Then Lucky sent Rachel a one-word text:

*Ready*

A few moments later, a black box Chevy turned onto the block. Rachel parked the stolen car in front of the house and hopped out. She spotted Lucky and T.A. on either side of the house as she walked upon the porch. Nervous energy flooded her body as she knocked on the door. No one answered, so she knocked again.

"Who dat?" A man called from behind the door.

"Black Barbie."

"I don't know no mu'fuckin' Black Barbie. Move around."

"I came over here from the club a couple nights ago. I need to talk to Flacco. He got my phone."

The door opened and B-Dog appeared. He frowned when he seen the lumps on her face. "Fuck happened to you?"

"Somebody jumped me after y'all put me out. Is Flacco here? I need my phone."

While she was talking, Lucky and T.A. began creeping from the sides of the house.

"Who dat, Blood?" Jordan asked, appearing in the background, holding a pistol.

"One of them hoes from the other night," B-Dog said, turning to look over his shoulder. "She wanna holla at Flacco 'bout her phone."

"Fuck that bitch, Blood. Make her move around."

B-Dog spun back to tell her to leave when T.A. made his move. The Detroit shooter ran in front of Rachel with his pistol sparking.

Clap, clap, clap!

B-Dog didn't know what hit him as hot lead tore into his face. T.A. ran into the house, putting Jordan in his sights. The Blood was ready and lifted his pistol first.

Clap, clap, clap!

T.A. went down as bullets tore into his chest.

Lucky ran in behind T.A. and began blazing at Jordan, hitting him in the chest with several shots. Then he turned to check on his li'l nigga when Jordan lifted his pistol and shot again.

Blocka, blocka, blocka, blocka, blocka!

Lucky caught a bullet to the stomach and fell into the door. He lifted his pistol and finished off Jordan with bullets to the face.

Lucky pushed himself up and turned to get out of the house.

Flacco came from the back with a chopper. When he saw Lucky, a vision of the shootout he had lost flashed into his head and he began shooting.

Tat-tat-tat-tat-tat-tat!

Two high-powered rounds tore into Lucky's back, knocking him out of the house and dropping him on the porch. Rachel was still standing on the porch when Lucky collapsed. She ran to help and looked up as Flacco was about to start shooting again.

Clap, clap, clap, clap!

Flacco ducked out of the way as T.A.'s gun barked. The Detroit shooter wasn't dead and he wanted to catch another body before death came to get him. But Flacco was battle ready. After dodging T.A.'s feeble attempt, the leader of the Bloods turned his chopper on T.A. and made sure he would never be able to get up again.

Tat-tat-tat-tat-tat-tat!

T.A.'s body jerked as the high-powered rounds tore into his face and neck, ending his life. During the distraction created by

T.A., Rachel took Lucky's pistol as she helped him up and took him to the car. She had just thrown him in the backseat when Flacco arrived in the doorway. Without thinking, she lifted the pistol and started shooting.

Boom, boom, boom, boom, boom, boom, boom!

Flacco ducked out of the way. When he looked out again, Rachel was climbing into the car. He ran onto the porch and let the chopper ride.

Tat-tat-tat-tat-tat-tat! Tat-tat-tat-tat-tat-tat!

High-powered rounds tore into the Chevy's frame and busted out windows as Rachel sped away from the bloody scene.

"Lucky, baby, are you okay?"

"I'm fucked up, baby," Lucky groaned, sounding like it hurt to talk. He was lying on his stomach across the backseat.

"I'm on my way to the hospital. Just hold on, baby. Hold on."

Lucky didn't respond. He was in too much pain.

"Lucky! Say something, baby. Keep talking. Keep talking," she told him.

"It hurt to talk," he mumbled.

"I know. But you gotta do it. You gotta stay woke."

"I think my phone ringing," Lucky mumbled.

Rachel reached over the back seat and dug into his pocket. Her name shone in the screen. She answered.

"Is he dead?" Flacco asked.

"You bitch-ass nigga! I swear to God, I'm killing you!" Rachel threatened.

"Turn around and come get me. I'm waiting on you," he taunted.

"Fuck you, bitch-ass nigga."

"Learn some more words, baby. But I didn't call for you. I wanna talk to Lucky. Is he still alive?"

Rachel looked in the backseat. Lucky looked like he was in bad shape. "Yeah. He still alive. And he fuckin' you up when he get better."

"Good. I'm not leaving Milwaukee until I kill both them niggas. Give Desmond this number and tell him I'm waiting," he said before ending the call.

"Lucky, you still woke, baby?"

Lucky grunted something that she couldn't understand. He sounded close to death.

"Lucky, hold on, baby! We almost there. What did you say?"

"Call Desmond, tell him I'm sorry and I love him," he mumbled weakly.

Rachel grabbed the phone and found Desmond's number. "Okay. I'm calling him now."

"Yeah," Desmond answered flatly.

"Desmond, this is Rachel. Lucky got shot!"

"What!" Desmond yelled. "Where is he?"

"He in the backseat. He can't talk. We on the way to the hospital."

"What happened? Who did it?"

"Those Blood niggas. His name Flacco. He got my phone. He want you to call him. He said he not leaving until he kill y'all."

"Gimme the number."

"555-3457."

"How is Lucky? Is it bad?" Desmond asked, pain filling his voice.

Rachel looked in the back seat again. When she spoke, tears began spilling down her face. "It's bad, Desmond. He said he's sorry and he loves you. He might not..." She couldn't finish talking. The thought of Lucky dying was too much.

"Move the phone so he can hear me."

Rachel held the phone over the backseat.

"Lucky, you betta hang on, nigga! I'm on my way. We Harrisons, nigga. We built to last. You bet' not die! You hear me? You bet' not die!"

◆◆◆

The guilt gripped Desmond as he sat in the coach seat aboard the 747-jumbo jet. He felt stupid for allowing what happened between Lucky and Lasonya to affect their relationship. Their entire life, it had been the two of them. The bond they shared was built on unconditional brotherly love. And then Lasonya came along and destroyed it. Never again, he told himself. Never again.

When the plane landed at Mitchell International Airport, Desmond took a cab to the hospital. He walked up to the nurse's station and grabbed the attention of the middle-aged black woman behind the counter.

"Excuse me. I'm looking for my brother, Larry Harrison."

"One moment, sir," she said as she typed the name into the computer. "Oh. He just came out of surgery. He's in the ICU."

When Desmond heard those words, a part of him was happy that Lucky was still alive. The other half was worried that his injuries might be too much. Anyone in the intensive care unit was in bad shape. After taking the elevator to the fifth floor, he followed the signs until he found the ICU. There was another nurse's station.

"How can I help you?" a pretty caramel-skinned nurse asked.

"I'm looking for my brother, Larry Harrison. They said he just got out of surgery."

"Oh, yeah." Her eyes lit up. "He's been up here for about an hour. The surgery was long and he suffered a lot of damage to his lungs and internal organs. His daughter and wife are already in the room. They're in room 6."

"Okay. Thank you." Desmond nodded before going to find the room. He steeled his nerves for what he might see as he walked up to the door. After taking a breath, he walked in. What he saw made him stop in his tracks.

Lucky was lying on the hospital bed, appearing to be asleep. There was a breathing mask on his face, an IV in his arm, a device on his finger that checked the oxygen levels in his body, and wires from his chest hooked up to a heart monitor. The machine next to the bed clicked and beeped every time he took a breath.

"Uncle Desmond!" Laronda shouted, running over and wrapping her arms around him. "Look what they did to my daddy," she cried.

Desmond wrapped his niece in a hug, unable to take his eyes off of Lucky. He had never seen his brother look so frail or weak.

"You gotta fuck them up, Uncle Desmond. You gotta kill all of them," Laronda continued.

"Hey, Desmond," Rachel said.

The sound of her voice pulled Desmond's attention away from Lucky. When he saw the bruises on her face, he gasped. "What's up? You good?"

She nodded, averting her eyes and looking at Lucky. "I'm good. It's Lucky that I'm worried about. He was in surgery for three hours and lost a lot of blood. He in a coma right now. His lungs got damaged and he can't breathe without the machine. I'm worried about him," she said, her voice trembling as she wiped tears from her eyes.

Desmond unwrapped himself from Laronda and walked to Lucky's bedside. He stared at his brother's face for a few moments. "Lucky, it's me. Desmond. I'm here now. We need you to pull through this shit, nigga. We Harrisons. We built to last. And I forgive you, brah. I'm not mad no more. I love you, nigga."

Lucky's heart monitor began to beep as his heart rate spiked. Then the machine began a high-pitched wail.

"What's happening?" Rachel panicked.

"Is he dying?" Laronda cried

"Lucky! Lucky, hang on!" Desmond screamed.

A few moments later, a team of nurses and doctors rushed into the room. Some of them began checking on Lucky. Two other nurses turned towards the family.

"I'm sorry, but we're going to need you guys to clear the room so we can work on him."

"I ain't going nowhere!" Laronda cried, fighting to get to Lucky. "Daddy, wake up! Wake up!"

Desmond wrapped his niece in a bear hug and carried her toward the door. "We gotta give them room to work, baby girl. They tryna save him."

Laronda continued fighting to get back to Lucky. "No! I want my daddy! Let me go! Let me go!"

The young woman's strength was no match for Desmond's. He carried her from the room and down the hall to the waiting room. After they were seated, Laronda cried on his shoulder. Desmond couldn't handle being around all the emotions.

"I gotta go, baby girl," he said before turning to Rachel. "Come hold her. I need to get out of here."

"Where you going?" Rachel asked.

Desmond looked in her good eye, allowing her to see the rage boiling inside of him. "I got a phone call to make. Do you got some heat that I can hold?"

Rachel gave him her house keys and told him the address. "It's a 10 millimeter in the kitchen drawer."

As soon as Desmond stepped outside the hospital, he called Rachel's phone.

"Yeah," Flacco answered.

"I'm in Milwaukee. Where you at?"

There was a momentary pause. "I been waiting for you to call, Desmond. Did Lucky make it?"

"Don't worry about my brother, nigga. You wanted me and now I'm here. Tell me where you at."

"You sound mad, Blood. Make sure you harness that anger. Don't let it cripple you and make you weak. I want you at yo' best."

"Quit talking, nigga, and tell me where the fuck you at."

"I'm in the abandoned building that used to be the Northridge Mall. Come get me."

After ending the call, Desmond searched the lot for a car to take. A Pontiac Bonneville speeding towards the emergency room got his attention. A man rushed from the driver's seat and ran around to the passenger side to help a pregnant woman from the car. Desmond moved quickly, trotting to the running car. He hopped in the driver's seat and sped away.

He went to Lucky and Rachel's house to get the pistol before heading to the abandoned mall. He parked the stolen ride a block away and walked in the dark the rest of the way. When he got to the building, he paused outside to look for signs of life. He wasn't sure if he was walking into a trap or how many niggas Flacco had in the building with him. But one thing was for sure. He wasn't leaving the building without killing Flacco.

After locating a way in through a broken window, Desmond entered the building. It was dark and he could hear pests scurrying around in the dark. He kept the pistol ready, staying close to the wall and taking slow measured steps. A noise behind made him spin around ready to shoot. A big-ass possum hissed at him before running away. Desmond continued to move with stealth as he searched the mall. A creaking sound coming from upstairs made him look up as Flacco took aim.

Pop, pop, pop, pop!

Desmond dove out of Flacco's line of sight, doing a tuck roll and coming up with his gun blazing.

Clap, clap, clap!

Flacco ducked out of the way as bullets whizzed past his head. Now that Desmond knew where his enemy was, he made his way to the broken escalator and moved upstairs slowly. He kept low and crept toward the spot Flacco had been, pausing to look around. That's when he felt a presence behind him. He spun just in time to see Flacco jump from his hiding spot about fifty feet away. Their guns fired at the same time.

Clap, clap, clap, clap!

Pop, pop, pop, pop!

Flacco let out a scream, his gun falling to the ground as he crashed into the wall. Desmond approached him slowly, keeping his gun trained on him.

Flacco began laughing. "Damn, Desmond. I didn't think you was that fast. You certified, Blood."

Desmond moved closer, pointing the pistol at his face. "Who the fuck is you? What's yo' beef with us?"

"Polo was my cousin. Which one of y'all did it? It had to be you."

"It was," Desmond admitted.

Flacco let out a harsh laugh. "If I had to go, it had to be by a nigga trained to do it 'cause can't no regular niggas fuck with me. Did I get Lucky? Did yo' brother die?"

"You should be worried about whether or not you gon' have an open casket, nigga."

Pop!

## EPILOGUE

One year later

Nervous excitement rushed through Desmond's body as he sat in the barracks with his new SEAL team. He had been waiting for this opportunity for almost two years, ever since he was blown off the building in India. As he looked around the room at the five men he had handpicked to be on his team, he got a good feeling inside. They were all young, battle ready and had tested high at the academy. With his leadership, they would all one day go on to lead their own squads. Hopefully. That's when the doubt crept in. As the team leader, Bravo One, he was responsible for all their lives. And they would all look to him for direction and guidance.

"You good, Desmond?" Kim Lee asked, popping up at Desmond's side.

"You think we got what it takes to lead them?"

Kim looked around the barracks at their team. "I do. And I think you are a good leader. You have what it takes to go far. Don't doubt yourself, brother. You were made for this."

Desmond nodded. "Thanks, brah. I'm ready for this debrief. I can't wait to get my hands on this muthafucka. I been waiting on this moment for two years."

"Me too. I can't decide if I want to bring Slayer back alive or kill him on sight."

"I had that same thought. Muthafucka tried to get us all killed."

A knock on the door interrupted the SEALS. When it opened, First Mate Amber Maldonado stepped into the room. "Colonel Jones is ready to brief your team, Desmond."

Seeing the brown-skinned Latin beauty brought a smile to Desmond's face. "Okay." He nodded before turning to his team. "Alright, Bravo Team. Let's get to the debrief room. Colonel Jones is ready."

The soldiers bounced from the room, eager to get on the mission. Amber turned to follow them when Desmond grabbed her hand.

"What?" she asked, spinning to face him.

He pulled her into the barracks and closed the door. "I wanted a good luck kiss from my fiancée," he said before leaning in for a kiss. The lovers shared a sloppy lip lock before she pushed him away.

"You better get out there before you get in trouble," she scolded.

"I wouldn't miss my team's first debrief. I just wanted a second alone with you to let you know that after I get Slayer, I want to take some R&R time to go back to your hometown. Get some more of your mother's cooking."

She looked down at the ring on her left hand for a moment. "Okay, soon-to-be-husband. 'Cause you know you can't go back to your hometown. You mess around and fall in love with another girlfriend from the past that turns out to be a hoochie."

Desmond looked hurt. "Damn, it's like that?"

"Yeah, it's like that. Now get to the debrief room before you get in trouble." She smiled before pecking his lips again.

◆◆◆

"Yo, Lucky! Lucky, hold on, li'l brah!"

Lucky was walking through the tall iron gate, but stopped to look behind him. A tall brown-skinned older man was hustling to catch up. "What's up, OG Mike?"

"You got it, baby boy," he grinned. "I wanted to walk back to the cell hall with you to holla."

"What's good, OG?"

"I just came from seeing my attorney. The courts accepted my appeal, man! I'm about to get a new trial!"

Lucky's eyes grew wide with elation. "Hell yeah, OG! That's what's up. Did you tell Rachel yet?"

"Nah, I just found out. I'm about to get the phone as soon as I go in here. Man, I'm so geeked up. I been fighting these muthafuckas for almost twenty years."

"That's what's up, brah. I'm coming out right behind you. I got one more year and it's over. You coming to Atlanta with us?"

"You know it, baby boy. Hit up all them strip clubs and make it rain on them hoes!" The older man laughed as they approached the Northwest Cell Hall. "A'ight, baby boy. Let me get in here and get this phone. I gotta call my daughter and let her know I'm on my way home!"

"Okay, OG. Love, fool."

"You know it. All day," OG Mike said before walking into the building.

Lucky walked twenty more feet and entered his temporary residence of the last year: The North Cell Hall. He hated being back in Waupun. The maximum-security prison brought back too many old memories from the beginning of his last bid.

"Harrison!" the sergeant called.

Lucky walked towards the cage. "What's going on, Sarge?"

"You got a visit. Hurry up and get ready."

Lucky ran up a flight of stairs and ducked into his cell to freshen up. After brushing his teeth and dabbing a little bit of pine-scented prayer oil on his neck, he grabbed the pass from the sergeant and headed for the visiting room. When he walked in, he gave the pass to the officer at the front desk before scanning the sea of visitors for his loved ones.

"Hey, Daddy!" Laronda stood and waved.

"Hey, baby girl!" He grinned, walking over to hug his daughter. "Where Rachel and Malik?" he asked, looking around for his girl.

"They in the bathroom. She had to change him. This was a surprise visit. Are you surprised?"

"Yeah. I didn't know y'all was coming. How is school?"

"Good. 3.9 GPA. I mailed you my report card yesterday. You said if I get a 3.5 you was gon' buy me a car. I want a Lexus."

Lucky frowned. "Damn. You jumped right to a luxury."

"I'm a princess. Princesses need to ride clean, Daddy."

Lucky was shaking his head when he noticed Rachel coming out of the bathroom carrying a three-month-old baby. He stood to receive the baby boy and a kiss from his girl.

"Hey, baby!" Rachel smiled. "We wanted to surprise you with a visit."

"Good surprise, baby." He smiled before turning to the child. "What's up, li'l man? How is Daddy's baby boy?"

The child reached out to touch Lucky's face.

"Hurry up and come home, Lucky," Rachel whined as she watched the father and son. "I want a baby too. Lasonya can't be the only one giving you babies."

"It's almost over, baby. Oh shit! I just ran into yo' pops right before I came out. He just came from seeing his lawyer and he finna get a new trial. If shit go right, he finna be coming home too."

Rachel let out a scream as her eyes bucked. "Ahhh, I can't believe it1 I'ma visit him after I visit you. Oh my God! I can't believe both of y'all coming home!" She beamed with excitement.

Lucky took a moment to look over his new family, surprised at how God worked. When he got out of prison the first time and went home to Melissa and her kids, it didn't work out and they were killed. But God had given him another chance and he got back everything he lost. When Lucky got out of prison this time, he knew things would be different. And most importantly, he no longer felt CHAINED TO THE STREETS.

**The End**

## Submission Guideline

Submit the first three chapters of your completed manuscript to ldpsubmissions@gmail.com, subject line: Your book's title. The manuscript must be in a .doc file and sent as an attachment. Document should be in Times New Roman, double spaced and in size 12 font. Also, provide your synopsis and full contact information. If sending multiple submissions, they must each be in a separate email.

Have a story but no way to send it electronically? You can still submit to LDP/Ca$h Presents. Send in the first three chapters, written or typed, of your completed manuscript to:

**LDP: Submissions Dept**
**Po Box 944**
**Stockbridge, Ga 30281**

*DO NOT send original manuscript. Must be a duplicate.*

Provide your synopsis and a cover letter containing your full contact information.

Thanks for considering LDP and Ca$h Presents.

**Coming Soon from Lock Down Publications/Ca$h Presents**

BOW DOWN TO MY GANGSTA

By **Ca$h**

TORN BETWEEN TWO

By **Coffee**

THE STREETS STAINED MY SOUL **II**

By **Marcellus Allen**

BLOOD OF A BOSS **VI**

SHADOWS OF THE GAME II

By **Askari**

LOYAL TO THE GAME **IV**

By **T.J. & Jelissa**

A DOPEBOY'S PRAYER **II**

By **Eddie "Wolf" Lee**

IF LOVING YOU IS WRONG… **III**

By **Jelissa**

TRUE SAVAGE **VII**

MIDNIGHT CARTEL III

DOPE BOY MAGIC IV

By **Chris Green**

BLAST FOR ME **III**

A SAVAGE DOPEBOY III

CUTTHROAT MAFIA II

By **Ghost**

A HUSTLER'S DECEIT III

KILL ZONE **II**

BAE BELONGS TO ME III

A DOPE BOY'S QUEEN II

By **Aryanna**

COKE KINGS V

KING OF THE TRAP II

By **T.J. Edwards**

GORILLAZ IN THE BAY V

**De'Kari**

THE STREETS ARE CALLING II

**Duquie Wilson**

KINGPIN KILLAZ IV

STREET KINGS III

PAID IN BLOOD III

CARTEL KILLAZ IV

DOPE GODS II

**Hood Rich**

SINS OF A HUSTLA II

**ASAD**

TRIGGADALE III

**Elijah R. Freeman**

KINGZ OF THE GAME V

**Playa Ray**

SLAUGHTER GANG IV

RUTHLESS HEART IV

**By Willie Slaughter**

THE HEART OF A SAVAGE III

**By Jibril Williams**

FUK SHYT II

**By Blakk Diamond**

FEAR MY GANGSTA 5

THE REALEST KILLAS

**By Tranay Adams**

TRAP GOD II

**By Troublesome**

YAYO IV

A SHOOTER'S AMBITION III

**By S. Allen**

GHOST MOB

**Stilloan Robinson**

KINGPIN DREAMS III

**By Paper Boi Rari**

CREAM

**By Yolanda Moore**

SON OF A DOPE FIEND II

**By Renta**

FOREVER GANGSTA II

GLOCKS ON SATIN SHEETS II

**By Adrian Dulan**

LOYALTY AIN'T PROMISED II

**By Keith Williams**

THE PRICE YOU PAY FOR LOVE II

DOPE GIRL MAGIC III

**By Destiny Skai**

CONFESSIONS OF A GANGSTA II

**By Nicholas Lock**

I'M NOTHING WITHOUT HIS LOVE II

**By Monet Dragun**

CAUGHT UP IN THE LIFE III

**By Robert Baptiste**

LIFE OF A SAVAGE IV

A GANGSTA'S QUR'AN II

By **Romell Tukes**

QUIET MONEY II

## Chained to the Streets 3

By **Trai'Quan**
THE STREETS MADE ME II
By **Larry D. Wright**
THE ULTIMATE SACRIFICE VI
IF YOU CROSSM ME ONCE II
By **Anthony Fields**
THE LIFE OF A HOOD STAR
**By Ca$h & Rashia Wilson**

## Available Now

RESTRAINING ORDER **I & II**
By **CA$H & Coffee**
LOVE KNOWS NO BOUNDARIES **I II & III**
By **Coffee**
RAISED AS A GOON I, II, III & IV
BRED BY THE SLUMS I, II, III
BLAST FOR ME I & II
ROTTEN TO THE CORE I II III
A BRONX TALE I, II, III
DUFFEL BAG CARTEL I II III IV
HEARTLESS GOON I II III IV
A SAVAGE DOPEBOY I II
HEARTLESS GOON I II III
DRUG LORDS I II III
CUTTHROAT MAFIA
By **Ghost**
LAY IT DOWN **I & II**

LAST OF A DYING BREED
BLOOD STAINS OF A SHOTTA I & II III
By **Jamaica**
LOYAL TO THE GAME I II III
LIFE OF SIN I, II III
By **TJ & Jelissa**
BLOODY COMMAS I & II
SKI MASK CARTEL I  II & III
KING OF NEW YORK I II,III IV V
RISE TO POWER I II III
COKE KINGS I II III IV
BORN HEARTLESS I II III IV
KING OF THE TRAP
By **T.J. Edwards**
IF LOVING HIM IS WRONG…I & II
LOVE ME EVEN WHEN IT HURTS I II III
By **Jelissa**
WHEN THE STREETS CLAP BACK I & II III
THE HEART OF A SAVAGE I II
By **Jibril Williams**
A DISTINGUISHED THUG STOLE MY HEART I II & III
LOVE SHOULDN'T HURT I II III IV
RENEGADE BOYS I II III IV
PAID IN KARMA I II III
By **Meesha**
A GANGSTER'S CODE I &, II III
A GANGSTER'S SYN I II III
THE SAVAGE LIFE I II III
CHAINED TO THE STREETS I II III
**By J-Blunt**

PUSH IT TO THE LIMIT

By **Bre' Hayes**

BLOOD OF A BOSS **I, II, III,  IV, V**

SHADOWS OF THE GAME

By **Askari**

THE STREETS BLEED MURDER **I, II & III**

THE HEART OF A GANGSTA I II& III

By **Jerry Jackson**

CUM FOR ME I II III IV V

An **LDP Erotica Collaboration**

BRIDE OF A HUSTLA **I  II & II**

THE FETTI GIRLS **I, II& III**

CORRUPTED BY A GANGSTA I, II III, IV

BLINDED BY HIS LOVE

THE PRICE YOU PAY FOR LOVE

DOPE GIRL MAGIC I II

By **Destiny Skai**

WHEN A GOOD GIRL GOES BAD

By **Adrienne**

THE COST OF LOYALTY I II III

**By Kweli**

A GANGSTER'S REVENGE **I II III & IV**

THE BOSS MAN'S DAUGHTERS I II III IV V

A SAVAGE LOVE  **I & II**

BAE BELONGS TO ME I II

A HUSTLER'S DECEIT I, II, III

WHAT BAD BITCHES DO I, II, III

SOUL OF A MONSTER I II III

KILL ZONE

A DOPE BOY'S QUEEN

# J-Blunt

By **Aryanna**
A KINGPIN'S AMBITON
A KINGPIN'S AMBITION **II**
I MURDER FOR THE DOUGH

By **Ambitious**
TRUE SAVAGE I II III IV V VI
DOPE BOY MAGIC I, II, III
MIDNIGHT CARTEL I II

By **Chris Green**
A DOPEBOY'S PRAYER

By **Eddie "Wolf" Lee**
THE KING CARTEL **I, II & III**

By **Frank Gresham**
THESE NIGGAS AIN'T LOYAL **I, II & III**

By **Nikki Tee**
GANGSTA SHYT **I II &III**

By **CATO**
THE ULTIMATE BETRAYAL

By **Phoenix**
BOSS'N UP **I , II & III**

By **Royal Nicole**
I LOVE YOU TO DEATH

**By Destiny J**
I RIDE FOR MY HITTA
I STILL RIDE FOR MY HITTA

By **Misty Holt**
LOVE & CHASIN' PAPER

By **Qay Crockett**
TO DIE IN VAIN
SINS OF A HUSTLA

232

# Chained to the Streets 3

By **ASAD**
BROOKLYN HUSTLAZ
By **Boogsy Morina**
BROOKLYN ON LOCK I & II
By **Sonovia**
GANGSTA CITY
By **Teddy Duke**
A DRUG KING AND HIS DIAMOND I & II III
A DOPEMAN'S RICHES
HER MAN, MINE'S TOO I, II
CASH MONEY HO'S
**By Nicole Goosby**
TRAPHOUSE KING **I II & III**
KINGPIN KILLAZ I II III
STREET KINGS I II
PAID IN BLOOD **I II**
CARTEL KILLAZ I II III
DOPE GODS
By **Hood Rich**
LIPSTICK KILLAH **I, II, III**
CRIME OF PASSION I II & III
By **Mimi**
STEADY MOBBN' **I, II, III**
THE STREETS STAINED MY SOUL
By **Marcellus Allen**
WHO SHOT YA **I, II, III**
SON OF A DOPE FIEND
**Renta**
GORILLAZ IN THE BAY **I II III IV**
TEARS OF A GANGSTA I II

233

**DE'KARI**
TRIGGADALE I II
**Elijah R. Freeman**
GOD BLESS THE TRAPPERS I, II, III
THESE SCANDALOUS STREETS I, II, III
FEAR MY GANGSTA I, II, III IV
THESE STREETS DON'T LOVE NOBODY I, II
BURY ME A G I, II, III, IV, V
A GANGSTA'S EMPIRE I, II, III, IV
THE DOPEMAN'S BODYGAURD I II
**Tranay Adams**
THE STREETS ARE CALLING
**Duquie Wilson**
MARRIED TO A BOSS… I II III
**By Destiny Skai & Chris Green**
KINGZ OF THE GAME I  II III IV
**Playa Ray**
SLAUGHTER GANG I II III
RUTHLESS HEART I II III
**By Willie Slaughter**
FUK SHYT
**By Blakk Diamond**
DON'T F#CK WITH MY HEART I II
**By Linnea**
ADDICTED TO THE DRAMA I II III
**By Jamila**
YAYO I II III
A SHOOTER'S AMBITION I II
**By S. Allen**
TRAP GOD

# Chained to the Streets 3

**By Troublesome**
FOREVER GANGSTA
GLOCKS ON SATIN SHEETS
**By Adrian Dulan**
TOE TAGZ I II III
**By Ah'Million**
KINGPIN DREAMS I II
**By Paper Boi Rari**
CONFESSIONS OF A GANGSTA
**By Nicholas Lock**
I'M NOTHING WITHOUT HIS LOVE
**By Monet Dragun**
CAUGHT UP IN THE LIFE I II
**By Robert Baptiste**
NEW TO THE GAME I II III
By **Malik D. Rice**
LIFE OF A SAVAGE I II III
A GANGSTA'S QUR'AN
By **Romell Tukes**
LOYALTY AIN'T PROMISED
**By Keith Williams**
Quiet Money
By **Trai'Quan**
THE STREETS MADE ME
By **Larry D. Wright**
THE ULTIMATE SACRIFICE I, II, III, IV, V
KHADIFI
IF YOU CROSS ME ONCE
By **Anthony Fields**
THE LIFE OF A HOOD STAR

J-Blunt

**By Ca$h & Rashia Wilson**

## BOOKS BY LDP'S CEO, CA$H

TRUST IN NO MAN

TRUST IN NO MAN 2

TRUST IN NO MAN 3

BONDED BY BLOOD

SHORTY GOT A THUG

THUGS CRY

THUGS CRY 2

THUGS CRY 3

TRUST NO BITCH

TRUST NO BITCH 2

TRUST NO BITCH 3

TIL MY CASKET DROPS

RESTRAINING ORDER

RESTRAINING ORDER 2

IN LOVE WITH A CONVICT

LIFE OF A HOOD STAR

**Coming Soon**

BONDED BY BLOOD 2

BOW DOWN TO MY GANGSTA

J-Blunt